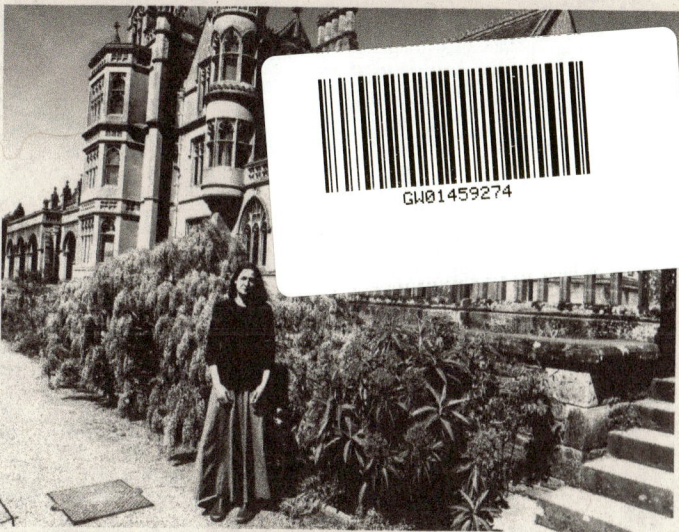

Dear Reader,

In 2002, the Gothic mansion of Tyntesfield near Bristol was acquired by the National Trust. Shortly afterwards, I went on a tour of the upper rooms and saw the bed in which the reclusive Baron Wraxall had died, a pair of ancient slippers beside it, and a tablet of coal tar soap on the washstand.

On my next visit, the bed, the slippers and the soap had gone, and the seeds of THE INFAMOUS GILBERTS were planted, a story twenty years in the making. Those twenty years were spent juggling a lot of jobs (waitress, cleaner, care home activity coordinator...) but I have always thought of myself as a writer.

So it is with great pride that I commend this proof of my long longed-for novel to you. I do hope you will enjoy it.

The photograph above is of me at Tyntesfield. Imagine, if you will, a warm breeze, the smell of wallflowers, and the bickering of rooks on the hillside behind.

With thanks and best wishes,

Angela Tomaski

UNCORRECTED PROOF COPY – NOT FOR SALE

This is an uncorrected book proof made available in confidence to selected persons for specific review purpose and is not for sale or other distribution. Anyone selling or distributing this proof copy will be responsible for any resultant claims relating to any alleged omissions, errors, libel, breach of copyright, privacy rights or otherwise. Any copying, reprinting, sale or other unauthorized distribution or use of this proof copy without the consent of the publisher will be a direct infringement of the publisher's exclusive rights, and those involved liable in law accordingly.

The Infamous Gilberts

ANGELA TOMASKI

FIG TREE

an imprint of

PENGUIN BOOKS

FIG TREE

UK | USA | Canada | Ireland | Australia
India | New Zealand | South Africa

Fig Tree is part of the Penguin Random House group of companies
whose addresses can be found at global.penguinrandomhouse.com

Penguin Random House UK,
One Embassy Gardens, 8 Viaduct Gardens, London SW11 7BW

penguin.co.uk

Penguin
Random House
UK

First published 2026
001

Copyright © Angela Tomaski, 2026

The moral right of the author has been asserted

Penguin Random House values and supports copyright.
Copyright fuels creativity, encourages diverse voices, promotes freedom
of expression and supports a vibrant culture. Thank you for purchasing
an authorized edition of this book and for respecting intellectual property
laws by not reproducing, scanning or distributing any part of it by any
means without permission. You are supporting authors and enabling
Penguin Random House to continue to publish books for everyone.
No part of this book may be used or reproduced in any manner for the
purpose of training artificial intelligence technologies or systems. In accordance
with Article 4(3) of the DSM Directive 2019/790, Penguin Random House
expressly reserves this work from the text and data mining exception

Set in 12/14.75 pt Dante Mt Pro
Typeset by Falcon Oast Graphic Art Ltd
Printed and bound in Great Britain by Clays Ltd, Elcograf S.p.A.

The authorized representative in the EEA is Penguin Random House Ireland,
Morrison Chambers, 32 Nassau Street, Dublin D02 YH68

A CIP catalogue record for this book is available from the British Library

hardback isbn: 978–0–241–75757–4
trade paperback isbn: 978–0–241–75758–1

Penguin Random House is committed to a sustainable future
for our business, our readers and our planet. This book is made from
Forest Stewardship Council® certified paper

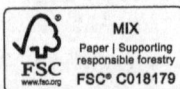

MIX
Paper | Supporting
responsible forestry
FSC® C018179

In memory of Kittgenstein,
who died while I was writing this book

Contents

I

The Bolt on the Blue-room Door

Thornwalk House, Somerset, 2002

Welcome to Thornwalk, home of the last of the Wynford Gilberts – Lydia, Hugo, Annabel, Jeremy and Rosalind. The downfall of this great family was once the subject of much tawdry gossip and many a sensational headline, and perhaps you hold in your heart some remnant, some echo, of this. If so, I ask you to let it go, and here, with me, meet them all anew.

You are entering through the servants' hall, as you see. The keys to the rest of the house have already been surrendered to the hotel people, but this one was given to me by Miss Annabel Gilbert herself and it shall not be relinquished to anyone but her. Since she is dead, that is unlikely to happen.

Come through, come through, but do not touch the door handles. The family's fingerprints are still upon them, and I have sworn that they shall remain.

'Max,' Hugo said to me, near the end, 'what will become of them all, after I am gone? What will happen to Annabel's dried conkers and the cracked Crown Derby shepherdess that

Rosalind hid under the morning-room dresser? I worry, because they're not the sort of thing people like these days.'

It broke my heart.

You find yourself now in the main hall. Pause for a moment, if you will. Breathe gently. A sensitive person will always breathe gently in a place like this, knowing the air to be a rare perfume.

But enough of that. Who knows when the philistines will arrive with their clipboards and their skips and their bottles of bleach? Until then, let us explore.

We shall start with Lydia, the eldest of the five.

Climb the staircase to the corner of the gallery. You will find a white door with a large crack in the centre panel, badly repaired with brown packing tape and paint. The crack was made by the swinging of an axe, but I shall tell you that story later.

For now, look up. Someone has fixed a heavy metal bolt to the top-left-hand corner of the door-frame. How ugly it is, you think, how incongruous – not an antique fitting, not in keeping with this glorious house – but no one asks why it is there. It is their fundamental flaw. Curiosity may have killed the cat, but it is the making of a man.

Now, open the door and go inside. There is a certain fragrance in the air. I wonder if you recognize it? Yes, it was lily of the valley she wore.

There is another scent, of course – oh, many – but do not despair. It is possible to untangle the threads. Take your time. There it is . . . a musty tang, like stewed nails. It is blood, very old blood, rubbed deep into the fibres of the pale blue rug at your feet. It was cleaned badly, even then, but that story too comes later.

There is a dressing table against the right-hand-side wall. Pretty, isn't it? White lacquered wood, perhaps late nineteenth century. Not valuable, certainly, but quaint. Surely it can stay.

Sit down on the stool and look into the glass. Can you see a face? A shadow of a girl with long, red-gold hair? Layer after layer it pressed there, this face, year after year, dark eyes boring into dark eyes, despairing at the passing days. She is beautiful, yes, but what will come of it? She has a banker's mind and expects a return on her assets. It is Lydia Gilbert, at the peak of her only mountain.

Open the drawer. Ah ha! A little bottle rattles towards you, a glass bottle with a daffodil-yellow smear at the bottom. Pull out the stopper and take a sniff. Yes, there it is. Lily of the valley. Almost seventy years ago she left, and you are the first person to touch this bottle, except me. Her fingers were the last upon it (before yours and mine). They hovered over it a moment before she closed the drawer. Mr Coldwell would buy her perfume, Lydia was thinking. Much better perfume. French scent. Buckets and buckets. But not yet. Go back to before I mentioned Mr Coldwell, before there was any hope of such a person, to the desperate face at the glass. It is this girl we are concerned with now.

Consider the five of them in the library below. No, wait, consider the four. Let us say that at this particular moment Hugo, the elder son, is away at school. There is not enough money to send the rest of them, or for a proper governess, and they are currently unchaperoned. The housekeeper has taken it upon herself to teach them to read, but that is the extent of her energies. She has gone back to her laundry.

Consider the mother, Margaret Gilbert, small and tired-looking. Something in the past has badly squashed her and you can still see it in her eyes. She stands in the doorway for a moment and watches them. Perhaps they need a little more direction, she thinks. Not much learning is taking place between the sprawling board games and dolls' houses. She wrings her hands and turns away.

There is an aunt who, now and then, sends someone to help, but they do not stay long. They get a rough reception, perhaps, from this little group. Rosalind, the youngest, cares nothing at all for books, only her cartoon magazines full of pony stories and fairy stories. Jeremy, the second youngest, won't be told what to do, not by these sorts of people. Lydia is too old, really. And the middle child, Annabel . . . poor little Annabel . . . well, the aunt has told them not to bother with her.

No, they do not stay long, these companions and tutors. They feel a definite uneasiness here. They do not want to be absorbed into this very special little vacuum. So they drift in and drag themselves out, leaving behind a favourite book or poem. Until Higgins.

Get up from the dressing table and turn to the bed. You may need to switch on the light. Lift up the blue-flowered flounce at the mattress's edge and slip your hand beneath. Halfway down, a foot deep, you will find a little wooden box. Control the fluttering of your heart! There is nothing of value inside – not the kind of value people look for now – only a string of amber beads, a pin with a tiny synthetic-pearl tip and a tarnished silver cross. But of what value to the dark-eyed girl? Let us see what price she has paid for them.

In 1928, when Lydia was fifteen, a man called Mr Higgins was employed as their tutor. He stayed longer than most and was slightly harder to get rid of.

I shall not go into details. You can imagine them all for yourselves – the nature rambles in remote corners of the garden, the deep, low conversations over books of dubious educational but rousingly emotional worth. He refers to her as a young lady . . . Yes, you can guess the rest.

Rosalind discovers them one afternoon in the old Chaplain's Cottage – sharp-eyed, birdlike, suspicious little Rosalind – and Mr Higgins is thrown from the house.

'I love him, Mother,' Lydia declares, over and over, with tears in her eyes. 'I love him, I love him, I love him.'

Mrs Gilbert can think of nothing to say. She has been caught off guard by this sudden leap from the precipice of childhood.

4

She does not recognize this wild-eyed, frantic creature, and marvels at the complete loss of her own power. She feels baggy, like a popped balloon.

She does the only things she might be expected to do. She has a bolt fixed to the outside of Lydia's door and calls Aunt Beatrice.

The next day, this formidable woman arrives. Pause for a moment to observe her. Large, satin-covered, creaking slightly, wearing one of those elaborate steel-grey bun wigs. There is a sly-looking brown dachshund under her arm, a hint of moth-balls around her handbag, and a tiny sugar crystal clinging to a corner of her lower lip from a biscuit hastily devoured in the back of the car. There, I think that will do.

'She says her heart is broken,' says Mrs Gilbert to her sister-in-law. 'She says she is dying.'

'She is not dying,' says Aunt Beatrice.

Mrs Gilbert marvels. How can Aunt Beatrice be so sure? How can anyone be so sure of anything?

'I love him,' declares Lydia, as Aunt Beatrice enters the bedroom.

'You do not love him,' says Aunt Beatrice, 'because the man is an idiot. How embarrassing, Lydia. Really.'

Lydia hesitates.

'I knew we ought to do better,' continues Aunt Beatrice, lowering herself on to the edge of the bed with a sigh, 'and said so to your mother, but she thought he might be adequate while Jeremy and Rosalind were still quite young. He was so much cheaper than the others.'

Lydia's face is suddenly very red.

'I have nothing against near-blindness,' continues the aunt, as the sugar crystal drops from her lip into the rug at her feet, 'nor facial features that remind one of a mole – though a compassionate woman might think twice before inflicting such things upon her offspring – but I draw the line at rancid breath. Breath of this sort is genetic, Lydia. It is endemic in the lower orders. I shall not go so far as to say it is characteristic of the class, but it has not been bred out of them so painstakingly. For obvious reasons, we do not often talk of it – it is a shame to have to do so now – but when one speaks of programmes of breeding, Lydia, it is partially the eradication of bad breath that is at stake. Thankfully, you have not gone so far as to allow him to touch you in any way . . .'

It is admitted that there has been a kiss. Perhaps more than one. That is how Lydia has earnt her little box of treasures.

'Well,' says Aunt Beatrice, examining the hoard, 'this is not without promise.' The objects themselves are worthless, naturally, but the reasoning is sound. The Gilberts are merchants after all, great captains of enterprise and exchange. In the absence of the children's father, her poor unfortunate brother, she sees it is up to her to harness such Gilbert-like proclivities and steer the family ship.

And so Lydia is taken to London, to Aunt Beatrice's own physician, where her mouth is examined, and swabs taken and cultured. She is directed in the use of an unpleasant-tasting medicine and various caustic soaps, and the lesson is learnt.

Higgins doesn't know this yet.

Cross the room to the window and look down into the darkness. I can almost see Higgins there now, a little round face, white in the light of the window below, blinking behind his spectacles, getting ready with his bits of Shakespeare.

But Lydia does not come to the window. She sits stiffly on the edge of the bed, her lips pursed, thinking of the indignity of the swabs, the smell of the caustic soap and her aunt's terrible words about breath . . . No, this last is so terrible that her thoughts cannot go anywhere near it. But the swabs and the soap are enough.

The peppering of the glass with clods of mud goes on. At last, Lydia lifts the sash.

'Go away,' she calls down.

'Lydia, my love,' Higgins cries. 'What is the matter?'

'Nothing is the matter,' says Lydia.

'Who has put you up to this?' says Higgins.

'No one. I just don't like you any more.'

'You don't love me any more?'

'No, of course not.'

Oh, the heartlessness of the girl! A woman scorned is nothing compared to the girl whose lover suddenly has a reputation for bad breath.

There are no more visits, no more letters. Higgins is gone.

Poor Mrs Gilbert weeps upon her bed as Aunt Beatrice, cold, looks on.

'So innocent she was,' sobs Mrs Gilbert.

'The innocence of children is very short-lived,' says Aunt Beatrice, 'if it exists at all.'

'She was so beautiful.'

'Beauty is as beauty does,' says the aunt.

'Really?'

'No. Thankfully, it is much less than that,' says Aunt Beatrice. 'Though, generally speaking, it is probably safer for beautiful people to do as little as possible. Just in case.'

There, that is the story of 'The Bolt on the Blue-room Door'. In fact, it is only half the story, less than half, depending on how you measure these things. The rest is connected to the crack in the door and the bloodstains on the floor, but all that will have to wait.

2

The Burn on the Library Rug

Let us go back downstairs to the library. You can sit for a while with a cup of tea and a chocolate Hobnob, and I will tell you everything you need to know. Yes, I know everything. I have absorbed it all like sphagnum moss. A surely disproportionate amount of knowing for so small a brain. A universe in my nutshell.

The library. You will stop, no doubt, and admire the vaulting, the original stencilling on the plasterwork, so bright, so vivid, after all these years. The rugs are by Crace, the upholstery by Holland & Sons and the bookcases by Jackson & Graham. There are plenty of books, the expensive brown ones that everyone admires, heavy on Gibbon and Ruskin and Carlyle. Yes, there are all sorts of things to catch the attention of the average mind, but they do not interest me.

Instead, I direct you to the rough wooden platform beneath the window at the far end of the room.

Poor, tragic relic. One of the first things to be lost, no doubt. The blue-room door must be repaired, the hotel people will say, and that odd little platform in the library removed. That will do a lot to improve things. Will it, indeed! Perhaps they are not aware that the platform is a stage, and that it was made by Jeremy Gilbert himself – the great explorer, the author, the invisible one – without glue or nails. The carpentry is crude but correct.

Look closer, there, at the spattered red marks along the back. No, no, how morbid you are! Blood does not look like that, not after seventy years. It is paint, dripped from the heads of Rosalind's dolls. All their plays included murder, guillotines and knives. There was a great deal of dripping red paint.

In the cupboard to the right you will find scripts, handwritten by Hugo for his brother and his sisters. Take them out. That is his handwriting there, broad and awkward but promising. The initials in the margin indicate the owner of the lines . . . Note that Hugo is always the king or the great detective, and Jeremy the miserable revolutionary or the stooge. Lydia and Rosalind take it in turns as queens and princesses, jilted lovers and wronged wives, while Annabel, rarely given any lines, represents the mindless rabble or the corpse.

Return them carefully.

That advice applies to everything from now on. It is tempting to become careless with things when there are lots of them. You must treat each object here as if it were the only one in the world.

Now, let your eyes stray to the other end of the room, to the dark circles of wallpaper above the morning-room door. Who knows what they plan to do about this, but I suggest putting up a plaque: formerly in this place: three blue-and-white sixteenth-century chinese dishes, monetary value immaterial, psychological value immense, the indisputable property of hugo gilbert, last lord of thornwalk, snatched by his sister lydia, renowned thief.

What else? So many things. You might open the cupboard there to the left of the fireplace and take a look at the board games. The *Monopoly* set is very ancient. One winter evening,

Annabel had a spectacular success with a hotel on the Old Kent Road and for the rest of her life tried to replicate it. She would race around the board trying to get back to the purple ones. She never minded losing, but it was sad to see.

Annabel's finger marks are all over the little dog. They always let her have him. Hugo's are on the top hat.

Beside the *Monopoly* set is a box of home-made Christmas tree decorations, some carved by Jeremy in the sawmill on the hillside behind the house, some knitted by Rosalind. Rosalind's are full of moth holes and dropped stitches. There are tears in them too, but those are less easy to see.

And now, something else you may not have noticed. See the small rug on top of the large rug in front of the fireplace? Lift up the small rug. There is a substantial burnt patch underneath it – the result of no tiny snuffed-out spark, surely, but an almost mighty blaze.

Picture it. Annabel is alone, playing with her dolls. She is perhaps five years old. The year? Let's say 1921. A spark flies from the fire and lands on the rug. Annabel continues to play. The spark smoulders a little and the rug catches alight. Still, she does not move.

It is Hugo who finds her, sitting there, a doll in each hand, staring blindly at the flames. Let me see . . . if she is five, he must seven. Old enough to whisk her up in his arms, throw her to Mrs Gilbert, who has come into the room behind him, and smother the blaze with a blanket.

Mrs Gilbert collapses into a chair, weeping. 'Gracious!' she says. 'Not again! What shall we do with her?'

'Hush, Mother,' says Hugo. He kneels down in front of Annabel. 'Annabel?' he says.

There is no response.

He waves a hand in front of her eyes. Annabel doesn't even blink.

'Well?' says Mrs Gilbert.

But, before Hugo can think of anything to say, Annabel sighs, the deep sigh of someone coming home from somewhere far away and not as nice. She looks up at him with her big dark eyes and smiles. 'Hugo!' she says. She wriggles away from her mother and holds out her arms.

Later, much later, Annabel told me that this was probably the beginning of the end for her. Mrs Gilbert had immediately recounted the story of the fire to Aunt Beatrice, and from then on, as far as the aunt was concerned, she had only four nieces and nephews – four whole ones, and one small leftover piece, about which, at some point, something would have to be done.

3

The Empty Bed

Where shall we go now?

I think I shall take you back upstairs to the bedrooms. There is something important I would like you to see.

On our way, pause for a moment on the stairs. The hotel people have already condemned the carpet, of course. They may have promised to keep the house unchanged, but a threadbare carpet is going too far. Apparently, the great swags of loose hessian would almost certainly trip a guest, who would then tumble to his death. It must be replaced, they say, but, fear not: from the remaining scraps and a series of old photographs, they will be able to make an exact replica.

An exact replica! How it makes me laugh. That carpet is fifty per cent sweat and skin cells – fifty per cent Gilbert DNA. There are tears in this carpet, poignant relics of joy and tragedy, and the scurf of fifteen beloved Labradors and one Miniature Schnauzer with dermatitis. They talk about Heritage and Authenticity but care nothing for nuance.

Up we go, back along the gallery to the smallest of the bedrooms, a funny little corridor-type room with a narrow bed against the far wall.

We shall just peek inside for a moment.

How quiet it is. How still.

Let your eyes rest upon the bed . . . the brown eiderdown, shiny and almost black at the edge, drawn up high over the pillows. The slippers beneath, squashed flat like dead hedgehogs. The toothbrush mug on the glass shelf above the sink, with a cracked tablet of coal-tar soap. But the toothbrush is gone. Someone has taken the toothbrush.

No, I think we will not go in just yet.

4

Everything in the Night Nursery

I have started this all wrong. I am thinking now that it would have been better to begin at the beginning. That is the traditional way, and probably so for good reason. We should go up to the top of the house, to the night nursery in one of the attics, where they played as children.

Yes, let us do that.

Go back along the gallery and up the narrow stairs on the right-hand side. You find yourself in a long, low room with three gabled windows, barred on the lower half. Two narrow beds and a cot in the far corner remain. The wallpaper has greyed, but the little sprigged pattern is still visible. There is a waft of carbolic soap in the air, castor oil, dust and resignation.

Take a moment to consider five small people here – five little nuggets of life, little kernels of person, who picked at this wallpaper, scribbled in these books, and clung to those bars, to press their smudgy little noses against the windowpanes.

Go to the bookcase and take out the small hardback copy of *Ivanhoe* from the top shelf. Turn to the flyleaf. There! That is the early autograph of Jeremy, perhaps seven or eight years old. He is trying to lay claim to something, but notice that he does so in pencil. It has been crossed out by a stronger hand and Hugo's name written there instead in black ink.

Now, carefully turn the page. A little hair is tucked inside. To whom the hair belonged, I cannot say for certain – it would need a microscope, some sort of laboratory analysis – but I think it is probably Hugo's. Tuck it back in, if you would, and return the book.

There are toys beneath the beds, including a little wooden dog held together by springs that wiggles and waggles its tail as it rolls along. The string is broken . . . there, you see . . . and a ribbon has been knotted to the end. How dirty it is! How much loved was this poor little dog. The paint is all coming off his nose from being kissed so many times, but his name is unknown, his future uncertain. Yes, put it back.

What else can I show you?

See those little black marks, there by the skirting board, where the paper is torn? No, it is not bat poo. It is beetles. Wallpaper beetles, I think they are called. Annabel would stare at them for hours. Woodlice too, in their little rotten pockets of the skirting. There is a gap between the floorboards under the washstand out of which a shrew would sometimes pop its head. Annabel would lie down on the floor and press her face to the hole. She longed to be a beetle or a shrew, to crawl all over the house on the inside.

Now, go to the window at the end of the room. Look closely at the bars. See where the paint has flaked away and there is a little dent in the metal beneath? It is the result of hours of work with a child's penknife. Yes, every time the nurse steps out of the room, Jeremy begins sawing at the bars.

He has plotted a path down on to the bathroom roof, then the drainpipe and the laurel bush. He thinks he will be able to make it to the stables before the alarm is raised. He has three shillings and a cheese roll in his pocket, and he is going to find their father.

'Father is dead,' says Lydia, nibbling the biscuits Jeremy has stolen from the pantry as the price of her silence.

'No, he's not,' Jeremy says. He glances at Rosalind, who has almost finished her cake. It is taking much longer than he thought, this bar, and Rosalind is not to be trusted any more.

'He died in the war,' Lydia says.

But Jeremy shakes his head.

Now, do not suppose that some clichéd family drama is being hinted at here. No, no, just a little childish hopefulness that Jeremy will soon grow out of. Their father is definitely dead and the drama (of which there will unfortunately be much) lies elsewhere, as you will see.

5

Broken Windows and Wardrobe Doors

Mighty Thornwalk. Nestled in a lonely cleft of the Wyn Valley, crested and turreted like a slumbering dragon, a long-slumbering dragon whose scales have grown dim and begun to crumble, whose fires have cooled to a curl of smoke from a single nostril.

In its massive walls, see the toil of generations. In its vast towers, see the rise of a dynasty, the legendary empire of Gilbert, Gilbert & Gilbert, flying its flag on a fleet of merchant vessels surging back and forth across the Atlantic, from Lisbon to Lima, from Cádiz to Valparaíso. Witness the audacity of its founding fathers as they plunge head first into a world of brigands and pirates, clinging to the motto *Intrepidi mundo corde* – fearless are the pure of heart, and battle their way to unprecedented heights of fame and wealth. In the London counting houses, they are called 'The Infallible Gilberts'. They can do no wrong.

See great-grandfather Nathaniel Gilbert – not the old man with the long white beard in the portraits around the stairwell but a young and wiry one, with a sharp discerning gaze. He is visiting a cousin in Nailsea in 1842 when he catches sight of a humble farmstead on the hillside above Wynford and determines to buy it for his beautiful new wife. A year later, the house and a thousand acres around it are his.

Now, see the house transformed by an army of builders and architects, men of vision, with their eyes on the elevation of the mind, the elevation of the soul . . . and Nathaniel in his study, sighing over the cost of so much vision and elevation . . . See all this, my friend, as you gaze upon the mighty remnants of Thornwalk.

When I was a child, it was a magical, myth-making place, a jewellery box of caged lights and stifled songs. I do not know how old I was when I first heard the name of Gilbert, but I was very young. The place and the name have been with me my whole life.

There were always stories in the village. How Mrs Gilbert had been left alone with all those children to look after. How paintings and bits of furniture were disappearing into auction rooms. How Hugo refused to allow the tenants at Wynford to be thrown out, even when they owed six months' rent, even when old Tom Stockley, drunk again, almost burned down the barn.

There was the night Hugo saved a pair of calves from flood water at Inscombe. He had jumped into the stream without a second thought, they said. Like a man possessed. He would rather have died than fail to save those calves.

One summer day, not long after this, there was a game of cricket in front of the house. From the village, you could hear the laughter and the heavy knock of the ball. I was no more than six years old, but I left my garden, crossed the road at the bottom of the valley and made my way up the meadows to peer through the bushes at the edge of the lawn.

From my hiding place, I watched them. The girls in white. The younger boy, Jeremy, stabbing the ground with the cricket bat and scowling. And Hugo, bigger and louder than anyone else, always laughing.

'Not like that, Jeremy! Loosen your grip.'

'I can hold the bloody thing any way I like.'

Jeremy hit the ball, and it sailed away, high into the air.

'See!' said Jeremy, as Hugo and his sisters set off after it.

Down came the ball, to land with a thud on the grass, roll into the bushes and stop at my feet.

'Well, well,' said Hugo, appearing between the leaves, 'what have we here? A spy or a handy outfielder? Come on, then, pick it up. Let's see how well you throw.'

I stayed with them all afternoon, playing cricket and eating cucumber sandwiches.

'He's a natural,' said Hugo, ruffling my hair.

At last, as the sun began to set, I slipped away again, but from then on I would often leave my books and my toys, and climb the hill to Thornwalk, where I haunted the edge of the garden and the woodland, looking for Hugo, and saw and heard many things.

Everyone liked Hugo then. They said he was sound, a good sort. They had high hopes for better days on the estate. But later, with everything that happened, they forgot. They forgot that he had ever helped the Stockleys or saved any calves, and when he got drunk and fell off his stool they laughed at him, and when he fell asleep at the bar they dumped him outside on the paving.

Many times, I found him lying out there, somewhere along the drive, and helped him get up and back to the house. Once, as he went in, he tripped over the boot scraper. I can see it now. I look down at the boot scraper – just a cheap one, very rusty and dirty – and see Hugo in a heap on the floor.

That is not what the hotel people see.

Victorian Gothic, they say, one of the finest examples of its type, a landmark acquisition. Almost unchanged, almost untouched. Perfect for an immersive historic experience . . . But still they plan their saunas, their gyms. I have seen the work of their heavy, heavy hands, and it chills my heart to think of them here.

But we are wasting time.

When they were older, one by one the five of them moved downstairs, to rooms at the back of the house, in the passage that links the East Wing to the chapel. It is called the green corridor, on account of the wallpaper.

If we are to go there, you must accept some risk. The fire caused a good deal of damage and not many years ago one of the skylights fell in.

But this is where they linger. There is a closeness in the air, a cold pressure against the cheeks that speaks of ghosts. The filmy residue of comings and goings, of thinkings and feelings, has given a misty softness to the light. Strong feelings leave strong marks, and fear and anger and disappointment are the strongest of them all, for these are the rusty little buckets in which we store our earthly loves.

Go to the last room on the right-hand side, opposite the archway to the chapel. There is a hole in the floorboards right in front of the door and you will need to skirt around it or leap over it. I leave that to your discretion.

Here it was that Jeremy plotted his better escapes.

It is a meagre room. All his real treasures were being stored elsewhere, in a secret little place, away from the prying eyes of his siblings – I will show you this soon. But that is the bed he slept in, and in which he spent so many long winter days and nights in his fearsome yearly battle with bronchitis.

Picture him there, pale and sweaty, shadowy under the eyes, clutching the edge of a rough woollen camping blanket. And there is Annabel, sitting on a chair beside the bed, reading to him from *The Adventures of Sherlock Holmes*.

Jeremy likes to have Annabel sit with him. She is good at reading aloud, doing all the different voices – and it is horrible to be ill alone, hour after hour – but there is a dreadful 'you and me' look in her eyes that Jeremy can't bear.

'That's enough now, Annabel,' he tells her. 'I think I'll go to sleep.'

That is the same blanket, damp and moth-eaten, tucked up tight around the sagging mattress, but the pillow and the chair have disappeared. Above the bed, the wallpaper is peeling in great sheets, and on the other side of the room the wardrobe doors are hanging on broken hinges and flapping in the wind. Three panes of glass are missing from the windows, as you see, and at night the air shrieks.

Between the windows, a nail has been driven into the wall. This was to display a military training chart: mornings building endurance; afternoons testing speed. When they finally sorted out his paperwork, Jeremy would be ready . . . But more of that later.

Go to the wardrobe. The shelves have collapsed and everything has tumbled to the bottom: survival books, Boy Scout magazines, dozens of pairs of rolled-up army socks – purchased from the Clifton Army Surplus Store with months of scavenged pocket money – tin plates and cups, cartons of dried food, a dirty canvas rucksack and a rolled-up canvas tent, black with mould.

Now and then, Jeremy sets up this tent on the lawn, with his little gas camping stove and a packet of dried soup.

'There's no need for cutlery when you're out in the wild,' he tells his sisters. 'Give me half an hour with a decent twig and I'll have whittled you a spoon.'

The next room on the right was shared by Annabel and Rosalind. Rosalind had the choosing of the decorations, I think – the silver flocked wallpaper, the pink-and-white satin flounces around the dressing table. Hers was the bed on the left, the eiderdown stained with little blobs of face cream and buttered toast. The one on the right, with the line of ancient, squashed teddy bears stuffed between the mattress and the wall, was Annabel's.

Mrs Gilbert's two rooms are opposite. Here she sat and sewed – a frantic stabbing at a poor miserable tapestry that would fall apart before it was finished – and talked to Mrs Miller, the housekeeper, about the state of the garden, and the roof, and the shortage of decent maids who were willing to work for less than the going rate for the privilege of living at Thornwalk. And outside this door, Annabel would listen. The best way, she had discovered, was to lie on the floor with her ear pressed to the tiny crack at the bottom. She was often found like this, asleep on the floor outside one room or another.

Look closely, then, at the carpet outside Mrs Gilbert's door. Is there a slight darkening? A suggestion of a head-shaped, ear-shaped flattening? Perhaps even a residue of ear wax?

It is not a nice habit, you say, this listening at doors. You are thinking badly of poor little Annabel. But she has her reasons.

Go inside. In the first room – Mrs Gilbert's sitting room – in the alcove to the right of the fireplace is a large wooden cabinet. The key is missing, but inside you would find row upon row of tiny, coloured jars, rusted tins and disintegrating cardboard packages, dozens of tonics and oils and syrups, Hugo's digestive pills and Jeremy's chest rub.

A tarnished spoon hangs from one of the door handles. Annabel's lips were the last upon it. They were almost always the last upon it. For years, they forced so many of these things upon her – first various bromide salts, then phenobarbital, which she would take in one form or another for the rest of her life.

Stop for a moment and listen.

'Can't you get her to change out of that dress?' Mrs Gilbert is saying, throwing aside her tapestry. 'It really is indecent now.'

Mrs Miller shakes her head. 'I've put it three times in the rag pile, and she just keeps on taking it out again.'

'Then burn it,' says Mrs Gilbert.

Mrs Miller shrugs.

'And her hair,' groans Mrs Gilbert. 'Surely something can be done about her hair?'

'It's a little late now,' says Mrs Miller. 'You'd have to shave off the lot.'

Mrs Gilbert puts her head in her hands. They come upon her every now and then, these moments when suddenly she sees her middle child.

'You'll have to keep her in the kitchen on Sunday,' she says. 'Give her a prayer book, of course.'

So, on Sunday, Annabel is given a prayer book and put in the kitchen under the care of Mrs Appleford, the cook, and for the next week they are assiduous with her medicine, the tarnished spoon and the cordial.

Annabel holds it in her mouth and glares at them.

'Swallow!' they command, prodding her cheeks, and at last she swallows, opens her mouth to show them and runs from the room with tears in her eyes.

'I should have helped her,' Hugo told me later. He loved Annabel, but there were times, near the end, when it was hard to look at her, knowing what they had done to her, seeing her wandering around, with all that terrible grey hair and the eyes of a child. 'I should have done something.'

'It wasn't your responsibility,' I tried to tell him.

'I was the man of the house,' he said. 'It was my job to protect her, and I did nothing. I did nothing to protect any of them.'

We were standing in the corridor outside Rosalind and Annabel's room, looking at the two empty beds. I remember a doll on the dressing table – naked and with the hair cut off – and a glass dome on the chest of drawers covering a pair of tiny stuffed canaries, but they are gone now.

'You didn't know what was happening,' I said. 'That awful aunt of yours . . .'

'No, Max,' he said. 'You can say that sort of thing if you like. It's kind of you. But in my heart I know the truth. I destroyed them all. I destroyed everything.'

6

Emma's Diaries

The next part of the story takes place on the night of a terrible storm, when the Gilberts woke in darkness, to bolts of electricity and hungry rumblings in the sky.

We shall turn off the light and stand here for a moment in the dark, as they did, and then try to find our way downstairs, like this, with only a little moon-glow through the skylight over the stairs.

Hear the rain against the glass. It is not a pattering of drops but an emptying of buckets.

'What if it falls in?' Mrs Gilbert says, squinting at the cavernous dome above their heads.

'Don't be ridiculous,' says Jeremy. 'It's just rain.'

'I don't mind if it falls in on me!' says Rosalind, dancing out into the middle of the staircase. 'It can if it wants to.'

'Come away, my darling,' says Mrs Gilbert. 'Stay close to the wall.'

In the library, fifteen-year-old Hugo quickly sees to the fire, then crosses the room to close the curtains. He stops there for a moment and looks out at the storm, at the silver cracks of lightning in the sky.

'One, two, three . . .' counts Lydia. 'Ooh, that means it's close, doesn't it, Mother?'

'Of course, it's close,' says Jeremy. He has joined Hugo at the window. 'You can see it right there.'

In the light of the moon and the flashes of lightning, they can see a smudge of white between the trees on the far side of the valley.

'That's Belmont, isn't it?' says Hugo.

'I don't know,' says Jeremy. 'I suppose so.' But he knows very well it is Belmont. He has been there many times – not inside the house but to the thick bushes at the edge of the garden – and its coordinates are marked very carefully on his maps.

Belmont is the home of the Asquills – Lord and Lady Asquill and their two children, Wilfred and Emma. They all remember, many years ago, the first proper afternoon tea they ever attended – the grim woman in the tweed suit, the uncomfortable chairs, the tiny cups and even tinier sandwiches. It was also the last one. No return invitation was offered by Mrs Gilbert – who agonized over it for a week, then forgot about it completely – and the acquaintance, generously offered by Lady Asquill, came to nothing.

Hugo peers into the night. There is something about the light at their windows. It isn't a steady electric glow but the sweep of torches.

'They've lost power too,' he says.

The lightning flashes again, closer this time. Rosalind screams and tries to climb on to their mother's lap, and a tall black shadow, a towering fir tree in the grounds of Belmont House, topples down upon the smudge of those soft white walls.

'Disaster!' cries Hugo. 'Mother, I must go!'

'Go? What do you mean, go?' says Mrs Gilbert. 'Look at the fire. I don't know what's wrong with it. The kindling must be damp again.'

'Jeremy, sort out the fire,' Hugo calls back from the hall. He is already pulling on his coat and boots.

'No chance,' says Jeremy. 'I'm coming with you.'

'Me too,' cries Rosalind, scrambling off their mother's lap and running out into the hall. 'Me too, please!'

Hugo grips his brother's shoulder. 'I'm counting on you to look after the girls,' he says, and dashes out into the storm.

'Oh, for goodness' sake,' says Jeremy. He rubs his shoulder, grabs Rosalind's hand and stalks back into the library, where he sets about fixing the fire.

But Mrs Gilbert is right: something is wrong with the kindling, and the fire is only just getting going when Hugo returns. Mrs Gilbert has fallen asleep, sprawled along the sofa with Rosalind tucked beside her, snoring and dribbling. Lydia is doing her improvement exercises on the stage, while Jeremy, trying to read by candlelight, says, 'If you're going to do that sort of thing, Lydia, can't you get dressed first? Or at least tie your dressing gown properly! . . . Mother, tell Lydia. . . Oh, for goodness' sake.'

And Annabel. . . what is Annabel doing? I don't know. Perhaps she is just warming her hands in front of the struggling fire, watching, listening.

The door opens, and in comes Hugo.

Jeremy stands up. 'Well, I looked after them,' he says. 'It's your turn now.' Then he notices Emma and Wilfred standing behind Hugo, and drops his book with a thud.

'Hello,' says Emma.

It is the first time Annabel has seen the Asquills. She sees a girl of about her own age, with straight, dark hair, a pale serious face and freckles. And a young man, maybe the same age as Hugo but much too tall, with long dangly arms, fine sandy hair and a spotty chin. She thinks they look nice.

Rosalind clambers off the sofa and wipes the dribble from her cheek. She stares at the girl with the dark hair, the wet hat, the ugly coat. Pretty, she thinks, but not as pretty as me. She looks at the young man. How handsome, she thinks. And then, perhaps, Mine.

*

Early next morning, Lady Asquill drives over to Thornwalk to fetch her children.

'It was no trouble at all,' says Mrs Gilbert. 'A pleasure. An absolute delight.'

Lady Asquill is a little stiff. She has not forgotten that her afternoon tea was never returned. Mrs Gilbert, beyond the first weeks when it ought to have taken place, has not given the matter another thought, but Lady Asquill has dwelt on it, stewed on it, made a whole cupboard full of chutney out of it, all these years.

'They can stay, if you like,' says Mrs Gilbert. 'They were going to put on a play, I believe. Hugo does write the funniest plays.'

But Lady Asquill does not wish to impose.

'Oh, you wouldn't be imposing,' says Mrs Gilbert. 'Not at all.'

Somehow, for all Mrs Gilbert's efforts, Lady Asquill cannot be convinced, and Emma and Wilfred are soon being driven away.

'A hero,' says Mrs Gilbert, standing at the library window, watching them go. 'That's what you are, Hugo.'

'I don't know about that,' says Hugo.

'Yes, a hero.' Mrs Gilbert looks quickly around to make sure Jeremy isn't listening. 'Just like your father.'

At the same time, in the sky-blue Austin 7 heading down the drive, Lady Asquill is saying, 'What, their electricity was off all night? Goodness. If I'd known, I wouldn't have let you go. Ours was only off for five minutes. The tree? Oh, nothing much. Just a lot of noise. Just a lot of silly fuss.'

Emma says nothing to that, and Lady Asquill looks at her sideways. 'I suppose you think you're in love now, do you?' she says.

'Oh, Mother!' says Emma.

'He won't do,' says Lady Asquill. 'Absolutely not. I'll tell you that right now.'

'Why not?'

'You'd soon see why not,' says her mother. 'You're too young to be able to tell, so you'd better just take my word for it. In fact, there's something decidedly off with the lot of them. There, that's all I'll say about it.'

They drive on in silence for a moment.

'I don't think there's anything off with them,' says Emma. 'Or, if there is, I don't mind it.'

'I see,' says Lady Asquill. 'That's how it is, is it? The more I tell you to stay away from there, the more you'll want to go. Just like your father. I tell him not to do something, and suddenly that's the only thing he's ever cared for in the world . . .'

Lady Asquill's voice fades to a wasp-like hum as Emma stares out of the window. She is thinking of Hugo, the smell of him, and the feel of his arm under her knees. She was wearing her nightdress and it was all scrunched up at the back.

'I can walk,' she had told him.

'You might have sprained your ankle,' he said.

'I don't think I did.'

'I'll carry you anyway. Just in case.'

Emma keeps her face turned to the window so her mother won't see how red it is.

'Well, I like them,' says Wilfred from the back seat.

Lady Asquill sighs. 'You're a sitting duck,' she says.

Wilfred laughs. 'I have no idea what that means,' he says.

That night, Emma writes the following entry in her diary:

12 February 1930

A tree fell on the house last night. It made a lot of noise and the lights went out, but Father says it's not too bad. The boy Hugo came down from Thornwalk to see if we were hurt, and said he thought Wilfred and I ought to go back up there with him, in case there was a fire or anything like that. It was so dark, I slipped on the grass and he caught me and carried me the rest of the way to the car.

We got to the house and it was all dark except for candles and even colder than here. We went into the library and I met Mrs Gilbert, who was very nice, and Rosalind, the youngest one. And then I saw a boy standing in the corner. 'Oh hello,' I said. I thought I recognized him, and then I remembered he was the boy I saw digging a hole to Australia in the field at the bottom of the valley. I often wondered who he was.

I stayed in one of the old nursery rooms, and when I had got into bed, Rosalind knelt down beside it and stroked my hair, saying, 'Poor baby,' which is strange because I expect I'm quite a bit older than she is. I said, 'I'm fine. It's not that bad,' but she just smiled and said, 'Poor baby.'

Anyway, they seem very nice. Mother says she doesn't think they're up to much and all that sort of thing, but I like them.

The diaries, what remains of them, are to be found in the attic of the West Wing, in the box marked 'E'. I have quoted here the most substantial of her surviving observations about Thornwalk. She is a diarist largely of the 'Tuesday: dentist, fish for dinner' type. Nothing was written from the start of the war right up to 1949, and much of what came afterwards has been cut out with a Stanley knife. Some of the volumes are nothing but the front and back covers, with the letters 'E. G'. on the spine.

7

Dancing Slippers

No, Lady Asquill does not think they are 'up to much', but she is wrong. Mrs Gilbert is perfectly capable of all sorts of things.

'We shall have a party!' she declares, as the Austin 7 retreats down the drive.

'A party?' says Lydia. 'What kind of party?'

'Oh, I don't know. A sort of ball sort of thing. You know, the type of party other people have.'

'Hooray!' says Rosalind. 'A party like other people have.'

Poor Mrs Gilbert. How lightly she throws up the idea. With what weight it falls back upon her head.

'A party?' says Aunt Beatrice, when applied to for help. 'Here? Really, Margaret, what an idea. But still, perhaps it would be something for Lydia.'

Poor Lydia. She has been to London three times, been dressed by Aunt Beatrice and paraded in front of rich men at various social events, but it has come to nothing. Beautiful though she is, there is a sort of washed-out look about her. It puts people off. 'Smile!' Aunt Beatrice says, and Lydia smiles. But that, somehow, is worse.

Yes, thinks Aunt Beatrice now, let her be seen in context.

Distract them with the frame, so to speak. It is an old trick.

And so the party is arranged. A menu is chosen, music organized, transport, accommodation . . .

'Goodness,' says Mrs Gilbert. 'I had no idea. No idea at all.'

Of course, with Aunt Beatrice in charge of the arrangements, her own way must be had regarding Annabel. If she is going to commit her friends to the occasion, a certain standard must be maintained.

'Yes,' says Mrs Gilbert. 'I understand.'

'There can be no repeat of this morning's exhibition,' says Aunt Beatrice. 'We can't have people finding her wandering around half-naked on the drive like some sort of gypsy.'

'That's her favourite nightdress,' says Mrs Gilbert, with a tiny, tentatively hopeful laugh. 'I know it's a little short, but I had no idea she ever went –'

'Has she no shoes, Margaret?'

'Shoes? Oh yes, she does. Somewhere –'

'And I suppose we are to add a soap allergy to the list of her charming ailments and idiosyncrasies?'

'Oh dear,' says Mrs Gilbert. 'I suppose at times –'

'This sort of thing reflects badly on all of us, Margaret,' says Aunt Beatrice, 'but the consequences for poor Lydia and Rosalind could be absolutely devastating. Now, I'm not saying she ought to be put into an institution –'

'Oh, Beatrice!'

'But there must be limits. Whatever standards you may or may not uphold in private, they cannot be allowed to spill over into the wider world.'

So, we come to the day of the party. Lydia and Rosalind are being bathed and perfumed by Mrs Miller. Annabel has been hunted down by Aunt Beatrice and dragged away to the big bedroom at the front of the house. She has been soaked in ammonia and scrubbed with salt, and is now tied to a chair in front of the dressing table.

'Naturally, you are to be allowed to attend,' Aunt Beatrice is saying, 'but it must be understood that if you start to feel unwell . . . you know what I mean by this, Annabel . . . if you start to feel unwell in any way, you are to come up here to Lizzie, who will take care of you. She will have lots of nice food and fun games to play, so you are sure to have a lovely time.'

Annabel scowls at her aunt in the mirror.

Lizzie is Aunt Beatrice's new maid. See them there in Aunt Beatrice's room – the one with the apricot-coloured walls and the walnut four-poster bed – as Lizzie brushes Annabel's hair. She is tugging it so hard, tears are running down Annabel's cheeks and dripping into her lap.

'Goodness,' says Lizzie. 'I've never seen anything like it.'

'Just do the best you can,' says Aunt Beatrice, and leaves them to it.

'Urgh,' says Lizzie, when the door is closed. 'Honestly, Miss Annabel . . .' She puts down the brush, picks out something from Annabel's hair and places it very deliberately on the dressing table in front of them. 'Well, look at that,' she says. 'A squashed leaf . . . or worse.'

Annabel presses her lips together.

Outside in the corridor, someone is calling Annabel's name.

'She's getting dressed, Hugo,' says Aunt Beatrice, who is standing guard.

'She's all right, is she?' Hugo asks.

'Certainly,' says Aunt Beatrice, and Hugo goes downstairs to help Mrs Gilbert.

Actually, that last part isn't true.

I should like to say that Hugo went looking for Annabel. I should like to use a little of that artistic licence I'm supposed to have, but I cannot. I am something of an historian at heart, with an innate and unshakeable reverence for the truth. No, he only wished he had gone.

He had heard the screaming and looked out into the corridor.

But then the sound had stopped, and he had gone back into his room and closed the door. It was another regret. One of the smaller ones, of course, but in later years he started to think of it again.

'Maximus,' he said to me, 'I wish I had a time machine. Not to see the pyramids being built or bet on the Grand National or anything like that, but to go back and tell Annabel that she looked very nice that evening. I could have done that, couldn't I? At the very least, I could have done that.'

And so, the party begins. It is indeed a terrible thing. Where on earth has Aunt Beatrice found these guests?

Jeremy looks at all the old men lined up around the edge of the room and grimaces. 'If this is the kind of party other people have,' he mutters, 'they can keep it.'

But then the music starts, and Emma and Wilfred are here – Emma in dreadful salmon-pink chiffon, Wilfred tugging at his collar and his cuffs. He can never find a suit that fits him properly. Jeremy greets them in the hall, but before he can say anything, apologize for all the old men, Hugo appears. 'Come and dance!' he says, and whisks them both away to the ballroom.

I have not shown you the ballroom yet. Let us go there now. It is the room at the far end of the inner hall. Pull back the sliding doors and step inside. Ignore the puddles under the windows and the mouldy smell of the curtains. Imagine instead a lively quartet in the far-left corner, framed by cascading ferns, a buffet table beside the fireplace, with a punch bowl and glasses, and small things to eat – not too crumbly, not too squishy – arranged artistically on silver platters.

See Jeremy standing in the doorway, watching Hugo and Emma dance. 'What a load of nonsense,' he says.

'Come on, Jeremy! It's easy!' says Hugo, with a wink at Emma.

Jeremy scowls and looks around for Wilfred. But Wilfred has disappeared.

There is Lydia, in a corset, looking very uncomfortable. She has been backed against a wall by a tall man with greasy-looking hair.

'I've got a good mind to go sort him out,' says Jeremy.

'You'll do no such thing,' says Aunt Beatrice, who is keeping a close eye on Jeremy.

Jeremy scowls, stuffs his hands in his pockets and stalks away.

Where is Rosalind in all this? She is standing beside her sister, tugging at the hem of her dress, staring up at the man with the greasy hair. She gets no response. Now, she is skipping off across the dance floor to see Hugo and Emma.

'Off you go,' says Hugo.

Rosalind looks around, and then heads to the morning room, where someone is playing the piano. She is quite good at playing the piano herself. She knows the whole first bit of 'Für Elise'. Perhaps they will let her show them.

Aunt Beatrice turns to Annabel, and looks her slowly up and down. 'You seem a little pale,' she says. 'Perhaps . . .'

Annabel doesn't let her finish, but turns and goes out into the hall. Here, she hesitates. She had meant to go upstairs, not to Lizzie, certainly, but perhaps the attic, but she changes her mind. Instead, she goes outside, to stand on the gravel with all the shiny, moonlit cars. Here and there, people are talking quietly together, but the mist is thickening and, one by one, they drift away into the house.

Annabel wanders down into the garden, between the tree-skeletons and the moon-shadows, and along the yew walk to the back of the house, where the maids and the gardeners are having a ball of their own.

There is Simon Greenway, the new gardener who is lodging with the Coneygars in one of the cottages below the stables. He is wearing a checked shirt, open at the neck, and old corduroy trousers. She watches as he dances with one of the maids, but the mist is almost a light rain now, and soon the maids squeal and run away.

'Hey, come back!' Simon calls after them. 'It's just a bit of mist!' With a sigh, he turns and looks out into the garden. And there is Annabel. He thinks for a moment, then holds out his hand. 'Want to dance?' he says.

And she says, 'Yes.'

She is fourteen years old and thinks he is the most beautiful thing she has ever seen. His hand is rough and warm, and he smells of soap and beer and hay.

Simon looks down into Annabel's eyes, round and dark like a baby cow's, and wonders why people talk about her the way they do.

So they dance, very badly, out on to the terrace, tripping over each other's feet, ignoring the music entirely, it seems.

The mist is falling even more heavily now. 'You won't leave me, will you,' Simon says, 'just because of a bit of mist?'

'No,' she says. 'I won't.'

Before we go, look up at the middle window above the ballroom. It is Aunt Beatrice's bedroom, where Lizzie is waiting for Annabel. Strumming the windowsill with her sharp little nails, thin lips clamped between sharp little teeth, Lizzie peers down at the moonlit garden and watches them.

I shall say no more. But if you feel a tremor of apprehension in your stomach, you will have judged the scene correctly.

Now, leave the ballroom, or Aunt Beatrice's bedroom, or the terrace at the front of the house, wherever you have got to, and go up to the attic, where you will find a box with party written on it in pencil. Inside, you will find a white envelope containing a piece of string and some brown dust. It is the remains of the chain of jasmine flowers Lydia pinned in her hair that night. Beneath the envelope are three pairs of soft white slippers. Annabel's are stained with mud from the yew walk. Lydia's and Rosalind's are full of dark misguided hope.

8

The Empty Linen Presses

Ah, hope. As deadly as fear, in its way.

For instance, take the following scene in the library: a Wednesday afternoon, a little past four, a ransacked tea tray, mangled crusts of egg sandwiches, a small dachshund snuffling under the table for a few sprigs of cress, and Aunt Beatrice and Mrs Gilbert discussing Cooper Coldwell, the man with the greasy hair who glued himself to Lydia at the ball.

'He's obviously taken with her,' Aunt Beatrice is saying. 'It's very promising because the Coldwells have plenty of money.'

In the last months, there have been frequent visits to London, short assignations under the watchful eye of Aunt Beatrice, and things seem to be coming along nicely. An offer of marriage has been almost made and almost accepted, but now there are hints that certain matters must be clarified before things are allowed to progress.

Aunt Beatrice understands. There were, naturally, similar negotiations before her own engagement, and she has never been any the worse for that.

'It's going to take careful managing,' Aunt Beatrice goes on, 'because he's a canny devil, but we'd better get it all done and dusted as soon as we can, because you know what Lydia is like.'

Mrs Gilbert is not quite sure what Aunt Beatrice means by 'what Lydia is like', but she murmurs her assent. Yes, it would certainly be best to get it done and dusted. She is quite exhausted.

Now, let us imagine the first time that Cooper Coldwell comes to the house after the party. We shall have to go into more detail with our description of him, now that we know he is significant: a thin man with a military bearing, well-oiled hair (not greasy, after all, but certainly grey above the ears), tight lips and a well-polished cane. He stops on the gravel outside the front door and looks up at the clocktower.

'Vast and incomparable Thornwalk!' he says. 'Even more impressive an edifice by day.'

'You must be joking,' says Jeremy.

'No, indeed,' says Mr Coldwell. 'Look at those gargoyles.'

Jeremy sighs and wanders away. He will not be seen for at least a week.

There is tea in the library, a quick walk around the garden for Lydia and Mr Coldwell, and then Lydia leads Mrs Miller on a tour of the house, collecting things for her dowry. See her rifling through the linen presses. 'French lace is the best,' she says. 'That's what Cooper says. Do we have any of that?'

Downstairs, Mrs Gilbert, Aunt Beatrice and Mr Coldwell are discussing almost the same thing.

'Is that all?' says Mr Coldwell, tugging at his moustache. 'I really thought you'd do better for her. I was certainly given that impression.'

'Oh dear,' says Mrs Gilbert, wringing her hands.

'Shouldn't all this be hers?' Mr Coldwell gestures vaguely around the room. 'I mean, it's 1931, not 1831. It's very old-fashioned, the way you people do things. It's not as though she wouldn't be able to manage the place, just because she's a woman. I would help.'

'Goodness!' says Mrs Gilbert.

'Well, I can't see how this is going to work out as it is,' he says. 'I'm very fond of Lydia, but I have to be sensible.'

'Sensible?' says Mrs Gilbert. She doesn't understand. What has being sensible got to do with love and marriage?

'Yes, I wish all this had been made more plain at the beginning,' Mr Coldwell says. 'You know, it's not fair play to drape a girl in jewels like that and only find out afterwards that they're borrowed. Not fair play at all. But, of course, she's in love with me now. It'd be a damn shame to have to disappoint her.'

'Oh, goodness!' cries Mrs Gilbert again, digging in her pocket for a handkerchief. 'Poor Lydia.'

'Hush,' says Aunt Beatrice. 'No one is disappointing anyone.' She turns to Mr Coldwell. 'There will be a great deal of money when I die.'

'But that's then, if you'll excuse my being so blunt,' says Mr Coldwell. 'What about now? That's the time I'm chiefly concerned about.'

At last, a deal is struck. Some of the outlying woodland will be sold and the money given to Mr Coldwell as Lydia's dowry. The wedding shall be scheduled as soon as the money is with his solicitor.

Outside on the lawn, Lydia is talking to Rosalind. 'Being twenty years younger, I shall always have the whip hand over him,' she is saying. 'That's what he told me. I shall like having the whip hand. I think it means he will do everything I ask.'

'But he's so old and ugly,' says Rosalind.

'That's the whole point,' says Lydia. 'He's bound to love me more than a better person would, because he will be so very grateful.'

That evening, Lydia looks down at her boxes of English lace and dented silverware. 'It's better to be loved than to love,' she says. 'I realize that now.'

'I'm so glad you're happy, my dear,' says Mrs Gilbert.

Lydia hesitates. There is a flicker of doubt in her eyes as she reaches out and clutches her mother's hands. 'That's right, isn't it, Mother?' she says. 'That *is* right?'

Mrs Gilbert hasn't even heard. She was thinking about her chickens. It is almost feeding time and she hates to disappoint them.

'Oh yes,' she says. 'I'm sure it is.'

Lydia doesn't let go of her mother's hands. 'I suppose anyone can be happy with anyone, can't they?' she says. 'If they try hard enough.'

'I'm sure they can,' says Mrs Gilbert.

'Even if . . . even if at first they don't really like them very much at all?'

'Anything's possible,' says Mrs Gilbert. She remembers a very feisty little bantam of whom she had ended up being extremely fond.

'Thank you, Mother,' says Lydia.

Mrs Gilbert watches her daughter walk slowly away, and feels a rare moment of pride. Parenting is not without its satisfactions, she thinks. Then, with a small sigh, she turns and goes out to the chicken coop.

And there is nothing more to be said about that.

9

The Shadow of the Taxidermied Moose Head

Now, let us turn to Wilfred Asquill, only son of Lord and Lady Asquill of Belmont, rescued with his sister, Emma, that dark and stormy night.

It is from Annabel that I have my description. She spoke of him often in those last years, when she was alone here with Hugo. A sad person, she told me. Quiet. An extra in a war film, sitting in a trench, talking wistfully about going back home to his girl. 'Doomed,' she said. But, of course, that was with hindsight. Who knows what he really looked like without all that history piled on top of him?

After the party, on weekends and holidays when they are home from school, Wilfred and Emma often walk across the valley and up the hill to Thornwalk, where there are games of croquet and badminton on the lawn, and trips out on to the lake in the leaky boat.

One afternoon, the curtains are drawn in the library and they put on their play of the French Revolution, with Hugo as the king, Jeremy as Robespierre, Lydia (still waiting for the sale of the woodland to go through) as the Princesse de Lamballe,

Rosalind as Marie Antoinette and Annabel, standing at the back with a broomstick, representing the savage proletariat *en masse*. She has not been given a speaking part, but she watches carefully and remembers everything.

'Bravo!' cries Wilfred, as the curtain closes, with Marie Antoinette sprawled weeping across the stage. 'I say, bravo!'

'I'm a good actress, aren't I, Mother?' asks Rosalind as they make their way in to dinner.

'Oh, wonderful, my dear,' says Mrs Gilbert. 'Absolutely wonderful!'

After dinner, Hugo, Jeremy and Wilfred retire to the billiard room to smoke cigars.

'Men!' says Mrs Gilbert. 'Let's leave them to it.'

But Rosalind returns a moment later, to listen in the doorway. She is sure they will be talking about her.

'You always make me sound like a complete idiot,' Jeremy is saying. He is fourteen years old, still can't smoke a cigar without choking, and scowls at Hugo, leaning back in his chair puffing away.

'It's nothing to do with my script,' says Hugo. 'It's that costume you insist on wearing. No one looks good in stripy pantaloons, Jeremy!'

'They're historically accurate at least, unlike yours. Honestly, did King Louis the Fifteenth really wear a tennis jacket and flannel trousers?'

'It's King Louis the *Sixteenth* and a *sports* jacket,' says Hugo, 'and he did indeed. But, even if he didn't, there's a lesson for you. Never sacrifice style for authenticity!'

'Oh, I see. That's a great maxim to live by,' says Jeremy.

But Wilfred is smiling.

'Next time, I'll write the script,' says Jeremy.

'Feel free!'

'I'll make you look like an idiot.' It is only an under-the-breath muttering, but Hugo has heard.

'You can try, dear boy!' he says, laughing. 'You can certainly try!'

Rosalind waits, but they don't mention her speech and soon they aren't talking about the play at all.

'A Purdey is seventy-five per cent less likely to jam than any other shotgun,' Hugo says.

'How do you know that?' asks Jeremy.

'Because they're the best guns,' says Hugo.

'But where did you get that number from?'

'It's called a statistic, Jeremy.'

'I know what it's called! But isn't it supposed to have something to do with facts? Why seventy-five?'

'It means it's a lot less likely to happen,' says Hugo.

At that, Rosalind gets up and goes back to bed.

But Rosalind isn't the only one interested in their visitor. As her younger sister saunters away down the corridor, Annabel slips out of the shadows and takes her place in the doorway.

That night, after they have all gone to bed, she will creep up the stairs to the guest bedrooms, let herself into Wilfred's room and stand by his pillow, listening to him breathe. She imagines there is a shallowness in his existence, a weakness in his grip, as of a dangling life on a caterpillar thread, and mourns (though she does not know why) as one would at the sight of a heavy shoe poised above a rare beetle, or a fine blue-green butterfly ambling, humming carelessly, along the brink of extinction.

Even as he plays billiards in the shadow of the taxidermied moose head, amidst the laughter and cigar smoke and the chink of whisky decanters, Annabel feels a great ache of future tears behind her eyes, and a terrible softness in her heart from a great future bruise.

'I think I'd like to go into farming,' Wilfred says. 'I'm happiest when I'm out and about – you know, outside. I'm not so good with people, really, not like Emma.'

You see? Doomed.

10

The High Hedge

Put on your coat. Let us go outside for a walk.

At the top of the drive, pause for a moment and survey the parkland. A herd of fine Devon Ruby cattle once grazed here. I can still see them, shining like conkers in the grass. Others, perhaps, will see nothing but the Great Storm of '87, a dozen mighty oaks toppled and rotting in the thistles, nothing but a number of hours with a chainsaw and a hefty bill. How sad.

Go down the drive, past the turning to the stables and the path to the Blacksmiths' Cottages, where Annabel's one true love, Simon Greenway, lodged with the Coneygars (more of this to come), past the arch to the kitchen garden and on to the south gatehouse. Step through the gate and at last you are on the other side of the hedge.

Have you been aware of a growing odour as you walk, a little niggly queasiness, a skin-cringing of the kind that occurs when one enters a mouldy shed or a rat-infested outhouse (where there are no visible rats, or even a ratty smell, but the body knows that something is not quite right)? In this instance, it is the reek of concrete, and as soon as we are beyond the hedge (which Hugo planted for this reason) you shall see the cause – a bungaloid mass, a sprawl of low, rendered semis in the grounds of what was once Belmont House.

I shall not go into this tragedy. We have enough of our own to contend with. But this story cannot be told without Emma and Wilfred, so let us turn back time, scatter the bungalows, and see instead a fine white Georgian manor, with a wide lawn flanked by flowering shrubberies. It is a lawn for garden parties and picnics, and the envy of the ramshackle Gilberts, who cannot plan ahead, whose idea of a picnic is standing outside with a sandwich.

Stop for a moment here, at the edge of the estate. The monkey-puzzle tree marks the border of the old garden. It is there that Hugo stood and wept, the day the wrecking ball came.

'Why?' he mutters. 'Why? They call it progress. Yes, it seems a logical progression, I suppose, but so is falling in a hole, once you have dug it.'

Now, look back at Thornwalk. See Jeremy in his army socks and khaki shirt and trousers, with the rucksack we found in the bottom of the wardrobe strapped to his back. He has chosen a stick from the woodland behind the stables and is coming down the hill towards Belmont. (There is no great fir hedge then, remember. You can see all the way up to the house.)

He arrives at the gateway, walks a little distance up the drive and paces back and forth, squinting at the ground-floor windows. Then he scowls and marches away through the side gate and into the field behind, where he sees Emma Asquill, Wilfred's sister, with her little dog, Muffin.

Jeremy is not particularly fond of dogs, not small noisy ones anyway, but he makes a show of admiring Muffin.

'I'm off to Drew Hill,' he murmurs, patting the little animal on the head. 'There's an old Roman settlement there and last time I found this,' and he pulls a battered coin out of his pocket.

'How interesting,' Emma says, peering at the coin. She is an ordinary creature, very pleasant, obedient. She is a year older than Jeremy – perhaps, at the moment of this meeting, she is fifteen – and always knows what to say.

'Would you like to come?' he asks.

She considers a moment. 'All right, then,' she says. 'But I'm afraid I can't be long,' and she tells him that they are all off to London that afternoon.

Mention of London cuts Jeremy to the bone, as does mention of any place to which he has never been (at this age, most conversations are agony for him), and for a moment he is silent. Then, with an effort, he regathers his strength. After all, there is no one who knows so much about mushrooms and birds' eggs as he does.

'See this,' he says, dipping suddenly into the earth at their feet and holding out a small, rounded stone.

'What is it?' Emma asks.

'It's a fossil, a seashell, from when this area was under water,' Jeremy says. 'It's called an ammonite.'

'How interesting,' Emma says again.

Jeremy is not used to such pleasantries. He blushes. 'If you like that,' he says, 'you'll love my collection. I've got dozens of them, better ones too, and belemnites.'

They walk on.

Emma says something about the weather.

'It's all right,' says Jeremy. 'But it probably won't last.'

'How are your sisters?' she asks him.

It is another pleasant nothing, but he scowls. 'Dreadful,' he says.

'I hear Lydia's getting married soon,' Emma says. 'Congratulations.'

'It's not congratulations at all,' says Jeremy. 'Not at all.' And he tells her about Mr Cooper Coldwell.

'It's Aunt Beatrice's fault,' he says. 'She only knows old people. He's probably one of her friends.'

'Oh, but Lydia must like him if she's agreed to marry him.'

'No,' says Jeremy grimly, 'I don't think she likes him at all. I think it's only because he's rich.'

'But that's shocking.'

'It is shocking,' agrees Jeremy with a shrug. 'But that's what they're like. Rosalind will be next. I mean, she used to be nice enough – she used to be quite sweet, really – before Aunt Beatrice got her hands on her. Mother does nothing to stop it. They tell her how wonderful she is all the time, even when she's being a complete pain. We have to let her win at hide-and-seek, just to keep her happy. You know, we're actually supposed to pretend we don't see her, when she's standing right in front of us. What good is that going to do? Honestly.' He shakes his head and lapses into silence.

Emma looks at him. He is very handsome, she thinks, with his messy, red-brown hair and his big grey eyes. When he talks about fossils, he is quite charming, but when he talks about his sisters, about his family, there's something dark and sort of empty about him that makes her cold inside.

'I have to get home,' she says.

'I'll walk back with you,' he says.

'But don't you want to go to the Roman settlement?'

'That's all right. I'll go tomorrow.'

They turn and walk back, and for a while neither speaks.

'One day I'll go all the way to Nailsea,' Jeremy says at last. 'I will just keep on walking.'

'And what will you do when you get to Nailsea?' Emma asks.

'I don't know,' he says, but there is a look about him as of plans being made, a look one might see in the eyes of a dog that moments later bites the postman's leg.

Standing at her gate, Jeremy offers Emma the fossil.

'But isn't it part of your collection?' she says.

'I can find another one,' he says. 'Take it if you want it.'

She hesitates. 'Well, thank you,' she says at last, and gingerly picks it up between her gloved fingers.

Carrying her fossil, Emma goes back into the house – see her stepping away across the lawn between Number 8 and Number 9 Belmont Crescent.

And here is Jeremy, lingering at the entrance to the drive, beside these gateposts with their big stone globes. They are much as they were then, no doubt. A few more snails, perhaps, lodged into a few more cracks.

When he goes home half an hour later, he finds that Rosalind is missing.

II

A Small Pile of Mouldy Hay

So, now we must talk a little about Rosalind, the youngest. Stop by the stables for a moment, on your way back to the house.

It was here, in the last stall, that Rosalind slept one night after the death of their father, curled up in a corner beside her little grey pony. Here she would come whenever she was unhappy, and lonely, and needed someone to talk to.

'I love you, Sparklefoot,' she would whisper into its mane. 'We'll be together forever, won't we?'

But that was when she was very young and ponies were almost enough.

Sadly, there is not much of any significance left to show you. Most of the mouldy half-eaten hay and the poo have already been removed. Next, they will repair the stable door. They will take out the broken bits, the bite marks of the long-dead pony, those little sticking-out strands of silver hair, give the whole thing a good polish, and then congratulate themselves on a job well done. It is almost unbearably sad.

Never mind, never mind. Let me see, where are we? The stables. Yes.

Now, it has been some years since the death of Mr Gilbert

and money is running low. One by one, the horses are sold, until only Rosalind's pony is left.

'Not Sparklefoot!' cries Rosalind, throwing herself on the ground and wrapping her arms around her mother's ankles.

'Gracious!' says Mrs Gilbert, who has almost been knocked over.

'I'll die without him,' says Rosalind. 'What else have I in all the world?'

'We shall talk about it in the morning,' says Mrs Gilbert, struggling to withdraw a foot from Rosalind's arms without leaving the shoe behind.

The next morning, they find Rosalind chained to the stable door. She has used Hugo's dressing-gown cord, which is quickly untied – and the door could easily have been opened and the pony removed even with Rosalind still attached to it – but it is enough for Mrs Gilbert to send the trailer away.

'Rosalind, my dearest, be sensible,' says Mrs Gilbert, stroking the sweaty orange curls from her youngest daughter's forehead. 'You never ride.'

'I ride all the time. All the time!' cries Rosalind.

Mrs Gilbert is flummoxed by this. Rosalind has not been near the pony in months. Occasionally, she attempts a tail plait, but it always ends in tears.

'We haven't the money to pay for it,' Mrs Gilbert murmurs, wondering if a few words of base reality might be beneficial.

'Take all my money!' says Rosalind. 'Have it all!'

Again, what can Mrs Gilbert say? Rosalind, as surely she knows, has not a bean in the world.

'Who is to care for it,' Mrs Gilbert tries again, 'now that Adam is gone?'

'I shall! I shall care for it.'

'What, feed it and groom it and clean out the stable?'

'Yes, yes,' cries Rosalind. 'Of course.'

And so it is settled.

'She loves so deeply,' Mrs Gilbert says to Mrs Miller that evening.

Mrs Miller only shakes her head and sighs.

Two weeks later, the topic is raised again.

'Rosalind, my dear, you are feeding and watering the pony?' says Mrs Gilbert.

'I said I would and I am,' says Rosalind. She is ready to be cross. She does not like to be doubted.

'It is only that I heard him whinnying as I passed on my way to the kitchen garden this afternoon.'

'He's so greedy,' says Rosalind.

'He was kicking at the stable door, my dear. You know you must take him out every day for exercise.'

'I do! I do take him out every day.'

'Well, then,' says Mrs Gilbert, 'just so long as you do.'

Mrs Gilbert walks away and Rosalind rolls her eyes.

'I'm sure the intensity of her love has not diminished,' says Mrs Gilbert that evening, 'but there's no denying she can be forgetful. I think perhaps it is too much to expect a child of thirteen to remember to feed a pony *every* day. It was unkind of me to force that kind of promise from her.'

Mrs Gilbert intends to ask Jupiter, the head gardener, to oversee things, subtly, from a distance, but by the morning she has forgotten.

Thankfully, it is not necessary, for the next afternoon the pony is gone. It is Annabel who discovers it, in the garden behind the Blacksmiths' Cottages where Simon Greenway has made it a little shelter under the apple trees.

'It's here if she wants it, Miss Annabel,' Simon says.

But Rosalind doesn't want it. She doesn't even seem to notice.

No, it is years before she thinks of the pony again – one day on location near Bristol, when a white pony is brought on set for a scene, and she stops dead for a moment and says aloud, 'What *did* happen to him? Goodness, where on earth did he go?'

She has that sudden clutched-stomach feeling of some essential, forgotten, undone something. He must be dead, then, she thinks, starved to death in his stable. It is a sickening little burst of reality, and for a moment she hates herself and wishes she were dead too. But just as quickly it is gone.

'Ready, my darling?' says the director.

'Ready!' she says.

But that is much later. For now, see her pacing up and down the library, growling like a tiger.

'Why can't I go to London with Lydia?' she is asking.

'You're too young to go to London,' Mrs Gilbert says again.

'I'm not too young. I'm not too young at all,' Rosalind cries. 'Why does no one believe me?'

When Lydia comes home, Rosalind follows her around the house.

'I need a dowry too!' she cries. 'Where's my dowry?'

On Saturdays, Mr Coldwell is here. See him and Lydia nibbling cucumber sandwiches on a tartan rug at the edge of the lake, with Rosalind under a tree a hundred yards away, weeping into a cupcake.

Lydia and Mr Coldwell go on trips to Bristol, shopping for wonderful things, coming back with boxes and boxes.

'Let me come!' cries Rosalind.

Mr Coldwell laughs lightly and hands her a shilling, which she throws on the floor.

When Mr Coldwell is gone, Rosalind leaps on to the library sofa. 'There's nothing to do!' she cries. 'Nothing to do!'

'Why not read, like Annabel?' says Mrs Gilbert.

Annabel looks up and frowns.

'I hate reading,' says Rosalind.

'Rosalind, don't bounce on the furniture,' says Mrs Gilbert.

'Urgh!' cries Rosalind. She climbs on to the back of the sofa and throws herself out of the window into the flower bed underneath.

*

'It was dreadful, the way she changed,' Hugo said later. He hated to think of it, the sweet little girl who used to write to him at school, ending all her letters with dozens of tiny hearts and kisses, getting smaller and smaller all the way down to the bottom of the page. And then how she was at the end, with no love left in her at all, with it all burned out of her like a used sparkler, which is just a stick.

12

Rosalind's Fashion Magazines

In the corner of one of the library cupboards, the one with the play scripts, is a stack of fashion magazines – *Harper's Bazaar*, *Vanity Fair* and *Vogue*. There were many more, once upon a time, but most of them got burned.

Yes, it was around this time that the cartoons and fairy stories were replaced with different cartoons and fairy stories. If you look inside these magazines, you will see that a number of heads have been cut out of the models and others scratched over with a pen. Large bottoms have been drawn on, and glasses and big noses.

Now, let us see why.

Two days after Rosalind throws herself out of the library window, Wilfred ambles up the hillside from Belmont to pay them a visit. He is whistling innocently and swinging a smart new cane. He has not given the idea much preliminary thought, and there is a pleasant, devil-may-care, spring-day attitude about him. Also, he is growing a moustache and it is coming along nicely. But that is enough about him. It is not his story, after all.

It is a subdued Rosalind who opens the door to him, one with a bandaged wrist and swollen eyes.

'You've hurt your wrist,' Wilfred says. He will have to abandon the whistling, he thinks, which is a shame.

'Yes,' says Rosalind with a sigh. 'I fell off my pony.'

'Oh no, how d . . . dreadful,' Wilfred says. Under duress, the slight stammer of his early childhood returns.

'I think he might have done it on purpose,' says Rosalind darkly.

'Surely n . . . not?' says Wilfred. He looks about for Mrs Gilbert to help challenge this shocking accusation, but Mrs Gilbert is not there.

'Why not?' says Rosalind with a shrug. 'He does it all the time.'

'Then you mustn't ride him,' Wilfred declares. He is not often certain about things, and it is reassuring to fasten on a matter that is quite clear.

'Are you worried about me?' Rosalind asks, looking at him closely with her head on one side.

'I s . . . suppose so,' he says. His big white face is suddenly a little pink.

Rosalind thinks for a moment. 'Let's have a picnic,' she says.

'A picnic?'

'Yes. I'll go inside and get all the food – there's all sorts left over from when that awful Mr Coldwell was here – and you can carry it down to the lake . . . and a blanket for us to sit on . . . and a parasol for me.'

'All right,' Wilfred says. He has not yet spotted the danger and is happy enough to oblige.

'Come along, then,' she says.

And so they have their picnic, down at the edge of the lake. They are just starting on the scones when the rain begins.

'Isn't this glorious?' says Rosalind, spinning her little paper parasol. 'What a beautiful day.'

'Well . . .' says Wilfred.

'Did you hear, my sister Lydia is engaged to be married?' says Rosalind, raising her voice above the sound of the rain.

'Yes, I did,' says Wilfred. 'That's topping news. Good for her. Many congratulations and all that.'

'I don't suppose I shall ever be engaged,' Rosalind says with a sigh.

'Of course, you will!'

'Do you think so? Really?'

'Of course! Why shouldn't you be?'

'Oh, Wilfred. How kind you are.'

'Not at all. Just telling the truth.'

'But you see,' says Rosalind, with another tragic exhalation, 'I'm not as beautiful as Lydia. That makes such a difference.'

'Yes, you are!' says Wilfred, smiling down at her little pink face, with its turned-up nose and halo of orange curls. It is not true, but he is all warmed up now, impressed by the effects of his chivalry.

'Am I? Oh, Wilfred, do you think so, honestly and truthfully?' She throws aside the parasol and clutches his arm. 'Oh, Wilfred.'

It is then that he feels the first twinge of misgiving in his stomach. Something has happened here, he thinks. At some point, somewhere, he has slipped off the straight and narrow.

'I'd better get home,' he says. 'I just popped by to say a quick how-do.'

'But you will come again tomorrow, won't you?' says Rosalind, hanging on his arm all the way up the lawn.

'I'm not sure . . .' says Wilfred, plucking his cane from the umbrella stand.

'Oh, say you will. Oh, please, please do. For me. Promise, Wilfred. Promise!'

Wilfred looks around desperately. What is happening? Where is Hugo? He had come to see Hugo, really, or Jeremy. But they are nowhere to be found. Only Annabel is there, watching sadly from under the stairs.

'Well, I'll s . . . see what I can d . . . do,' Wilfred says, tripping over the doorstep as he backs away.

'Hooray!' says Rosalind.

The next day, see her waiting with her picnic basket and her parasol. The minutes tick by, the hours. The pastries go soft and sweaty. Rosalind's face is stricken and grey.

'He promised,' she whispers.

'He'll come tomorrow, I'm sure,' says Mrs Gilbert, ushering Rosalind inside.

But he does not come tomorrow, or the next day. He does not come for another two weeks, and they are long, long weeks at Thornwalk.

'Where is he? Why doesn't he come?' cries Rosalind each afternoon. 'He said he would. He promised he would. Why do people lie?'

'I'm so sorry,' whispers her mother. 'So sorry.' Yes, people lie, she thinks. They lie and cheat and deceive, and leave others to pick up the pieces. Oh, it is heartbreaking for the young to have to learn such cruel lessons.

'I don't understand,' Rosalind says. 'If he loved me, he would come.'

'There's your answer right there,' says Jeremy. 'Face facts, Rosalind.'

'Hush,' says Mrs Gilbert. 'Of course, he loves you, my darling. You're both so young, that's all. You just have to be patient.'

'It's no wonder she is the way she is,' says Jeremy. 'You don't see the Asquills talking such a load of bloody nonsense. That's why Emma's like Emma and Rosalind's like this.' And he packs up his rucksack and disappears.

Jeremy is right. But it has been going on for years and years – this talking of nonsense – and it is too late to do anything about it now.

'He probably thinks I'm ugly!' Rosalind says.

'No, no, my dear,' says Mrs Gilbert.

'Then why isn't he here? If I were beautiful he would be

here, so you must have lied when you said I was beautiful. I hate you all.'

Hours are spent poring over her fashion magazines.

'Am I as beautiful as this one?' she asks.

'Absolutely,' Mrs Gilbert replies. 'You are to me.'

'Just to you?'

Mrs Gilbert sees the problem. 'No, no,' she says quickly, 'to anyone, I'm sure.'

'Could I be an actress, then?'

'Well, I don't know about that,' says Mrs Gilbert.

'Why not? Why not, if I'm as beautiful as them? You said I was. Was that a lie?'

It is exhausting. Mrs Gilbert's nerves are in tatters. But what is to be done? They have so little family, so few people to go to for help. She almost wishes she had written to her mother, as she promised, and kept up with her old friends, even though they weren't quite the thing. If only she'd known how quickly her husband would be gone, how soon she would be left almost entirely alone.

For three days, Rosalind refuses to eat.

On the fourth day, she is found in the kitchen at midnight, tears running down her cheeks, devouring a whole, cold steak-and-kidney pudding.

'Why doesn't he come?' mutters Mrs Gilbert each evening, pacing up and down her sitting room. 'It's terrible to play with a girl's affections in this way. Shame on him!'

Mrs Miller doesn't look up from her mending. 'Hmm,' she says.

'She's a lovely girl,' says Mrs Gilbert. 'She really has the sweetest temperament, the purest, most open nature.'

'Hmmm,' says Mrs Miller.

'He'd be lucky to have her,' says Mrs Gilbert.

Mrs Miller clears her throat. 'Hmmmm,' she says.

Mrs Gilbert turns to her companion with a scowl. 'I think I shall retire now, Mrs Miller,' she says.

Mrs Miller gathers up her basket and leaves the room, stepping over Annabel, who is asleep in the corridor outside.

It is around this time that Rosalind disappears.

13

The Little Black Address Book

Let me explain how this came about.

Go to the study at the top of the stairs, at the front of the gallery – the one with the tarnished handle, the half-drawn curtains and the desk overlooking the lawn. There is a large map over the fireplace, a bare patch in the middle of the mantelpiece where a model ship may once have stood, and an empty display cabinet behind the desk of the sort that usually houses a collection of war medals.

It is their father's study. That is their father's desk. It is a shrine you are entering.

One by one, they crept here, sat in this chair, ran their fingers over the leather top of this desk. It was dusty even then, because Mrs Gilbert, a long time ago, asked for it to be left, and no one had cleaned it since.

Annabel has been here many times, stealing pens and sheets of paper. And at night, she sits here under the desk.

She likes the night-time. She does not sleep well, not for more than a few hours at a time, and has become comfortable with darkness. If it is cold, she will stay in bed and stare at the ceiling, thinking about things, listening to Rosalind snore. If it is warm, she will leave Rosalind and wander around the house, her bare feet, slightly sticky, *pat, pat, patting* against the floorboards and *pad, pad, padding* against the carpets.

She likes the smell of the house. She knows it so well. She knows the difference between the smell of rosewood and the smell of mahogany, and walnut is different again. She knows old paint and new paint, foreign paint and famous paint. One notices these things in the dark.

By day, the house breathes in, she thinks, and at night it breathes back out. This is the moment that each day leads to, not the other way around. This is the time when things are weighed and absorbed. This is what the daytime is for.

Jeremy haunts the study too, in the dead of night, rifling through the drawers, the diaries and letters, looking for clues, because once, a long time ago, when they were talking about the war, Mrs Gilbert hesitated as she said to Mrs Miller, 'The war took the best of them,' and he saw the look that passed between them.

From then on, Jeremy has tested his mother, saying, 'How proud I am that my father is a war hero,' and, out of the corner of his eye, watched her face redden.

'So you should be, my dear,' she says. 'Absolutely. Yes. Quite right.'

'And you must be proud to be a war widow.'

'As I am,' she says. 'Of course.'

'Where are his medals, I wonder?' asks Jeremy.

Mrs Gilbert searches too long for her answer, and Jeremy's final doubts are dispelled.

'No, Annabel,' he says. 'Mark my words – father isn't dead.' His dreams are full of adventure, of the coincidences and good fortune of Rider Haggard and John Buchan. The truth, somehow, is in these maps, these letters . . . perhaps this half-made ship. One day, he shall bring their father home to them.

'You're such an idiot,' says Lydia.

But Rosalind throws her arms around his neck and kisses him.

Ah, poor Jeremy.

Hugo has read the letters and the diaries too. He knows all about the plans their father had. There is an architect's sketch for a tower on Wynford Hill, like the one Lord Meer has on the other side of Wraxley. Hugo writes down the details in his notebook and swears that he will see it built.

He is making a list of the things he will do when he has money. There are three sections in his notebook: the people he will help, the Christmas presents he will buy for his brother and his sisters and his mother, and the changes he will make at Thornwalk. He will buy back Jessop's Farm, for instance, and the North Wood, and stop them cutting down the trees.

Plan of action, he writes. *1. Make money. 2. Invest the money. 3. Make my father proud*.

He guards their father's memory like the curator of a museum. Whenever he is mentioned, which is almost never, Hugo speaks in a whisper, and frowns until other people do the same. When Jeremy tries to question their mother, Hugo says, 'Hush, Jeremy, can't you see how it upsets her?'

'But it was ages ago,' says Jeremy.

'One never gets over the death of such a man,' says Hugo. 'Never.'

'It's true, Jeremy,' murmurs Mrs Gilbert. 'I would rather not talk about it.'

And Rosalind, it seems, has also been here.

On the morning she disappears, Mrs Gilbert's much-admired red leather travelling bag is found to be missing, as well as all the egg money from the tin in her sock drawer. But that is not all, for the door to their father's study is open, the desk drawer pulled out, and the little black address book gone.

'Why should she take that?' Mrs Gilbert asks. 'I have no idea who's in it. I never knew any of your father's friends.'

Luckily, Jeremy has made a facsimile.

'But who are these people?' says Mrs Gilbert in despair. Poor Mrs Gilbert. She is not sure what has absorbed her all these years, but absorbed she must have been. She realizes suddenly that she knows nothing at all.

I shall not go into the details of that sordid affair. If it is of interest to you, pursue it at your leisure. Now that you know what to look for, the material will not be hard to discover.

Let us only glimpse Rosalind rifling through her father's desk. She finds the book and flicks through it hungrily. What is this? The words 'Terence Aslet – film man' are scrawled somewhere in the margin of the third page. At that, the matter is decided. Armed with an impressive resumé of bit parts in various productions – hadn't she played Marie Antoinette herself in their dark retelling of the French Revolution? – thirteen-year-old Rosalind sets off to find the film man.

Jeremy is quick to point out who is to blame, as Mrs Gilbert, close to collapse, is ushered to her bedroom.

'I said this would happen,' says Jeremy. 'But no one listens to me.'

'What is wrong with them all?' Annabel hears her mother groaning that night. 'I'll have to let Beatrice know. What will she say? After Lydia and that awful Mr Higgins . . .'

'All children run away now and then,' says Mrs Miller, but her tone is not convincing.

'I've done my best,' cries Mrs Gilbert.

'Of course,' says Mrs Miller. 'Absolutely.'

The next morning, Hugo is sent for.

'What are you going to do?' Mrs Gilbert asks him.

'I don't know, Mother,' he says. He is bewildered. It is his first real test, and he senses the possibility that he may fail it.

'Find her, Hugo! Find her!'

If you do go off in search of further details, I shall say here that the newspaper articles are misleading and you must take them with a handful of salt. There was no real suspicion of kidnapping, no ransom demand was ever made, and Rosalind was found unharmed, certainly not murdered.

Yes, the facsimile of the little black address book is given to the police, Rosalind is soon discovered and returned home, and Mrs Gilbert is swift to recover. So long as Rosalind promises never to do it again, her mother is prepared to forgive her, to be amused by it even, and see it as a show of spirit, quite endearing in a way . . .

It is Annabel who is forced to listen, night after night, to 'The Truth'.

'You remember that man at the party?' Rosalind whispers to her sister. 'The man playing the piano? That was him . . . That's what Aunt Beatrice used, you know, to find people for the party. It was our father's address book. I knew it was.'

'Oh,' says Annabel.

'I said I didn't find him,' Rosalind says, 'but I did. One day I will tell you all about it, but for now I've promised to keep it a secret.' There is an odd expression on her face, and she has a new habit of looking over your shoulder, of never quite meeting your eyes. It is all for someone else, you think. This isn't for me at all.

Night after night, Rosalind clutches her stomach. 'I'm pregnant,' she says. 'I'm having a baby.'

'You've probably just eaten too much,' says Annabel.

14

Jeremy's Attic

It is around this time that Jeremy, the second youngest of the five, makes his first significant retreat.

Let me take you back upstairs to the nursery. You will remember I mentioned the rotten skirting and the hole in the floor beneath the washstand where the shrew lived? Look closer. Between the mirror and the left-hand edge of the washstand there is a section of panelling slightly darker than the rest. Touch it. Push it gently to the left. You will see that it moves, revealing a narrow gap behind, a passage between the new Victorian walls their great-grandfather built and the old square farmhouse Thornwalk had been before.

For some time now, Jeremy has busied himself with this discovery, scrabbling along a network of narrow brick tunnels to hidden attic spaces, the largest of which he has turned into his storeroom.

'What is he doing now?' Mrs Gilbert says, standing on the landing outside the green corridor, peering up at Jeremy, who is sawing a hole in the ceiling. 'Jeremy, my dear, not the ceilings.'

Jeremy ignores her.

'I don't know why he does these things,' says Mrs Gilbert. 'I really don't.'

'Boys will have their fun,' says Mrs Miller. But her expression is doubtful.

Jeremy builds shelves in the gable eaves, and each day is seen scurrying up a ladder with boxes and piles of books to add to his collection.

The first time Emma visits after the storm, he invites her to see it.

'I've got all my things up here now,' he tells her, 'where I can keep an eye on them.'

Emma looks around. There are cabinets of narrow drawers marked fossils and coins and insects, and a microscope with a stack of boxes next to it marked botanical slides and biological slides. Along the right- hand side of the room, she sees a series of shallow, glass-topped cases filled with tiny animal skeletons. 'Goodness,' she says.

'That's what they look like on the inside,' says Jeremy. 'So do we, you know. No one thinks about these things except me.'

Emma shivers.

Jeremy turns to his boxes of antlers, but he has only just started on the third when Hugo's head appears at the top of the ladder.

'Jeremy, my dear boy, what is that interesting aroma? I think perhaps one of your carcasses is underboiled! Leave all this, Emma. Come and play croquet instead.'

Jeremy is appalled. They never play croquet. They never do anything, except when there are visitors. It is another pretence, like that ridiculous party, and Lydia and that awful Mr Coldwell.

Unfortunately, things are only going to get worse, as we move swiftly through these long, tedious years of board games, embroideries and restless wanderings around the estate, to 1934, when Rosalind finally turns sixteen and once more Aunt Beatrice comes to the rescue with another terrible old man.

I shall pause here to describe the scene when this is arranged. They are all sitting in the library when a car pulls up outside. That's him,' says Rosalind. She puts down her embroidery and looks at Annabel. 'You don't like him, do you?' she says. 'Nor do I. He's so horrible. But I think he's going to ask me to marry him. Oh, Annabel, what shall I do?'

'Say no,' says Annabel.

'I can't!' Rosalind cries. 'Oh, Annabel, you don't know what it's like to have someone love you so much. It's such a burden, such a responsibility. Only I can make him happy. Poor Mr Simms. Poor ugly fat old man!' Out she runs.

Half an hour later, Mr Simms drives away again, and Rosalind rushes back into the library, her cheeks flushed, her orange hair full of static and standing on end.

'We've had our picnic,' she says, 'and now I'm engaged!'

'You must be crazy,' Jeremy says.

But Rosalind is staunch. 'Anyone can love a young handsome person,' she says. 'But that's not real love. A really loving person can love anyone. I'm like that.'

'What a load of rubbish,' says Jeremy. 'You can't love someone who looks like him. Look at his sweaty nose. Look at his spotty head.'

But it's not the sweaty nose and spotty head that Jeremy most objects to. It's the hungry look in the old man's eyes, the look of the fox that thinks it has the rabbit fooled, and the way he walks behind her, with his hand drifting towards her bottom.

'I think it's disgusting,' says Annabel.

Rosalind's eyes narrow. 'Just because you like servants,' she says. '*That's* disgusting.'

'Ignore her,' says Jeremy. 'You do what you want, Annabel.'

That evening, he drags a camp bed up through the hole to his attic.

'Goodnight, Jeremy,' says Annabel, watching from the landing below as he pulls up the ladder.

'Goodnight,' says Jeremy. The ladder disappears. The hatch shuts with a snap. For a while there is a dull thudding and shuffling above, and then silence.

15

The Sawmill Loft

Jeremy is not the only one who has found a place to hide.

Let us go outside again. This time, take the path up the hill away from the stables, past the chapel and the pet cemetery, towards the dairy. A few hundred yards above the house, turn right on to the narrow track up the hillside.

The building at the top is the sawmill. Go inside – the door is unlocked. See all the old tools, speckled with rust, piled up against the walls, and the circular saw in the bench in the middle. It has not turned for years. But it was here that Simon worked. Those, perhaps, are his gloves. No, perhaps not. They look reasonably new and this was all a long, long time ago.

Look around. Feel free to explore. I have commandeered the table at the back for a small project of my own, but otherwise the room is entirely as it was left.

The sawmill is Annabel's special place. For some time now, she has been visiting the pony in the garden behind the cottages, and following Simon here, where she sits in the doorway with a bread roll or a book, and watches him work.

It is another world, high up between the pines and the rhododendrons. The house below is almost hidden. Now and then, someone will pass along the drive, but no one looks up into the trees.

One day, Annabel climbs the path and finds the sawmill empty. She is about to leave when she hears a tiny shuffling sound in the loft above. She climbs the ladder and sees Simon asleep on the hay. There is a moment of indecision, a teetering on the brink, followed by an act of such miraculous audacity that she marvels at it in the years to come. She creeps up the ladder, lies down next to him, and falls asleep.

It is the same ladder that you see there now, propped against the wall to the left of the saw table. Its rungs are soft and worm-eaten, but climb it if you like. That is the same pile of hay they lay on, there in the room above, shrunken now and almost turned to powder, the same window through which the sunlight fell on to his face, lighting the pores in his nose, the dust in his eyelashes, the little chickenpox scar in his cheek.

A few months later, on a hot summer day, the air filled with the hum of insects and the scent of pine, she finds him there with his shirt off. This time, she puts her head on his chest, and from then on they lie like this.

Over the years, whenever Annabel is in pain, she goes to the sawmill.

'Are you going to lie down soon?' she asks him, standing in the doorway wringing her hands, shifting from one foot to the other. There are days when she aches all over, deep and everywhere.

Simon puts away his work and climbs the ladder.

'Are you going to take off your shirt?' she asks.

So he sits up again and pulls off his shirt, and she tucks herself against his chest and sighs and falls asleep.

Sometimes, if he is busy, he will wait a few minutes after she has fallen asleep, then carefully pull his arm out from under her, cover her up with his jumper and go back to work. And when she wakes, she listens to the whir of the saw and the thud of his gloved hands. The smell of sun-warmed hay and newly cut wood will haunt her all her life. When she is dying, she imagines she is here.

'Simon,' she whispers, 'what are you thinking about?'

He is thinking about his dinner, and what needs to be done in the cottages. He would like to put in a proper bathroom, like they have in the big house.

'Are you thinking about me?' she asks.

So he begins to think about her. He remembers the first time he saw her, one afternoon when he was working in the flower beds at the edge of the lawn.

He remembers the warmth of the sun, the chatter of guests, the vicar and his wife, perhaps, and the elder son home from school – 'No, no, Jeremy, like this. Back straight! Knees bent!'

He sees the girls in their white dresses, running back and forth. And then Annabel, dark hair streaming, both hands outstretched for the ball. She is no more than twenty yards from him when she stops, her eyes roll back in her head and she drops to the ground.

Hugo reaches her first, then Jeremy, then Lydia and Mrs Gilbert.

'The cricket ball hit her on the head,' says Lydia.

'No, something happened before that,' says Jeremy. 'It's that thing she does. I've seen it before.'

'Never mind, Jeremy,' says Mrs Gilbert.

Hugo scoops Annabel up in his arms, and Mrs Gilbert ushers them across the garden and back into the house. 'She'll be fine!' she calls to her guests. 'Just a little bump on the head!'

'It wasn't the ball,' Jeremy says. But the door is closed.

Yes, Simon knows all about it, how they hide her away in the kitchen now when anyone comes, and the terrible medicine they make her take.

'One day, I won't take it,' she tells him, her little hands in fists, 'but then I'll die.'

'Who says you'll die?'

'They all say it. Mother and Aunt Beatrice.'

'I bet you wouldn't. What is it anyway? It just smells like liquorice to me.'

'It isn't liquorice,' she says.

'They don't treat you right,' he says, rubbing her hands, smoothing out the stiff little fingers. 'You should come and live with me.'

She says nothing.

'What about that, then? I can do up the cottage next to the Coneygars. It doesn't need much,' he says, but looking down he sees that she is asleep.

One day, not long after this, Annabel wakes to find the aching in her hands has stopped. She lifts them up in front of her face and scrunches her fingers.

'Simon,' she whispers. 'Wake up.'

The clock chimes the quarter-hour. They have not been asleep more than ten minutes and Simon is not in a hurry to move. He stretches his arms up over his head and yawns.

'What are you thinking about?' Annabel asks, picking up a wisp of hay and beginning to twist it.

Simon shrugs. 'I reckon it's steak-and-kidney pudding for dinner tonight,' he says. He smiles. 'Mrs C's a really good cook. I'll bring some for you tomorrow, if you come.'

The twisted hay is bent downwards into a loop. Annabel reaches for another wisp, thinner this time, twists it and pulls it into a thread, and with this thread the loop is caught to make a little oval head.

Over the months, the wisps of hay become a family of dolls, lined up on one of the rafters. There is a mother and a father and a series of babies that grow smaller and smaller until Simon laughs and says that the last one is not a baby at all but only a tangle of nothing, and throws it back into the hay.

It is the only time she is ever angry with him, and they spend an hour searching through the hay until they find it.

That will do, I think. You get the general idea.

16

A Silver Spoon

Now, let us skip ahead. No, not ahead, but to a moment in the middle of this time. It must be, because Lydia is here, though perhaps she is only visiting, and Rosalind.

Aunt Beatrice is helping to oversee the sale of some land and has come to stay for a few days. Marbles, her chauffeur, is helping to unload the children's gifts from the car. Here is Lydia's. She snatches it up, hovers for a moment in case there is another, then kisses her aunt and hurries into the library. Rosalind grabs hers and tears off the paper right there in the hall. Jeremy's is left in the porch, for whenever he appears. Then Marbles goes back to the car to fetch the last gift. It is Annabel's, and so she is at his elbow when he collapses.

Aunt Beatrice hears the crash and comes out into the hall. She stares at the upturned hat stand, the scattered hats, the body of Marbles, face down, arms outstretched, and then at Annabel.

'What did you do to him?' she says.

It is soon understood that Annabel did nothing. Aunt Beatrice remembers that Marbles had a weak heart and often forgot to take his medication.

'Oh, never mind,' she says to Annabel, and waves her away. Of course, she will always have a lingering suspicion that Annabel killed Marbles, but it hardly matters. He was old, could only ever carry one thing at a time, which was becoming tedious, and she had been wondering for a while now how she was going to get rid of him. When a servant has been in the family for more than fifty years, it is impossible to jettison them without appearing hard. It is perhaps best practice, she considers, to terminate such engagements after around fifteen years, as a precautionary measure, before one starts feeling the pressure of any obligation.

They take their tea in the library as usual, with the body of poor Marbles lying under a woollen travel blanket in the hall.

Aunt Beatrice's expression is very definite. They all understand that this is a test, as things often are. Those with character will not pretend to feel unduly sad. Those with spirit will still be able to enjoy their tea.

'Cake is still cake,' is all Aunt Beatrice says. But they understand.

'Yum,' says Rosalind, her eyes very round and fixed on the door.

'He would have wanted us to go on as normal, wouldn't he, Aunt?' says Lydia. 'Dear Marbles.'

She has misunderstood, thinks Aunt Beatrice, but it is good enough.

Only Annabel says nothing. The moment before Marbles fell, he had patted her on the head, and she still feels it burning in her hair.

The remains of Marbles are swiftly dispatched to the remains of his family, and when next Aunt Beatrice comes there is a young man with her whose name is Randall.

How shall I describe him? Dark tousled hair, a little too long, blue eyes and a boyish grin. No, that is not enough. There is electricity in his eyes, and his smile turns the heart like a pancake flipper.

He hangs around the kitchen. The maids get sore throats from all the giggling they do when he's there. Mrs Appleford bakes him special things, and Aunt Beatrice makes special allowances for him, secretly.

'How's Randall coming along?' Mrs Gilbert asks.

'Dreadful,' says Aunt Beatrice. 'I've never known anyone so undisciplined, so tardy and careless in his dress.' She thinks of how his tie is always hanging loose, his shirt open at the neck, the sleeves rolled up high on his arms . . .

Mrs Gilbert commiserates. It had been a good idea to get someone younger, she says, someone with a bit more energy, but perhaps age comes with some advantages. They all miss poor Marbles.

'Oh yes, I admit that I had high hopes for him, on those grounds,' says Aunt Beatrice with a sigh, reaching for another biscuit, 'but it has been a sore disappointment. I don't know why I put up with him.'

Annabel is sitting in the corner of the room with a book. They have forgotten she is there. She has forgotten she is there.

'Probably because he's so handsome,' she says. It is a mistake – Annabel feels this instantly. Her aunt's hand pauses on its way to the biscuits and all sound stops.

'What did you say?' Aunt Beatrice says.

'Never mind, Beatrice,' murmurs Mrs Gilbert.

Aunt Beatrice's eyes grow small and her lips tighten as she turns to her niece. 'You look unwell, Annabel,' she says. 'I think it's time you went to bed.'

'I feel fine,' says Annabel.

'Bed!' says her aunt.

Annabel runs out of the room, past Randall, who is leaning against the wall outside, laughing.

I shall take you to see the place where he slept. You will need to go back through the servants' hall and out into the courtyard.

In the middle of the storerooms is a door to a flight of stairs, at the top of which is a small flat – one room to the right, as you see, and to the left a sink and WC. It has long since been taken over as another storeroom, but beneath the boxes of old glass lampshades and moth-eaten rugs, and disintegrating binbags full of dirty bedding, you can see the bottom of the old bed-stead he slept on, and there beneath the window the armchair and the rug and the little chipped Chinaman that Mrs Miller gave him to brighten the place up a bit.

Yes, they all love Randall . . . but none more than Lizzie, Aunt Beatrice's lemon-haired, lemon-hearted lady's maid.

Lizzie loves and hates to come to Thornwalk. She loves the distance between the chauffeur's quarters and Aunt Beatrice's room at the front of the house, and that no one is watching to see a light at his window. But she hates to share Randall with the maids and the cook, hates to come into the kitchen to find him telling them jokes that she hasn't heard yet, hates how his eyes pass over her, with no special something in them to tell of all the time they have spent alone together, just the two of them. It doesn't matter how hard she stares at him, they pass over her just the same.

And now, there is something else. She has begun to notice one of the daughters hanging around the kitchen too. The middle child. The odd one. She knows all about Annabel and looks at her with something like disgust, certainly contempt.

There she is now, standing in the doorway to the courtyard, clutching the door-frame, staring at Randall.

How dare she! thinks Lizzie. She fixes Annabel with a steely glare, but Annabel, so insolently, does not notice.

There is some sort of joke under way. Everyone is laughing and looking at Randall. Lizzie smiles inanely until she under-stands. Ah, the little stray cat has been bringing in birds again. Gifts they seem to be, that's what Mrs Appleford thinks, and it always happens when Randall is here.

'Perhaps they're for you,' giggles one of the girls.

'Well, take 'em away, then, please do,' says Mrs Appleford. 'I keep scooping 'em up and chucking 'em out. This morning's are in that bowl there. Take it away, if you will.'

'Now, now,' says Randall, picking up the bowl. 'Don't pretend you didn't mean to add them to the pie! Why not, I say. You'd do wonders with a couple of robins and a blue tit, I'm sure, same as you do with everything else.'

He swirls the bowl, and there is a soft scratching sound of beaks and claws against metal.

One by one, he offers the bowl to the maids, one hand behind his back like a waiter. 'Songbird anyone? Anyone for a small songbird?'

The maids draw back, pressing their hands to their mouths. Lizzie reaches in her hand, saying, 'Don't mind if I do!' before snatching it out again with a squeal.

And then Randall turns to Annabel. He considers her for a moment before holding out the bowl.

'Songbird, Miss Annabel?' he says.

Annabel shakes her head.

'No? Hmm.' He lowers the bowl and slaps at his pockets, before pulling out a spoon. 'Spoon?'

She smiles, but again shakes her head.

'No again? Oh dear. Is there anything I have that you might want?'

It is a long moment, as Annabel stares at Randall. One of those ear-muffled, time-tunnel ones that go on and on in one direction, while everything else in the world goes on in another. The maids sigh, heave themselves off their stools and go about their business. Mrs Appleford demands to see the spoon.

'Ha!' she says. 'I knew it. One of mine.' And she slaps it down on the table. 'I'll thank you to leave my teaspoons be. Now, take your bowl, and your muffins if you want them, and let me get on with my work.'

Randall laughs, snatches up the plate of muffins and saunters away.

As Mrs Appleford disappears into the pantry, Annabel walks through the kitchen into the house, slipping the little silver spoon into the pocket of her dress as she passes.

17

A Button between the Floorboards

Over the months, it goes on in this way. When Aunt Beatrice is here, Annabel haunts the kitchen. When she leaves, Annabel returns to the sawmill.

'Where have you been?' Simon says.

'Busy,' she says. 'Tired.' And she hovers under the opening to the loft until he sighs and climbs the ladder, pulling her up after him.

'My hands hurt,' she says.

He picks up her hands and starts rubbing her fingers.

Day after day it goes on, month after month.

At night, when Aunt Beatrice is away, Annabel sits on the floor under her father's desk, or wanders up and down the passage outside her mother's room.

When Aunt Beatrice is here, she follows Lizzie through the house and into the courtyard and listens at Randall's door.

'Oh, it's you, is it?' she hears him say.

'Of course, it's me,' Lizzie says, half cross, half coy. 'Who else would it be? The cook?'

'Very funny,' he says.

'Or maybe that little runt you seem so fond of,' says Lizzie, more cross than coy.

'She's not a runt,' says Randall.

'She is too. Goodness, isn't she funny, in her little patched-up dress. Someone ought to sort her out.'

Annabel, peering through the keyhole, sees her pacing nonchalantly up and down the little room, brushing the head of the chipped Chinaman with the tips of her well-groomed fingers.

'Why don't you, then?' Randall says.

'Not me! I'm not about to start helping the competition!'

'Oh, hush up and come here.'

She is like one of the little black beetles after all – Annabel, I mean – small and insignificant, skimming a thin layer of existence. The beetles never give a thought to the vast shapes moving in and out of focus in the big world around them. It might be a child chasing a ball, or an exterminator approaching with a can of bug spray, but until the critical moment it is just a scudding cloud in an immense and unfathomable sky. So it is with Annabel. She thinks she is invisible, but, of course, she is not.

'Where have you been?' Simon says. 'With him, I guess?'

'Shh,' Annabel says, burying her face in his shoulder.

'You know he's nothing but a flirt, don't you . . . just a lad,' Simon says. 'He hangs out with all the girls. He's always in the pub. Every night when he's here.'

'No, he's not,' says Annabel.

'Where did you think he would be?' he says. 'Tucked up in bed next to your aunt?'

'That's disgusting!' she says.

'I meant in the room next to your aunt,' says Simon. 'I didn't mean in her bed . . .'

Annabel presses her hands to her ears. 'That's enough,' she says. 'I don't want to hear anything else you have to say.'

Simon sighs and shakes his head.

After a moment, Annabel lowers her hands. 'Will you take off your shirt?' she says.

Simon sits up and tugs at his shirt, and a little button flies off and drops between the floorboards.

'Goodness,' says Mrs Coneygar that evening. 'Another one? Well, I've run out of those ones now, so it'll not match.'

Yes, the button is still there, and there, I think, it ought to remain.

18

The Broken Vent in the Morning-room Wall

Let's go down to the morning room.

It is late spring, 1936, not long after Rosalind's marriage. Two weeks have passed since the previous scene, with Annabel listening at Randall's door. Aunt Beatrice has been gone all that time, and now she is coming back.

Annabel is in the tower bedroom as the car rolls down the drive, pressing her nose against the window, trying to see Randall in the driver's seat. When a moment later she comes downstairs, it is just in time to hear the thud of the library door. She pauses, then crosses the hall to the morning room, closing the door very softly behind her.

Now, perhaps so far you haven't believed my account of Annabel's eavesdropping. What evidence have we besides a possible ear-shaped mark on the carpet outside Mrs Gilbert's sitting room? Perhaps this is not enough to convince you? Well, then, go to the armchair beside the door to the library and look behind it. Pull out the chair, if you must. See two small red-leather volumes, hidden beneath the grandfather clock? *Wuthering Heights*, I think, and *Jane Eyre*. This was Annabel's reading matter for when she was camped out, waiting. Waiting for what? Look to the right, under the marble-topped occasional table. There is a small vent in the wall. Look closely. See how the screws have been removed and badly returned? In the library, on the other side of the wall, the vent has been slipped to the open setting, while, on this side, the whole grille can be smoothly and soundlessly removed in a moment.

See Annabel squeeze behind the chair now and settle herself on the floor with her head close to the vent. If anyone should happen to come in, she will not be seen.

'I warned you,' comes Aunt Beatrice's voice from the other room. 'I made it quite clear that if you didn't do something about it, I would.'

'I have tried, Beatrice,' replies Mrs Gilbert. 'I really have. But she doesn't listen to me. None of them do.'

'You need to be more forceful, Margaret,' says Aunt Beatrice. 'You need to dominate the household. Lead or be led – that is the essence of parenting, just as it is the essence of social design. The strong and virtuous have a duty to impose their will upon the weak and morally defective. It is all part of the greater plan . . .' And she directs her sister-in-law to some literature on the subject – some of which she has penned herself – which Mrs Gilbert ought to read.

In the morning room, Annabel picks up *Wuthering Heights* and begins to flick through the pages. She has heard this sort of thing before.

'Which leads us to the matter in hand,' says Aunt Beatrice. 'You'll be pleased to know that it is all arranged.'

'All arranged?' says Mrs Gilbert. 'Oh no, Beatrice. I never said to make any arrangements.'

'What are you talking about, Margaret?' says Aunt Beatrice. 'Of course, I've made arrangements. That's the logical progression of a good idea. I made enquiries and everyone agreed that it is not only the best course of action but the only one. It's a commonplace procedure in Europe. In such circumstances as these, they wouldn't think twice.'

Annabel puts down her book and shuffles closer to the vent. She can't make any sense of it so far, but something is clearly afoot.

'I envy them,' Aunt Beatrice goes on. 'They are people of conviction, while we are famous the world over for a lazy libertarian prevarication. Our society is sullied with the result – stained and weakened and befouled.'

There is a muffled murmur from Mrs Gilbert. She must have walked away to the other side of the room, the way she does. She will be wringing her hands, with that weak little frown on her forehead. It is a look of appeal, this frown, an invitation to be convinced. When seen on the face of a so-far-innocent would-be accomplice in a crime drama, the viewer has reason to be concerned.

Aunt Beatrice is ready to oblige. There is a creak as she lowers herself into a chair, followed by the clink of a cup. She leans back and prepares to besiege.

'The cook tells me there is a problem with stray cats around the kitchen,' she says.

Though she has not yet identified an angle of attack, Mrs Gilbert knows better than to relax. 'They keep away the rats,' she says slowly.

'One cat is enough for that,' says Aunt Beatrice. 'Or, better still, a small dog. There is no need for twenty.'

'Not twenty. I don't think it's anything like twenty.'

'Lizzie says yes. She has counted them.'

'Oh.'

'And now one of them has had kittens,' says Aunt Beatrice. 'That is another six.'

'I think Rosalind used to feed them,' Mrs Gilbert says. 'She has such a caring –'

'Six, Margaret! Hideously deformed. Jupiter has taken them away to be drowned.'

'How horrible, Beatrice. How horrible,' says Mrs Gilbert.

'But you see my meaning.'

Mrs Gilbert hesitates.

'I should not like to have to spell it out,' says Aunt Beatrice.

In the morning room, Annabel presses her ear to the vent.

'She's not a cat, Beatrice,' Mrs Gilbert says at last. 'She's just a little girl.'

'Not so little any more, Margaret,' replies the aunt. 'It does you no good to pretend not to notice. Never in the whole course of human history has any good come from the not noticing of important things.'

'I don't know, Beatrice,' says Mrs Gilbert. 'I can't get it clear in my mind.'

'Perhaps you are thinking of your obligingly undiscerning gardener?' Aunt Beatrice says. 'Perhaps you think she might simply be swept away into a convenient rustic idyll?'

'Why not, Beatrice?' says Mrs Gilbert, with a last surge of spirit. 'Why shouldn't she have something, like everyone else?'

'Why not?' Aunt Beatrice slaps the arms of her chair, and for a terrible moment it looks as if she may even rise.

Mrs Gilbert retreats. 'I don't know. Perhaps not, then. I don't know.'

'Even if I thought such degradation suitable for my brother's daughter, which I do not,' says Aunt Beatrice, 'I am obliged to tell you that it is simply not an option. It seems she is no longer content with the gardener. She has now been seen coming out of the chauffeur's quarters . . .'

'No!'

'Yes. I have spoken to Randall and naturally he knows nothing about it,' continues Aunt Beatrice. 'So far, it seems she has gone no further than the staircase, but I must point out the implications here –'

'It could be perfectly innocent, Beatrice,' says Mrs Gilbert. 'She is so often awake at night.' But her voice is tired. Her last ramparts are quivering.

'Oh, Margaret, what a fool you are,' says Aunt Beatrice. 'She grows more audacious, more shameless, with each passing day. What next? The village? What do you say to a litter of deformed kittens behind the tavern bar?'

And so the defences are breached. The siege is over. 'Very well,' says Mrs Gilbert, bowing her head. 'When?'

'Today,' says Aunt Beatrice. 'This moment.'

Now turn to see poor Annabel, who has listened to all this without a sound. Lift your hand to her forehead and feel the damp chill of her skin. Her legs are weak, as soft as the bones of one of Jeremy's overboiled skeletons.

So, then, she thinks, here it is at last – the danger she has sensed all these years, unseen but undeniable, like the spores of a certain death-scented fungus that haunts the darkest corners of the woodland. Aunt Beatrice is taking her away to be drowned.

Her next thought is of Simon. He will protect her.

It is a short sprint she manages, out of the morning room, across the hall, along the kitchen corridor and into the courtyard, heading towards the sawmill. She does not get far. Here, at the mouth of the courtyard, Randall catches her, hooking his arm around her middle and lifting her off the ground.

'Calm down, Miss Annabel!' he whispers into her hair.

'Ah, there she is,' says Aunt Beatrice, appearing in the doorway behind. 'Hold tight, Randall, or she will be off into the brambles and we'll never get her out again.'

Somehow, bags have already been packed and in a moment they are flung into the boot of the car.

'Do I hold her or do I drive?' says Randall.

Aunt Beatrice looks at her niece. She sees a wild animal, with an open mouth and bared teeth, damp hair streaked across phlegm-wet cheeks, and shudders.

'Hold her,' she says. 'I'll drive.'

19

The Blacksmiths' Cottages

The exact date of Simon's leaving is unknown. Annabel was never able to talk about it. To the day she died, part of her was convinced he had never left. Either he had never left or he was just about to come back.

Mr and Mrs Coneygar stayed at Thornwalk for many years afterwards, finally leaving in 1962, and their cottage behind the stables has been almost entirely empty ever since.

Let us go and see it. We must take the opportunity while we can. Yes, it is on the hotel people's list as a potential self-catering unit. They have already worked out how much they will be able to charge for it, peak season, as soon as it is equipped with sage-green shutters, bespoke kitchen units and a roll-top bath. They are extensively familiar with such sordid reckonings.

It will not be worth looking at then.

Think of Simon here, working away at the garden in the dusk, with the pony tethered to a wooden post beside him. It has grown a little fat, the pony, and whinnies when he touches its nose. It hasn't bitten anyone in months.

The air is cool and clear. The sun is setting in a way that suns no longer set. Evenings like this, one pictures the sun swinging beneath the earth and up the other side, not sinking into the ground with a thud as it does now.

Look deep beneath the weeds and see a square lawn, a little border to the right-hand side with comfrey and wild white asters. There is a metal trough of herbs outside the front door, raised on piles of bricks to keep it away from the cats.

There are three apple trees in the middle of the lawn, ancient now, thick with lichen and propped on crutches, dropping their fruit, year after year, to rot in the grass. One has died. But they were well loved then, well-tended, and Mrs Coneygar made all sorts of pies and jams and chutneys. The air was sweet with the possibility of such things, not thick and sour and heavy with wasps as it is now.

And the privet hedge. It must be ten feet high now at least, maybe twenty. Numbers are not my strong point. But you can see nothing of the drive, can you, as it weaves down to the south gate and the Bristol Road below? Then, it was much lower, and anything passing on the drive could be spied by Mrs Coneygar as she stood at the kitchen sink, or by someone working in the garden.

So, we return to the car, with Randall and Annabel in the back seat, and Aunt Beatrice driving, gloved hand clawing at the gear stick. What a noise it makes – engine roaring, brakes screeching – as it bounces down the drive. It rounds the corner and Aunt Beatrice sees a pair of estate workers standing by the cottage hedge. Her face reddens, but she keeps her eyes on the road. She knows they will be staring, uncouth rustics that they are, and scowls at Annabel in the mirror.

Annabel sees the men too. One of them is Jupiter. He is facing in their direction but not looking at them yet. The other one has his back to them, but she would recognize him anywhere. His hands are in his pockets, the collar of his checked shirt is sticking up on one side, and there is a piece of hay in his hair.

Turn around, she thinks. Turn around!

But he doesn't turn around.

As the car passes, Annabel scrambles up in her seat and reaches out to knock on the rear window.

'Randall!' calls Aunt Beatrice.

'Hang on there, Miss Annabel,' says Randall. He grips both her wrists and drags her back into her seat.

'Shameless!' cries Aunt Beatrice as the gears scream. 'Absolutely disgusting. I only hope we are not too late.'

20

The Ash in the Kitchen Range

What more is there to say about that? One last thing, I think. Let us stand for a moment in the kitchen. The cold white too-big kitchen with its long wooden table. How it echoes. The traces of a long decline are here – the odd little packets of ready-meals, tinned things, for all the years that followed the leaving of the cook, when the fire in the range went out at last, and the microwave and the rickety little electric cooker took its place. We shall come here again later and I will tell you about these things. We will look closely at the man standing there, struggling to open a packet of dry soup, in his green velvet dressing gown and squashed hedgehog slippers . . .

But leave that for now.

Let us go to the range. Open the door to the fire – the top left-hand door. It glowed night and day then. In the morning, the maids would stoke it up and take out the ash, leaving a little puddle of dust on the floor. During the day it was the fat hot heart of the house, and at night it was a soft relentless pulse, a reassuring little hiccup of life. It was a sad day when it finally went out.

Look down into the opening. You can still see the ashes of the last fire that burned there, of all the fires that ever burned there.

Who knows what tiny precious somethings are lingering in the corners, shrivelled and blackened as they are? Hope, I think. And possibility. A whole yellow brick road to the great unknown.

Annabel was gone for three months.

For most of her life, until almost the end, she said nothing about what had happened to her, but she would often wake in the middle of the night, struggling to breathe. She could feel someone's arm around her waist, she told me, someone's hands gripping her wrists.

See Aunt Beatrice's car pull up at the front of the house and Annabel climb out. For a moment, she doesn't know what to do. She stares at her aunt, standing on the other side of the car. Then she turns and walks away.

'Annabel . . .' says her aunt.

Annabel starts to run, up the path towards the dairy and the little track between the trees to the sawmill. There is Simon, standing at the bench in the middle of the room, frowning at a piece of wood, a saw in his hand and a pencil behind his ear.

'Annabel,' he says. 'Where on earth have you been?'

She doesn't answer, but runs to the ladder and scrambles up.

Simon climbs up after her, and watches as Annabel scoops the little dolls from the rafters and stuffs them into the pockets of her dress.

'Too old for dolls?' he says. He is actually smiling.

She looks at him then, with an expression he doesn't understand. He will think of it often in the years to come, even dream of it, but will never know what it means. When she climbs down the ladder a moment later, she trips on the last two rungs and stumbles away.

She brings them here, the dolls, stuffs them into the fire and watches them burn. All except the littlest one, the little tangle of nothing, which stays wedged in the corner of her pocket with the bits of fluff.

As I say, she never spoke of it, but now and then in later years Hugo would see her sitting on the edge of her attic bed, with a small wooden box open on her lap. It was her own collection, her own little box of treasures, inspired by Lydia's perhaps, but its contents were very different – a splinter of wood from the dining table, a tiny white sock from a chest hidden in the attic (more of these things in a moment), the little tangle of nothing and the silver spoon.

For months after this, she doesn't go near the sawmill, but at last she can bear it no longer. It has been a bad week, a terrible week. Her legs are aching, deep in the bones. She pauses in the lane, then climbs the path, slowly, one step at a time, and stands in the doorway.

He doesn't look at her. He just sighs. The *thud, thud, thud* of his gloved hands goes on without a pause.

'I'm tired,' she says.

So at last he tugs off his gloves and climbs the ladder. He takes off his coat, spreads it out on the hay, lies down and holds out his arm to her.

With a long sigh, she lies down next to him, and settles her head on his chest.

They are silent for a moment. She is almost asleep.

'What about Randall?' he says.

'I don't want to talk about it,' she says.

It is the same the next time. He climbs the ladder and lies down without a word, but doesn't hold out his arm or rub her hands.

She reaches over, lifts his hand and puts it on her head. He leaves it there but doesn't stroke her hair, so at last she shrugs it away.

'What's wrong with your shoulder?' she says, propping herself up on her elbow and prodding him.

'Nothing's wrong with my shoulder,' he says.

'It's the wrong shape today,' she says. She prods it some more, then lies down. But still she can't get comfortable.

'Marry me,' he says.

Annabel is silent for a long while. But at last she says, 'No.'

Outside, the sun is shining, just the same, and the birds are still twittering in the trees, but the sawmill loft has grown cold and quiet.

'Why not?' Simon says. 'Mrs Coneygar says no one is ever really sure until they have a few babies, and then –'

At this, Annabel presses her hands to her ears. 'No!'

Simon leans over, pinches her face and kisses her mouth. She is too tired to fight him, so she closes her eyes and goes dead in his arms, and at that he drops her back on to the hay and rolls away. She waits a few moments before tucking herself against his side again. He hugs her briefly, tightly, then strokes her hair until he thinks she is asleep.

But she isn't asleep. She is still awake when he gently rolls her over and slips his arm out from under her. Still awake as he climbs down the ladder and goes on with his work in the sawmill beneath. She hears the whir of the saw and the clack of the timber, the pad of his gloved hands, and every so often a deep, sad sigh.

It is the last time she goes to the sawmill.

Three months, six months, maybe a year later, Simon comes to see her instead, knocking on the kitchen door and sending one of the maids to fetch her. They stand in the courtyard, just there.

'I'm a simple person,' he tells her. 'Maybe there's something you need me to do or say.'

'No, there's nothing,' she says.

'Maybe I did something wrong.'

'No.'

Annabel's head is bowed, her eyes fixed on the cobbles. He doesn't know, she is thinking. He doesn't know what has happened. She is amazed. Furious. It should be impossible, because the hollow they made inside her has grown so big and so dark, she is sure there is only the hollow, and nothing left of her at all.

Simon stares at her for a long while, but for all the staring he still can't see it.

'I'm thinking of going away,' he says at last. 'Back to my sister's.'

'Go, then.'

'I came to ask you if I should. If you don't want me to go, I won't.'

'I don't care,' she says. 'I don't care what you do.' And with that she runs into the house and slams the door.

The next day, he is gone.

That evening, knowing he is gone, she stands in the courtyard waiting for him to come back. It has started to rain. It is just a little light rain for now, but the sky is dark and it threatens to rain for a long time.

21

The Bump in the Lawn

We will leave Annabel standing in the courtyard and turn our attention to Jeremy. It is 1939, which needs no explanation.

Hugo and Wilfred go to the recruitment office in Clifton together. Hugo is twenty-five years old. Wilfred is twenty-six. They have their posting papers, and then they are gone. Half the men on the estate go with them. Only Jeremy remains.

'A mix-up with the paperwork,' says Mrs Gilbert. 'Nothing to worry about.' But at night Annabel hears her talking to Mrs Miller about the medical examination. 'He never was very strong,' she says. 'Poor Jeremy.'

The next months are hard. When Mrs Gilbert talks about 'our brave boys abroad', Jeremy scowls. When postcards arrive from Hugo, Jeremy leaves the room.

'Just you wait,' he tells Annabel. 'I'm biding my time, honing my skills. You'll see.'

He sets himself drills – marching around the estate, going on manoeuvres – and digs a trench at the bottom of the front lawn.

Let us go there now. Stand for a moment on the south terrace and look down the hill towards the lake. Perhaps you had already wondered about the incongruous contours of the ground? Not much good for croquet now.

He plans his response to dozens of mock invasions, marking hand-drawn maps with red and green lines and pinning them all over his bedroom walls. Over the years, they have fallen down and been swept into the corners like the chicken feathers in the scullery.

See him in his home-made camouflage gear, charging down the hill. 'Attaaaaaack!' he shouts, wielding his grandfather's old sabre.

Mrs Gilbert watches sadly. 'Come in now, darling,' she calls.

Jeremy ignores her. 'Thrust, parry, thrust, parry, thrust.'

Annabel is watching too. It has grown dark and Jeremy is still digging his trench. She goes out and stands on the edge, looking down at him. His face is all smeared with mud, but beneath the mud he looks pale and he has started to cough.

'You've got a cough,' she says.

'No, I don't,' he says. 'It's only a bit of peanut that went down the wrong way.'

'Won't you come in?'

'No.'

The next morning, they find him lying in the bottom of the trench. For a moment, Mrs Gilbert thinks there has been a secret invasion. She looks around for the enemy, but the enemy, if it has been here, must now be in hiding. When she turns Jeremy over, she expects to see a bullet wound. But Jeremy has not been shot by the enemy after all. He is only ill.

Together, Mrs Gilbert and Annabel drag Jeremy back to the house and put him to bed.

The doctor comes every day for the next fortnight. 'His lungs are weak,' the doctor says. 'Very weak.'

'It's just a peanut,' Jeremy murmurs, but they all know it is not.

For a while, it is hit and miss, touch and go. Mrs Gilbert and

Mrs Miller take it in turns to sit beside Jeremy's bed. Mrs Gilbert stares at her youngest son, and realizes that she hardly knows him. Here is another thing that she has not really seen. She has spent all her time knowing Hugo and Rosalind, and there was Jeremy, and now he is about to die.

But Jeremy does not die.

'Out of danger,' the doctor says at last.

'Out of danger?' says Jeremy, with tears in his eyes. 'Just where do they think the danger is?'

22

The Work-basket

A lot more could be said about those years, no doubt, but I shall not say them. If you want that sort of thing, you must go to the library. There are sections all about it in *West Country at War*, *Women at War*, *Heroes of the Home Front*, etc., etc. In some of them there are photographs of Belmont, which was requisitioned as a hospital, with ghostly bandaged men all over the lawn.

Instead, I will take you through the kitchen to the still-room.

I know what you are thinking, but ignore the jam jars for now, if you can. We shall come to them later.

In the wide cupboard to the left of the sink, you will find a wicker work-basket. Take it out. This was the work-basket of Mrs Miller and then of Mrs Gilbert. Lift the lid and look inside. What a mess it is! A huge ball of tangled wool on top, dozens of colours together, mainly brown. That was Mrs Gilbert's contribution.

Yes, it is around this time that they lose Mrs Miller to her family in Portishead and Mrs Gilbert goes on alone.

In 1941, a displaced family from a bombed-out part of Filton lives for some time in the old servants' quarters until they decide to go elsewhere. The house is cold and uncomfortable. They are pretty sure they can do better.

In 1942, a bomb lands in the lake but fails to explode.

'I can't help thinking,' says Mrs Gilbert, 'that it was out of respect for your father that it didn't land on the house.' She thinks this is a very clever thing to say, but she will always remember it and regret it, because it is deliberately dishonest, in a way that most of her other lies haven't been.

'What?' says Jeremy. 'How on earth would that have been managed?'

'I don't know,' says Mrs Gilbert. 'It's just one of those mysterious things, isn't it?'

'Oh, for goodness' sake,' says Jeremy. He packs up his tent and disappears for a month.

At the same time, the main downstairs rooms of the house, including this one, are commandeered as army stores. The rugs are hastily rolled up and put away. If you look beneath them now, you will see that the floorboards are badly scratched.

See poor Mrs Gilbert standing in the middle of all this, wringing her hands. Her face has a desperate look, a wideness in the eyes that does not bode well.

She joins the Clifton Women's League and begins to knit, but her first batch of socks is returned. They have not passed basic quality control, they tell her, and she is advised not to try again, since in all likelihood any further efforts would also need to be returned and the postage would be better spent on the war effort.

Lift up the tangle of wool and you will see a pair of these rejected socks – khaki, a little moth-eaten. The toe parts are too wide and the openings too narrow. One would think that Mrs Gilbert had never seen an actual human foot.

Mrs Appleford is still here, very red in the face, digging in the kitchen garden, doing her best with cabbages and potatoes, and, now and then, there are hampers from Aunt Beatrice's estate in Kent.

I would have brought them in person, writes Aunt Beatrice on the accompanying cards, *but my charitable work leaves me little time for leisure. I wish I could give less of myself sometimes, but from those who have been given much, much is expected.*

'Oh dear, that is a shame, isn't it?' says Mrs Gilbert. 'It would have been lovely to see her.'

Annabel is deeply absorbed in a book and doesn't reply.

The hampers are filled with wonderful things – meats and cheeses and home-made jams and chutneys.

'Oh, Annabel, you must try this ham,' says Mrs Gilbert.

But Annabel isn't hungry.

Most of Annabel's time is spent in the dairy, where only old Jupiter remains to care for a dwindling herd.

She doesn't go near the sawmill.

Afterwards, when it is all over, some of them return and some of them, including Wilfred Asquill, do not. There's not much more to be said about that. And on they go as before.

Hugo's homecoming is something of a disappointment. He walks past their banners and their outstretched arms, goes straight into the library and closes the door, at which point Mrs Gilbert bursts into tears and runs upstairs to her room. That evening, Annabel begins work on a piece of embroidery. It is the front of the house, but back to front, with the chapel on the left and the tower on the right.

After a week alone in the library, Hugo begins walking around the estate with Annabel, very slowly, round and round, past the chapel and through the little pet cemetery. There is a shrapnel wound in his leg and he walks with a limp. 'So much death, Annabel,' he says, looking down at the little pet headstones. 'So much suffering.' He is twenty-nine years old, perhaps thirty, but, what with the limp and all the talk of suffering, he seems like an old man.

Then, at last, it is spring – dogwood flowers and hawthorn leaves, new grass blown shiny by an April wind. The daffodils come up and flower, relentless, oblivious. Never has nature seemed so blind.

It goes on for months, this silence, this walking and staring at graves, until suddenly it stops and Hugo announces that he will be taking over the family business. The manager, who has failed them miserably all these years and is probably guilty of gross misconduct if not actual embezzlement, will be sacked.

Picture the scene: Mrs Gilbert, Hugo, Annabel and Jeremy in the library (Lydia and Rosalind safely married, of course, and somewhere else). Annabel is working on her backwards embroidery. Mrs Gilbert is perched on a stool with this mending basket on the floor beside her and a sock in her lap. Jeremy hovers at the edge of the room, his eyes on a book or the window.

Hugo is standing with one hand resting on the mantelpiece, staring down into the fire. 'All this has got to stop,' he says. 'All this miserable darning of socks and eating of potato soup. I won't stand for it any more. I intend to take over the business.'

Jeremy lowers his book. 'What do you mean, take over the business?'

'Isn't that obvious, brother?' says Hugo. 'When I say take over the business, I mean take over the business. There, it's quite simple when you think about it.'

'What about Mr Tilney?' asks Jeremy.

'Mr Tilney will naturally be leaving.'

'But you've never set foot in the office,' says Jeremy. 'Or the warehouse. You don't know anything about running a business.'

'Am I not my father's son?' demands Hugo.

'What's that got to do with it?' says Jeremy. 'You don't automatically learn –'

'Am I not my father's son?'

Mrs Gilbert is more sensitive to atmosphere than she used to be. She quietly begins rolling up her wool. 'I only do it for relaxation, Hugo,' she murmurs. 'I actually quite enjoy it.'

But the damage has been done. It sickens Hugo to see socks with holes in them. How disgusting it has all become!

'It ends now,' he declares.

'How?' asks Jeremy. 'How do you intend to –'

'It ends now!'

'Oh, Hugo,' says Mrs Gilbert, clutching the sock.

'You can leave it to me, Mother,' Hugo says.

'Leave it to you, Hugo? What, everything?' She is thinking about the sale of the east meadows, and the renovation of Failand Farm, and all that trouble with the man who was hit by a falling tree.

'Yes. Leave it to me,' Hugo says.

'Can I, Hugo?' Mrs Gilbert gazes up at him, a sudden spark in her tear-stained eyes. It is the light of hope. Like sugar water on a Chelsea bun, it quite transforms her. 'Can I really?'

'You don't need to worry any more,' he says.

'Oh, Hugo,' she says again, 'that would be wonderful. It would be wonderful not to worry any more.'

It is at that moment that Annabel begins to cry. Everyone stops what they're doing and stares at her.

'Why are you crying?' asks Hugo. He crosses the room and stands by her chair. He hates to see women cry. It is worse than seeing them darn socks.

Annabel looks up. 'Because Hugo is dead,' she says.

It is a flicker of her old audaciousness, but it doesn't go down well in this instance.

Mrs Gilbert falls off her chair. 'Don't listen to her, Hugo,' she cries. 'She's not well. She doesn't know what she's saying. You're not dead, Hugo. Obviously, you're not dead.'

'I'm here, Annabel,' says Hugo. 'It's all right. I won't be going away again.' But his voice is hard and his hands are clenched.

'You don't have to go away again,' says Annabel, coughing on her tears, wiping her nose with the back of her hand. 'You're already gone.'

23

The Tree Stumps in the North Wood

How well I have managed this, after all. It is almost in order and beginning to form quite a coherent little story. It is better than I had hoped.

Now, come with me to the western edge of the north wood. Do you know what I mean by west? So many people do not. The compass is no longer a fashionable pocket accompaniment and no one studies the stars. But I am something of an adventurer. A little like Jeremy in that regard. It is an instinct with me, a sensitivity if you will. As a child, my success at Blind Man's Bluff was legendary. Later, I was like a homing pigeon. Drop me in the middle of nowhere, I would always find my way back. And when danger threatened those I loved, I could smell it like smoke in the air from the other side of the world.

The western edge is the one nearest the dairy. There is a little copse of Nordmann firs there, from which they would choose their Christmas trees.

It is another place that may soon be lost. Yes, apparently they plan to clear it for a car park. Their justification for this blatant reneging on their promises? That the trees are not native! What fools they are. It is almost funny.

Look down, deep in the grass and the undergrowth, at the ragged stumps. See Hugo's hand upon the axe, upon the saw. See Rosalind clapping her mittened hands. See her little cherry nose and chapped forehead. She is at her best in these moments, before she has time to think. She runs ahead, chooses wildly.

'This one!' she says. 'It has to be this one.' She has fallen in love with it, she says. She loves it the best of them all and her heart will be broken if they don't have it.

'It's Annabel's turn to choose,' says Jeremy. 'Go on, Annabel. You choose.'

'Choose this one, Annabel!' cries Rosalind. 'Choose this one. Don't worry, Norman. She's going to choose you. She won't leave you behind. Norman wants to come home with us, Annabel. I heard him say so.'

'You didn't hear him say so,' says Jeremy, 'because trees can't talk.'

But Hugo says, 'Hush, Jeremy,' and then, 'Well, Annabel?'

Annabel shrugs, and Rosalind claps her hands together again. 'Hooray! Norman is coming home!' And Jeremy sighs and shakes his head at Annabel . . .

It is the same every year.

But what about after the war? Let us see.

Christmas 1946, and here is Aunt Beatrice, paying her last visit to Thornwalk.

Mrs Gilbert, welcoming her sister-in-law into the library, is amazed at the transformation. Gone the great satin-covered bulk. Gone the iron jaw and stony brow. Gone even the formidable, irrepressible appetite, and the customary tea tray sits untouched on the table between them.

Perhaps something terrible happened to her, thinks Mrs Gilbert. Perhaps poor Beatrice was hit by a bomb or trapped in a collapsed building. Or perhaps the rationing has hit her very hard – in the past, she has been used to a great deal of food. But then Mrs Gilbert remembers the cards and the hampers.

'My dear,' says Mrs Gilbert at last, 'aren't you feeling well?'

'Well?' says Aunt Beatrice. 'Certainly, I'm well! I am never ill. Never.' And she reminds Mrs Gilbert that she is one of the chosen ones, blessed with good fortune and sound health as an acknowledgement of her moral superiority and pivotal position in the social progress of mankind.

'Didn't you read my last pamphlet?' Aunt Beatrice says. 'It's all in there.'

'Oh yes,' says Mrs Gilbert. 'Of course.'

'No, it is clearly not illness that afflicts me,' says Aunt Beatrice, leaning back and closing her eyes. 'Clearly not. But I have been worn out. I simply gave too much of myself – mainly to you and the children. No, don't apologize, Margaret. I did so willingly, for my brother's sake, for the sake of our great and noble family. But one is only human. One can only do so much.'

When Aunt Beatrice opens her eyes, she sees Annabel standing in the doorway, watching them. There is a close, knowing look on her face, and for a moment Aunt Beatrice wishes she had never written any pamphlets.

Then Annabel turns and wanders away.

'I shan't come again,' says Aunt Beatrice.

Rosalind is here too, with her husband, the terrible Mr Simms. He stands in the corner of the library, scowling into a small glass of watered-down sherry. Whenever he says anything, Rosalind rolls her eyes. Every time he comes near her, she winces and moves away.

Christmas 1947. Rosalind has left Mr Simms at home with his mother and spends hours in the morning room with Lydia, crying.

'We made a terrible mistake, didn't we, Lydia?' says Rosalind, dabbing at her eyes with the corner of a handkerchief. 'Jeremy was right.'

Lydia frowns. She objects to this assumption that her husband is somehow as bad as Mr Simms. He's two years younger, at least, much less sweaty and, as far as she can tell, considerably richer. She has a big white London town house and a neat little weekend estate outside Warminster, lots of wonderful jewellery and plenty of fine food – always the best of everything. If anything, Rosalind should be jealous.

'There's nothing wrong with Cooper,' Lydia says. 'I'm perfectly happy.'

'Are you? Are you really?' says Rosalind. 'But I suppose it's different for you. Men don't adore you the way they adore me. That's the problem. It's so hard to break their hearts, Lydia, just because of Mr Simms. What if it kills them?'

Lydia scowls. 'Perhaps if you had some children,' she says. 'I'm extremely happy with mine. Everyone says they're incredibly promising.'

'And be trapped with Mr Simms forever?' says Rosalind. 'I'd rather die.'

In the library next door, the two Coldwell babies are making a terrible noise, fighting over an empty cup.

'Nanny, please!' Lydia calls out. 'Isn't it time for another turn around the garden?'

Christmas 1948. Mr Coldwell and Hugo are talking politics. 'There are great opportunities out there,' says Mr Coldwell. 'New ideas –'

'I'm a traditionalist,' says Hugo. 'What we need is for things to go back to how they were before. That's when they were good.'

'That's never going to happen,' says Mr Coldwell. 'We have to forge ahead, make the best of what we've got.'

'The best of what we've got is what we had,' says Hugo.

That afternoon, Jeremy arrives. For months he has been coming and going, unannounced, never staying more than a few days. He is tanned and has the air of the cosmopolitan hobo about him.

He comes into the library and looks around at all the gifts, the toys scattered all over the floor for the little Coldwells, the plates on the side tables and the mantelpiece, covered in bits of cake.

'So the business is doing well?' he says.

'It will succeed,' says Hugo. 'Do not think for a moment that I shall allow it to do otherwise.'

'What does that mean?' says Jeremy. 'Is it doing well or not?'

'What ridiculous questions!' Hugo says. 'Why, Jeremy, why? Have you any intention of helping? No, of course not. You despise all responsibility. You wish me to give in, as you have given in, walk away, shirk, as you have. I will not do it. I shall persevere, and in the end I shall prevail.'

'This isn't some bloody epic poem,' says Jeremy. 'If you're losing money and you keep persevering, things will get worse, not better. That's just common sense. I heard from Mr Tilney –'

'When have you spoken to Mr Tilney?' Hugo says. 'How dare you speak to Mr Tilney! Do you think for a moment that I am interested in what he has to say? He is a saboteur. Yes, a saboteur. Never was a business handed over in a state more ruinous. The mess I was left with! You want the truth, Jeremy? The man is a traitor, an embezzler, a thief, who has as good as starved your mother. If I had any proof of it, I would see him hang. My brother fraternizing with the man who wishes to murder his family! Of all the low-down things you have done, this is the worst.'

At that moment, Mrs Gilbert slips forward, fondling a silk scarf. 'Oh, Hugo, it's so lovely,' she murmurs. There are tears in her eyes, but at the sight of them Hugo grimaces.

She reaches out a trembling hand and strokes his face. 'Just like your father,' she says. 'So kind, so generous, just like your father.'

'It's nothing, Mother.'

'Nothing to you, perhaps. Everything to me.' And with that she slips away again.

'You see?' says Hugo. 'It matters not what I would wish to do. Some of us have responsibilities to fulfil, examples to live up to.'

After dinner, Jeremy tries again.

'If it's all so hopeless, for God's sake get out of it,' he says. 'Do something else.'

'How ridiculous you are! Do something else? Do something else!'

'Would you like to do something else?' persists Jeremy. 'What? What would you like to do? You are free, Hugo. You have a choice.'

'No,' says Hugo. 'It is too late.'

And now, perhaps, I had better say something more of myself, for it was around this time that Hugo and I finally became friends.

They were restless years for Hugo. I can still see him striding around the estate, swiping the air with his walking stick and muttering to himself.

In the evenings, he would often come down the hill to the village pub and sit at the end of the bar with a pint of bitter, his collar turned up against his chin, the brim of his hat pulled down low over his eyes. He imagined he was in disguise, I think, but the villagers would nudge each other and wink.

'Thank you, my good man,' Hugo would say to the barman when he got up to leave. Then he would turn to the villagers. 'Gentlemen,' he would say. They would nod, but, when he stumbled in the doorway, they would laugh.

Many times, I followed him out, and stood at the bottom of the drive as he ambled up the hillside, stopping every so often to smell a flower or gaze at a flock of birds passing overhead.

Once, he fell over on the paving, and then I took him home with me.

I will mention, just briefly, this little village house of mine. It is the last at the end of School Lane, some distance beyond the edge of the village, on the border of the Belmont Estate. A low thatched roof, whitewashed rubble walls and an old yellow door. I will go into more detail later, for it will feature again in this story.

What matters is that, for a while, this house of mine was something of a haven for Hugo. He would sit there, in a green velvet armchair in front of the fire, hour after hour.

Sometimes he spoke of Wilfred, poor Wilfred, lost on the battlefields of Normandy with so many others. Sometimes his schooldays. Never Thornwalk. Never his family or the business. Almost never. Not then.

He was interested in poetry. Few people know that. And art. He planned, on his retirement, to paint, and was envious of my little watercolour set, but, when I tried to make a gift of it, he drew back as though I had offered him a scorpion. There was plenty of time for all that later, he said. Later.

Well, that is probably enough for now, but in the pages to come, whenever Hugo disappears for a moment, between the 'I shall prevail' and the 'Do something else? How ridiculous you are!', you might safely envisage him there with me – in front of the fire, his eyes watering as he stares into the flames, saying, 'Maximus, when did life get so damned hard? When did it all get so heavy?'

Now, where were we? Ah yes, 1949 . . . Hugo in the library at Thornwalk, his hands grasping the vast marble mantelpiece, staring down into the cavernous fireplace beneath. But the fireplace is cold. No one has lit it. No one has brought in any wood. Amongst the stumps at your feet, there is none marked 1949.

'What is wrong with the world?' asks Hugo. 'What fundamental error in its organization is indicated by the fact that a man such as myself, who has devoted his life to his country, to his society, who simply wishes to carve for himself a modicum of success, a rightful reflection of honest worth, must struggle as I must? How can it be that I fought for a world, was prepared to give my life for a world, that is now so mismanaged as to no longer be able to sustain me?' He clenches his fists and there are tears in his eyes. 'Men died for this world. Damned good men. And for what?'

'It's a terrible time,' says Jeremy. 'I was speaking to Mr Fisher down at Home Farm. You know both his sons –'

'How is this relevant to me?' Hugo says.

'I thought we were talking about the way society has changed –'

'How can the trivial miseries of Mr Fisher of Home Farm possibly be of interest to me?'

At this, Jeremy stands up and leaves the room.

'Now he sulks!' says Hugo. 'And yet all I did was ask him to explain the relevance of his observation, if there was one. Is that unreasonable? I ask you all, is that unreasonable? Once more, I am punished. He makes me out to be a tyrant, because he is a fool.'

24

A Tuft of Wool

I must stop here for a moment. There is something else I need you to see.

We will go back a little . . . to 1932, perhaps. No, earlier than that. Hugo has just turned sixteen, so it is 1930, early spring – the middle of April, I think – and there are sheep in the field at the bottom of the valley, mother sheep with their tiny baby lambs, so tiny that the little dangly bits of dead tail are still attached.

It is early morning. Hugo is out walking when he hears a plaintive bleat. He stops. Even at this young age he can perceive that the long, high mew, swiftly repeated, over and over, is a cry of distress.

He comes closer, through the gate to the lower meadows, and soon sees a single lamb running back and forth along the wrong side of the fence.

He hurries to the farmhouse to inform Mr Golledge, the owner of the sheep. There is no answer to his knock. There is no answer to his calling in the courtyard at the back of the house. He looks up into the fields behind, but the horse and cart are nowhere to be seen.

So it is that Hugo must head back to the meadow to rescue the lamb himself. I shall keep my description short, but it is a good hour that he spends there, crossing the strip of woodland behind the field, wading across the channel that runs through the woodland, clambering up the bank on the other side, and then chasing the little lamb up and down along the fence. Now and then, it hurls itself against the wire, but whatever hole it managed to squeeze out of, it cannot find it now to squeeze back in.

At last, Hugo notices that one square of the fence is broken, making it the size of two squares, width wise. Back and forth, Hugo ushers the lamb towards the broken square. Back and forth, back and forth. The lamb rushes past each time.

Hugo is starting to get sweaty. He takes off his coat. Somehow, he must get the lamb to stop in front of the gap. He begins dragging dead branches out of the woodland and propping them in the fence, just after the gap. His plan is that the lamb will run along the fence, meet this barricade, stop to think for a moment, notice the gap and (seeing Hugo hovering in its peripheral vision) try to squeeze out through it.

'It's not going to work,' says a voice.

Hugo looks up to see Jeremy clambering up the bank of the stream.

'I can't think of anything else,' Hugo says.

'Right. Well, let's give it a go,' says Jeremy.

So Jeremy herds the lamb, with Hugo standing by, just in front of the gap, ready to usher it through.

Here comes the lamb . . . racing along the fence . . . and slipping between the branches of the barricade.

They rebuild the barricade, thicker this time.

Here comes the lamb . . . bouncing along the fence . . . and swerving around the barricade.

They are just rebuilding the barricade again, longer this time, when the lamb hurls itself so hard at the fence that its head gets stuck.

It doesn't take long to extract the lamb and drop it back into the field.

'We're a pretty good team,' says Hugo, as they watch the lamb go racing away to find its mother.

'Not bad,' says Jeremy.

Hugo lays his hand on Jeremy's shoulder. 'A bit of a hero there,' he says.

'Ha!' says Jeremy. 'You too.'

'Number 39,' says Hugo, peering after the lamb at the painted number on its side. He plucks a little tuft of wool out of the fence and puts it in his pocket, and they make their way back up to the house, with Hugo's arm around his brother's shoulders.

There.

I should have put that bit first, before Hugo said, 'He makes me out to be a tyrant, because he is a fool.' But you can see what has happened.

Sadly, it is only the beginning.

As for the tuft of wool, it can be found at the back of the top drawer of Hugo's bedside cabinet. It still smells of an April morning and a tiny lost lamb.

25

The Film Reels

Now we can move on.

In the previous scene (the one before the sheep, I mean), we glimpsed Rosalind in the morning room with Lydia. Let us go back there now and linger awhile. See her prostrate upon the velvet chaise longue. She is an expert at reclining in this manner, one arm flung back. Her hair has been pulled straight and rolled up. Her face is narrow and doll-like, well-powdered, with shiny red lips that all these tears somehow do not disturb.

Under the name Rosie Sparke, she was a familiar face in the war. With Mr Simms trailing along behind, dipping his hand frequently into his pocket, she toured the posting stations. She charmed them all, threw extravagant parties for everyone she met, and eventually found her way into the movies. Not Hollywood, of course, just the little British studios with their cheap romances and gaslight thrillers.

She sent them to Hugo, every one. You will find them in the attic, in the box marked 'R'.

She sent him a projector too, and a screen for him to watch them on, both of which you will also find in that room. Feel free to have a look. You might set up the screen in the library, if you are curious.

Start with the one titled *Death by Desire*. That was her first part. No, she is not the statuesque blonde on the train. To see Rosalind, you will have to wait until halfway through, when the blonde is at the café with the murderer. A woman in a fur coat walks past. That is Rosalind. It is in black and white, which you will not be used to, and the quality is poor, but it is unmistakably her. See, just before she exits the screen, how she glances to the side, almost into the camera. What strange expression is this? Pause it, if you can. Examine and remember . . . But it was not a good film, and it has not kept well. If it starts to flicker, do not persevere with it.

Watch them all, if you like. Or, if you have had enough of such things – they are none of them masterpieces – skip to the one marked *Castle of Death*. It was her only starring role, and you will see from the box that not many came after it. The industry was cruel to her, as it has been cruel to so many others. It heaved her up and flung her down.

Jeremy is quick to diagnose the problem.

Her eyes are too close together, he says. Her teeth are too small. There is a suggestion of the rodent about her, every time she opens her mouth. She does not trust her beauty as Phyllis Calvert does. She cannot afford to be 'natural' and that is her downfall.

But it was enough to live on for a number of years. Psychologically, I mean.

In the spring of 1949, around the time of *Murder by Madness* (three canisters to the left of *Castle of Death*), Rosalind leaves Mr Simms, who arrives at Thornwalk one afternoon not long afterwards, his hat in his hands.

He tells Hugo that he is almost bankrupt. Rosalind has spent all his money on clothes and screen tests. He had to pay to get her those first parts, he tells Hugo. He had to pay through the nose. What does Hugo have to say about that?

Hugo has nothing to say about that.

'She's been seen out with a man called Terence Aslet,' Mr Simms says. 'And there's talk that she knew him already.' He wants to know if they had been carrying on before the wedding. If so, Rosalind was sold to him under false pretences and he wants his money back.

'She's not a box of biscuits,' says Hugo. He looks at Mr Simms's sweaty nose and spotty head, and remembers the eager eyes and the hovering hand. 'Besides,' he says, 'I think you got more than you paid for.'

26

The Scrapbook

Now, we must move ahead a little. Time is ticking on and there is much more to say.

For this, you will need to go to Hugo's study, beside the morning room.

He spent a great deal of time in this room, in the early years, engaged in matters of business. Hence, the two large metal filing cabinets, much dented. Hence the rather dishevelled look of the place, though Annabel did a reasonable job hiding most of the damage to the walls.

In later years, he took it upon himself to alert various food manufacturers to shortcomings in the quality of their products. Once, Annabel found him asleep here, the desk scattered with envelopes addressed to Cadbury, Warburtons and Heinz. The unfinished letter beneath his arm was addressed to Mr Kellogg, informing him of a piece of plastic found in his cornflakes that morning and his decision to notify health and safety.

But that is not for some time yet.

In the bottom-right-hand drawer of the desk you will find a dried-up Pritt Stick and a faded scrapbook. Open the scrapbook carefully, because some of the sheets are loose.

The woman in the pictures is Emma Asquill. She went on to mix in the highest circles, socially I mean, and was often featured in the society pages of newspapers and magazines. She was something of a philanthropist, founded a charity for victims of domestic abuse in Zimbabwe, and was even slightly political for a while, until she realized it was hopeless. Anyway, articles were written about her, and Hugo would find them, cut them out and put them in his book.

Of course, all these photographs were taken after Emma left Thornwalk, so in this next scene you will have to imagine a younger face. There was not always that hardness about the lips, that haunted look in the eyes that you see here.

See her fairly young and confident instead – thirty-four or -five, I think – her hair in a neat, unfashionable little bob, stepping out of a taxi in front of the house. It is perhaps 1950.

Mrs Gilbert almost weeps at the sight of her. It is wonderful to think about the past, when things were good, instead of thinking about now, when they are so awful.

'Has it been very difficult?' asks Emma.

'Dreadful,' says Mrs Gilbert. 'I can't tell you how dreadful.' She has forgotten about poor Wilfred. She doesn't ask how it has been for Emma.

They go to fetch Hugo from his study, where he is sitting at his desk, staring at a pile of papers.

'You'll never guess who's here,' says Mrs Gilbert.

'Neither do I imagine I will ever care,' says Hugo.

'Oh, Hugo, how funny you are,' says Mrs Gilbert. 'It's Emma. Emma Asquill.'

A moment later, Hugo appears at the study door.

There is something about the way Emma looks at him. Even Hugo can see it. He suddenly remembers the games of croquet, the games of badminton, the little trips out on the lake in the leaky boat.

'Emma,' he says.

'Hello, Hugo,' she says.

Mrs Gilbert looks at Emma, and then back at Hugo. 'How wonderful,' she says. 'How wonderful for us all to be together again.'

'I came to see Belmont one last time,' Emma tells them, sipping tea a few minutes later in the library. She glances towards the window, and then quickly away again. 'They're going to sell it.'

'Oh, how awful,' says Mrs Gilbert. 'Everything is so expensive now, isn't it? No one can afford to keep on a place like this. Not really. It's just dreadful.'

'It's not that,' says Emma. 'Father's terribly clever about money so we've come out of it pretty well. No, they just can't bear to be there. To think about Wilfred.'

Mrs Gilbert remembers Wilfred and blushes. 'Oh yes,' she says. 'Yes, of course.'

'But I hate London,' continues Emma. 'Besides, I want to think of him, and that's where I remember him. And here.' She looks around the room, and at Hugo, standing in front of the fire, one hand on the mantelpiece. His face is heavier, she thinks. His eyes are red and damp-looking, as though he's just been crying.

'Stay, then,' says Hugo. 'Stay as long as you like.'

27

The Library Request Slip

Pause for a moment in Hugo's study. Put back the scrapbook and open the middle drawer. You will find a bundle of post-cards held together by an ancient rubber band. They are all from Jeremy.

At around this time, he begins the first of his great disap-pearances, ones where he is gone for months and months. He sends home postcards from all over the world, with a few hasty words scribbled on the back: *View of the Matterhorn over Lake Stellisee, quite magnificent . . . The Lauterbrunnen Valley, exceptional in May . . . The medieval church of Santa Maddalena – I stayed in a small pensione just to the left of the picture . . .*

At Christmas and birthdays, sometimes a package will arrive containing wonderful things wrapped in layers of fluffy tissue paper: hand-painted wooden toys, a tiny tin music box playing Mozart's Minuet in F major, a stack of leather-bound note-books for Annabel. *Will these do?* he writes. *You didn't specify a size.*

But of Jeremy himself there is almost nothing. Now and then, there will be a clatter of boots and bags in the hall, and the ladder to his attic space will come down. For a few hours, there will be footsteps back and forth across the gallery, up and down the ladder, but the next morning, before anyone else is up, he will be gone again.

Under the postcards is a little pink piece of paper. It is a library request slip. See, Hugo has filled it in. He was going to request a book, a travel work by Wilson J. Wilberforce: *Me and My Penknife: A Whittling Journey*.

I have never seen this book, but there are still some copies in libraries, I believe. Probably in the archives. Most likely you will not have heard of it before, or its author, Mr Wilberforce. His work is not fashionable now. Even with the tragedy of his demise, most people do not know about him. A tragic demise is not sufficient to retain interest these days. There are too many of them around. To retain interest now, one must die a thousand deaths. One must be tragic each week, on demand, in entertaining new ways, like an episode of a cheap soap opera.

But this was the age when hard work, intelligence, sensitivity and talent were enough. Critics at the time observed his ironic style. There is no sentiment in it. That was once admired. These days, we want emotion. We want cameramen to stand weeping in front of orphans. Jeremy (you will have guessed that Wilson J. Wilberforce is one of the pen names of Jeremy Gilbert) would not have been able to do this. He would have thought it was stupid.

Now, let us picture his next homecoming. It is six months after the return of Emma Asquill – the spring of 1951. There is a familiar thud in the hall as a rucksack hits the Minton tiles, then a few moments of silence as Jeremy pauses to take off his boots. In the midst of this, the library door opens, and Jeremy looks up to see Emma standing in the doorway.

'Emma!' he says, dropping his boot. 'What on earth are you doing here?'

Hugo appears behind her. 'We sent you an invitation, Jeremy,' he says, 'to the last address we had for you. It was a great disappointment to us all that you chose not to attend.'

'An invitation?' says Jeremy. 'To what?'

Hugo's face reddens. 'Our wedding, of course.'

Jeremy looks from Hugo to Emma, and back again. 'You're joking,' he says.

It is a subdued tea they give him. There is a strong odour of dismay in the room.

Then it is time for the afternoon walk. Annabel goes on ahead with Emma, while Jeremy walks behind with Hugo.

'Listen, Hugo,' says Jeremy, 'about all this –'

'I shall provide for her,' Hugo says. 'You needn't worry about that. I shall make this a palace for her. Together we shall produce an heir and resurrect our fortunes. And so shall my duty be satisfied.'

Jeremy shakes his head. It is too much. He doesn't know where to begin. 'But you don't love her,' he says.

'What gives you that impression?' says Hugo. His eyes are wide and hard. 'Just because this isn't the sort of wild oat-sowing you indulge in. There are deeper loves than that, Jeremy. Substantially superior loves.'

Jeremy sighs. 'I don't know what you're talking about,' he says.

'No? That doesn't surprise me in the least.'

Hugo strides ahead, with Emma clinging to his hand, and Jeremy is left with Annabel.

'What on earth is going on here?' Jeremy says.

'Didn't you know about it?' says Annabel. 'It was three months ago. He did send a letter. He did try to find you.'

'I've been away,' Jeremy says.

'Where?'

But Jeremy doesn't answer. 'Is that love?' he asks instead. 'Is that what love looks like to you?'

'I think so,' says Annabel, looking ahead. Emma has slipped on a tree root and Hugo is trying to scrub the mud from her skirt with a paper handkerchief. 'I think they do love each other.'

But Jeremy shakes his head. 'This will end in disaster,' he says. 'People are ridiculous. Honestly, I can't bear it.'

28

Coldwell's Cane

After the wedding, counter to Jeremy's predictions, there is a rare period of calm at Thornwalk, and Mrs Gilbert thinks that perhaps this is what people call happiness.

She wakes one morning in early June to find the sun shining, the birds singing. Yes, surely, happiness. There is only one small thing spoiling it all – a letter from Dr Lennox, asking if there has been any change in Annabel's condition.

At breakfast, Mrs Gilbert looks across the table at her daughter. Change? Well, no, there is never really any change. There is the same dull, faraway look on Annabel's face that has been there for years . . . the same look Mrs Gilbert used to see on the faces of her beloved chickens, before she set them free.

Mrs Gilberts shifts uneasily on her chair. She feels her happiness wavering.

After breakfast, Mrs Gilbert goes out to feed the chickens. This now consists of throwing toast crumbs and potato peelings around at the bottom of the garden. It is much less trouble than going to the coop had been, with all that opening and closing of doors. There is much less smell too.

She begins to toss the breadcrumbs, and three French Marans

and a pair of Dorkings skitter out of the bushes. Ah, there are Fatty and Spotty, notes Mrs Gilbert happily, but where is Mrs Pecky? Surely that is three days now she hasn't seen her beautiful little Barnevelder. She is probably in a tree somewhere. Or perhaps she has joined Gertrude and Edwina in whatever golden cornfield they have discovered. What adventures there were to be had by spirited and enterprising poultry!

She thinks again of Annabel.

Perhaps . . . perhaps she didn't need the medicine any more. How was Mrs Gilbert to know? Certainly, there hadn't been as many unfortunate episodes recently. Not that she had noticed. Perhaps they ought to stop the medicine and see . . . But what if it made things worse? What if Annabel suddenly got upset and refused to take it ever again? She was very peaceful now, no trouble at all.

Feathers are scattered everywhere under the trees. Mrs Gilbert picks one up and absent-mindedly strokes her face with it as she continues to think. Generally speaking, she thinks, chickens ought to be free . . . but, then again, after all, Annabel wasn't a chicken.

Mrs Gilbert sighs and goes inside, where she sits down at her bureau and writes to Dr Lennox: *No change. Please send box of the same.*

In this time of happiness, Lydia and Mr Coldwell are often at Thornwalk. Mr Coldwell is hoping that Emma will invest in a new business venture he's planning.

'She's just what your family needs,' he tells Lydia. 'A bit of sense.' But, of course, he means money.

Lydia and Mr Coldwell have two children, whom we have already briefly glimpsed. Two sons.

I have been fortunate enough to make their closer acquaintance. Yes, one night about a month ago, they came here, letting themselves into the servants' hall and scouring the place for the last little bits and pieces that Lydia might have overlooked in her lifelong campaign of thievery.

The things they took! They were not interested in Jeremy's collection of fossilized shark teeth, or Annabel's pens, only silver spoons and nasty gold clocks that can be bought at any jeweller's in Paris.

The hotel people are just as bad, obsessed as they are with the roof.

'Three million pounds!' they cry. 'Just the roof. We'd never have taken it on if we'd known!'

There is no romance in any of them. No heart.

But enough of that.

It is after the wedding, then. The boys are small, only just exhibiting those inexplicable traits for which they will become so well known in the family: Cooper Junior's overeating (Mrs Appleford has nothing but contempt for a child who cannot wait an hour for a good dinner, but instead steals half a round of cheese and eats the lot squatting in the coal store). And Sydney's habit of referring to himself cryptically in the third person: 'Someone is feeling sad. Someone has done something bad for which he is now feeling ashamed.'

Lydia has grown large. Determinedly large. Superficially, one might diagnose in both Lydia and Mr Coldwell a certain bigness of self that demands physical expression. He wears a hat and swings a cane. She eats. But there is more to it than that.

'Do you remember the first time you came here?' Lydia asks Mr Coldwell, as they drive away from one of these visits. She has had a good lunch, the sun is shining, and she is feeling nostalgic, almost as though she might reach over and put her hand on his knee.

'I do indeed,' says Mr Coldwell. 'Things haven't worked out quite as I'd hoped, but that's not your fault.'

Lydia's hand stays where it is. There is a hollow feeling in her stomach, despite the good lunch, and she suddenly feels very alone.

Turning in her seat, Lydia looks at her two sons. Cooper Junior is frowning at a pair of tin soldiers, muttering a savage battle scene under his breath, from which only the words 'damn' and 'bloody' are audible. Sydney is drifting off to sleep, clutching a dreadful little shred of his favourite blanket.

'Mummy . . . Mummy loves you,' Lydia says.

Sydney blinks. 'Does she?' he says.

'Well, of course,' says Lydia. 'Of course, she does.'

'Yay,' says Cooper Junior, not looking up from his soldiers. 'Does that mean we'll go somewhere nice for tea when we get back?'

Lydia sighs. 'I suppose so,' she says. 'Yes, why not.'

Unfortunately, the peace and happiness do not last long, for someone else has also started visiting Thornwalk more often. Things are not going well for Rosalind. She has discovered that Terence Aslet is a bad man. A violent man. There are stories in the newspapers – the usual noisy public scene between the movie star and the film director – until one day she is found unconscious on the altar steps of a West End church.

'Have you any idea of the identity of the attacker?' the police ask.

'I didn't see him clearly,' she says, 'but moments before it happened there was a familiar smell in the air. I had a familiar feeling.'

They are quick to pick up the crumbs. 'You think you knew your attacker?'

'I wonder if I did know him. Perhaps I knew him very well.'

The newspapers are happy to make suggestions. Terence Aslet gets ready to sue. Then the next day there are pictures of them together on a cruise ship . . .

But now it seems it is finally over.

'He has hurt me once too often,' Rosalind says, sprawled face down on the hall floor. 'He has destroyed me one too many times.'

Yes, Rosalind often comes back to Thornwalk now, to be comforted by Emma. She is so good at it, Emma I mean. She never gets angry. Never contradicts anything.

'I only ever loved one person,' Rosalind says. 'Only one person really and truly. Oh, Wilfred, why did you have to die and leave me?'

Emma listens in silence, a little crease on her forehead.

'Yes,' says Rosalind, 'that's where it all went wrong. Oh, I know he didn't love me. But why didn't he? Why?'

Emma only shakes her head.

One spring day in 1952, the Coldwells stumble into one of these scenes. They have come for afternoon tea. Emma is famous for her afternoon teas. They are all looking forward to it very much and Lydia stares with dismay at the little yellow sports car parked at an odd angle in front of the house.

'Oh no,' says Mr Coldwell, stopping the car halfway down the drive. 'It's her.' He looks around. For all he knows, there may be photographers crouched in the rhododendrons. So far, no one has connected his wife with the notorious Rosie Sparke, and he would like to keep it that way. 'I don't think this is a very good idea,' he says.

'Someone is very hungry, Mummy,' says Sydney. 'Is he not getting any tea?'

'Not getting any tea?' says Cooper Junior, sitting up with a start. 'Why not? I'm having some anyway. You bet I am!'

'Hush, boys,' says Mr Coldwell.

But Lydia is hungry too, which makes it three against one, and in they go. Mr Coldwell's expression says much, but Emma doesn't seem to notice. She is dividing her time between the library, where the Coldwells sit stiffly with their cakes and sandwiches, and the front terrace, where Rosalind is curled up on a bench, wrapped in a blanket, weeping loudly.

The Coldwells eat quickly and leave as soon as the cakes are finished.

'She's getting ridiculous now,' Mr Coldwell says. 'We had better not come here again.'

'Not come again?' says Lydia. She is thinking about the little wafery chocolate biscuits and regretting not slipping one into her handbag for later. 'That's a little drastic surely?'

'People in my position cannot be too careful,' says Mr Coldwell.

(And in the end, of course, Mr Coldwell was proved right. When, in 1961, he was accused of fraud, embezzlement and sundry other acts of financial misconduct, it was only because his wife was a Gilbert. He had been hounded, he said. Hostile forces, paid by the opposition, probably Communists, had scrutinized his business dealings to an unfair degree, actively looking for criminal tendencies, and he blamed Hugo and Rosalind for that.)

The car is halfway down the drive before Mr Coldwell realizes he has left his cane in the umbrella stand. He stops and thinks about it, the engine dawdling. He is very fond of his cane. He glances back. Can he quickly nip in again? No. Something is happening. It seems Rosalind has come out on to the drive to see them off, tripped on the edge of her blanket and fallen over.

Emma is kneeling beside Rosalind, looking up the drive after the Coldwells' car. She is just about to raise her hand to beckon them back, perhaps, when Mr Coldwell puts the car into gear and roars away.

Take a look in the umbrella stand. Mr Coldwell's cane is the one with the big green glass top. He never came back for it, and I expect no one has touched it since.

29

The Cracked Balustrade

We shall stay with Rosalind for now. Imagine her sitting at a table on the front terrace with Emma and Annabel. It is a fine summer afternoon, and she is telling them about the new man in her life. He's nothing to do with the film industry, she says. Goodness, no! He's just a simple man. An ordinary man. That's what she loves best about him.

'He saw me in *Murder by Starlight*,' Rosalind says, 'and admired me, of course, but he isn't excessively concerned about all that. He isn't one of those dreadful *followers*.'

She smiles, lifting a hand to shield her eyes from the sun.

'He's an engineer of some sort,' she says. 'An engineer! How wonderful to finally be part of the ordinary world – just to have what ordinary people have, and feel what ordinary people feel. It's such a relief.' She turns to Annabel. 'You've never really wanted anything, Annabel, so you don't know how terrible it is.'

The man's name is Nicholas Middleton. He is walking in the garden with Hugo, his hands behind his back, looking thoughtful.

Hugo is talking loudly, gesticulating and tugging his moustache. He is trying to make a good impression. It is all he can do not to shake the man's hand. 'Thank you,' he wants to say. 'Well done, you.' But he does not.

'I shall tell you how we met,' says Rosalind, 'because I think it illustrates exactly what kind of person he is. I was in a little café in Soho where no one was likely to know me, and the man I was with – I shan't say who it was. I shall not even utter his name – got up and left me. Just walked out on me. Well, naturally I had no money to pay the bill. I never carry any money, and he knows that. It's just the sort of thing he does, this man. How dreadful he is. How dreadful.

'You can imagine how upset I was. I was quite beside myself. The waitresses tried to comfort me, and the proprietor too, but I couldn't speak, could hardly breathe, and my arms and legs had started to shake so terribly that they were scared to come anywhere near me.

'Well, into the midst of this strode my wonderful Nicholas. He just came up to me, helped me up off the floor, picked up all my things and put them back in my bag, apologized to all the people who had accidentally got hurt and asked if he could do anything to help. Isn't that wonderful? That's real heroism for you. That is the kind of thing I admire these days. I've changed so much.'

Annabel looks at her sister. There is something different about her, she thinks. The orange hair is less stiffly waved – a little curl is coming down, like it used to, soft and wispy beside her face – and her lips are unpainted.

'Where's Mother?' asks Rosalind, looking around. She would like to tell her about this love – how happy Mother will be for her.

But Mrs Gilbert has a new hobby. She is down in the village, giving their excess potatoes to the poor people.

'Ah,' says Rosalind, but she has nothing to say about poor people or potatoes. Instead, she says, 'You know, we never talk about love, Nicholas and I. He just loves me – it's as simple as that. How wonderful it is. How refreshing! Oh, Annabel. Real love! Here it is, at last.'

It is late in the evening when they leave, Rosalind leaning out of the car and waving, all the way down the drive.

A month later, they receive a newspaper clipping of a wedding announcement. For five months after that, nothing, At dinner, now and then, when there is any mention of Rosalind, Hugo will sigh and say, 'Thank goodness for Mr Middleton.'

And Emma will say, 'Yes, quite.'

Then Emma starts to get letters: *How dull it is, after all, to be ordinary!* Rosalind writes.

> *It's a different kind of effort, isn't it? To be a little less like your-self and a little more like everyone else every day.*

Then:

> *I don't know how you have put up with it all these years. I try to do it, I really do. I try to think less, feel less, just sit around doing nothing the way everyone else does. But for some reason it isn't enough for me. My soul is in turmoil, Emma. What shall I do?*

And then:

> *He's like a dead person. He has no emotions at all unless I give them to him, no words or ideas. I write it all for him like a script. He's like one of those dead frogs Hugo used to bring home from school and try to make come alive again. He's nothing at all.*

'I think there's something wrong with Rosalind,' Emma says, lowering this last letter on to the breakfast table with a sigh.

'Everything is wrong with Rosalind,' says Hugo.

Now, let us go outside on to the drive. Look at the balustrade above the steps at the edge of the terrace. You may already have noticed the large crack there, and the small chunk of stone that has fallen on to the gravel. Look closely at the crack. Can you see tiny flecks of yellow paint embedded in the edges? No? You may have to use your imagination.

It is five o'clock in the morning. The valley is filled with mist, and Hugo and Emma are awakened by a crash as Rosalind's little yellow car skids across the gravel and smashes into the balustrade.

They rush downstairs to find the car door open and Rosalind in a puddle on the ground . . . a bodily puddle, I mean. There is no blood or anything like that.

They carry her up to Aunt Beatrice's old room at the front of the house. See her there, very tiny in the four-poster bed. She is throwing her head from side to side and whispering something about frogs.

The doctor is called. He can find no physical malady, he says, but something is obviously wrong. It is some sort of nervous collapse.

'Has anything been upsetting her?' he asks.

'Nothing in particular,' says Emma.

'Everything,' says Hugo.

There is a sudden rustling of bedclothes. 'Wilfred, where are you?' cries Rosalind. 'The only man who ever really loved me. Why, Wilfred, why?'

'Who is Wilfred?' says the doctor.

Emma doesn't answer. She thinks of Wilfred at the ball, standing at the edge of the room with Jeremy, watching them dance . . . and setting off with Hugo to the recruitment office, his face newly shaved, very red and bleeding slightly from a spot on his chin . . . and in the back of their mother's car heading down the hill to Belmont. 'You're a sitting duck,' says their mother. And Wilfred laughs. 'I have no idea what that means.'

'Can he be fetched?' says the doctor.

'No,' says Emma. 'He can't.'

'Well, then, she must be kept very quiet,' says the doctor, turning back to Rosalind. 'Distracted from causes of anxiety. She must eat good, simple food at regular intervals. No coffee. No cake.'

For the next week, Mrs Gilbert neglects her poor village people and stays at home to look after Rosalind. See her coming upstairs with a bowl of chicken broth on the little brown tray that Hugo and I would later use for our cocoa.

'Oh, Mother, you have saved my life,' whispers Rosalind. 'How wonderful, this silence. How wonderful to be home again, to be alone and free . . . and quite, quite alone.'

She asks for the windows to be opened so that she can hear the birds. 'They too are free,' she says. 'How wonderful it is.'

On the second day, the room has got a little cold and Rosalind asks for the windows to be closed. She wonders where all her old magazines went. She could do with something to read.

'Has Nicholas come?' Rosalind asks on the third day.

'No, my love,' says Mrs Gilbert, sitting at Rosalind's bedside, watching her flick through the pages of a magazine. 'No one has come.'

'Good!' says Rosalind. 'I told him not to and he has finally done as I've asked. Oh, I couldn't bear it if he were to come. He stifles me. This is the first time I have been away from him, the first time I have been free to think and to breathe. Thank goodness he has not come.'

It is a long day. Rosalind is restless. Now and then, she gets up, wanders around, opens and closes the windows.

That night, she cannot sleep. Mrs Gilbert wakes at two in the morning, shivering, to find Rosalind sitting on her bed, wrapped in her eiderdown. Her hair is wild and her eyes are red and wet with tears.

'I thought it would be different this time,' Rosalind says. 'But it's just the same. I thought it was love, but it wasn't.'

'I'm so sorry, Rosalind,' says Mrs Gilbert, sitting up and reaching for her dressing gown.

'No one loves me,' says Rosalind. 'No one at all.'

'Oh no,' says Mrs Gilbert. 'I'm sure they do. Of course, they do.'

'Well, if they do, I can't feel it. I don't know why. It's like I'm trapped in myself. That's what it feels like. It doesn't matter where I go or what I do, I can't get out.'

'Oh, Rosalind,' says Mrs Gilbert. 'My poor sweet girl.'

'Never mind,' says Rosalind. 'It doesn't matter. It's probably the same for everyone. They just don't mention it.' And with that she clambers off the bed and wanders away, taking Mrs Gilbert's eiderdown with her.

The next morning brings with it a thunderstorm. Rosalind sits in the window, watching the banks of rain sweeping across the valley. The last flowers in the borders have been bent over into the mud.

'I marvel at the weakness of men,' Rosalind says. 'Their love is so paltry a thing compared to a woman's. I tell him not to come, so he doesn't. Has he no will of his own? Has he no desires of his own? Have I been his puppet master all this time?'

'Men!' says Mrs Gilbert.

At last, the telephone rings.

'I don't want to speak to him!' Rosalind says. 'See him hounding me. He will not let me alone. I am so sick of this relentless pursuit. I have been a victim of it all my life. You are so lucky, Annabel, to be as you are. It has been my doom to be so attractive to men.'

The next day, Nicholas calls again. This time, Rosalind gets up and goes downstairs, closing the morning-room door behind her.

'Well?' says Mrs Gilbert, when Rosalind emerges two hours later.

Rosalind shakes her head. She will say nothing about it, but the next morning Nicholas arrives and is shown into the bedroom.

He has the look of a condemned man, this Nicholas Middleton, as he closes the door, and for the next three hours they hear nothing from him but a subdued murmur. It is Rosalind they hear.

'I can't live like this. I can't. After all your promises, Nicholas! You said you would love me, but this isn't love. You said you would take care of me. But look at me! This isn't being cared for.'

It goes on and on. How can there be so many things to say? Annabel wonders. How can it all take so long?

It is growing dark when they finally emerge and climb into his car, Rosalind stiff and silent, Nicholas white-faced and trembling. Rosalind's little yellow car sits on the drive for a month before someone comes to tow it away.

30

The Onion Basket

But, besides these Rosalind-shaped interludes, what of life generally here at Thornwalk at this time?

Well, Hugo is much occupied with the business, every weekday climbing into his coal-black Austin 16 and disappearing to the office in Clifton, and every evening and weekend sitting in his study with his piles of paperwork.

While he is working, Emma must amuse herself as best she can around the house and garden. She grows dahlias, which takes a great deal of determination, and attempts to eradicate the moles and ants on the lawn. There are battles with a nest of shrews in the old night nursery, and perennial altercations with wool moths and woodworm.

The servants require a little guidance, and the cook has grown temperamental in her old age and needs some soothing and encouragement, but still there are moments, every day, when she finds herself at something of a loss.

Occasionally, very occasionally, she writes to her mother:

Dear Mother,

I have taken your advice about the custard and am very happy with the results, so must offer you my thanks. Hugo sends his also, for custard is, as you know, quite a favourite with him.

With reference to your suggestions regarding foot powders, I am experimenting with a number of remedies using ingredients from the kitchen garden. So far, lemon balm has been the most effective.

The asters are quite wonderful this year.

With love from
Your daughter, Emma

The reply, written on the back of Emma's letter, is dated three weeks later:

Dear Emma,

So pleased about the custard.

Love,
Mother

Emma stuffs the letter back into the envelope, throws it into a dresser drawer and resolves to write no more letters to her mother.

Six months pass before she tries again:

Dear Mother,

I wonder, since you were so good as to share your thoughts about the custard, whether you might have a little advice for me regarding Hugo. He spends such a lot of time at the office or in his study, and sometimes when I go in, I find him asleep on his desk. There are some days when I hardly see him at all. Of course, there is a great deal to be done around the house and I am quite able to busy myself productively, but I wonder sometimes whether I might do more, or if I am doing things quite right, for Hugo I mean.

With best wishes from
Your daughter, Emma

The reply arrives the next day:

My dear daughter,

*Every new wife is responsible for finding her own ways to
interest her husband. Numerous books have been written on
the subject, I believe, and there are frequent articles in certain
women's magazines, though I do not, for obvious reasons,
have first-hand knowledge of them myself.*

*It is only left for me to remind you that I said you should
find this to be the case, but you would have your own way
in it.*

Mother

Emma's reply is swift, and tight with restrained indignation.

Dear Mother,

*Thank you for your letter of the 4th. I am not quite sure
what you mean by saying that I 'should find this to be the
case'. I don't recall your saying anything of that sort at all,
but never mind.*

*As for 'interesting my husband', I think we are talking at
cross-purposes, and it was not quite what you have in mind
that I was referring to . . .*

At this, Emma stops for a moment and rubs her bottom lip
with the end of her pen. Perhaps it is, she thinks. Perhaps, after
all, that is actually what I mean. With a sigh, she goes on:

*It's nothing like that at all, only that he's so busy with the busi-
ness, and I wonder if I might do something to help. I always had*

a flair for accounts and such like and I do seem to have a good deal of time on my hands.

If you have time on your hands, Lady Asquill replies, *you are almost certainly doing something wrong.*

As for your wish to involve yourself in the running of Hugo's business, it seems to me that what you are saying is that you have fallen out of love with each other and are looking for some other occupation to justify the union. If that is the case, you might do better to admit it, but really it makes little difference. You have made your bed, and now you must lie in it.

Please direct further correspondence to Mr Bainbridge at the Exeter house. Your father and I are going to France.

And that is the end of that.

Now and then, there are visits from Jeremy. When he is here, they always take a walk around the grounds in the afternoon and Hugo tells Jeremy his plans for the house and the land.

'The vision comes first,' he says, 'then the execution. You've got to be clear about the vision.'

'I see,' says Jeremy. 'So, how is Failand coming along?'

'Farms take a great deal of thinking about,' Hugo replies. 'A great deal of arranging.'

It is the same thing he says every time.

After dinner, as they sit together in the library, Jeremy notices how red Hugo is and that he always has a glass in his hand. He takes it with him to answer the telephone and to go to the toilet. He notices how quiet Emma is, how tired she looks.

'Have you . . . have you all been well?' he asks.

'Oh yes,' says Emma. 'Oh yes, perfectly well.'

'What about you, little brother?' says Hugo. 'How goes it in the big wide world?' But it's just something to say. He doesn't want to know how it goes.

'Different,' says Jeremy. 'I think most people hardly recognize it.'

Hugo pulls a face.

'How goes the business?' asks Jeremy.

Hugo shrugs. 'As you say, difficult times. But we shall weather them. Shan't we, Emma?'

Emma blinks. 'Oh yes. Of course.'

'What we cater for are traditional values that transcend these superficial alterations,' says Hugo. 'When the world has finished changing, we will be right here waiting for it.'

'When the world has finished changing, it will no longer want you,' says Jeremy.

'Nonsense,' says Hugo.

'I think Hugo's right,' says Emma. 'The best things, the best feelings, never change.'

Jeremy looks at her and feels a great lurch in his stomach. She used to be so clever, he thinks. She used to mind what she said. He grieves for the girl with the gloved hands to whom he gave his fossil.

'But let's not argue about it,' Emma says. 'It's so lovely to have you home.'

They ask him what he's been doing. He admits he's writing a book but will tell them no more about it for now, except that it's a travel book. Have they been to Patagonia? The Andes?

'I would love to have travelled more,' says Emma. 'I've been to Paris a few times, obviously, once to Madrid, and then there was that trip to New York . . .'

'All this jet-setting is rather unnecessary,' says Hugo. He reaches for the whisky decanter. 'The real things, the fundamentals, are the same the world over. A wise man sees all in a blade of grass, Jeremy. And, as you can see, we have plenty of grass.'

Jeremy never stays for long.

★

Meanwhile, now that all the chickens have gone to live in trees and golden cornfields, Mrs Gilbert is busier than ever with her poor people. Every morning, she hefts a vast wicker basket into the crook of her arm and she and Annabel set off down the hill to the village.

You will find this basket where it was left all those years ago, in the cupboard beneath the still-room sink. It still smells of onions. So many things fade, but the smell of onions, sadly, is not one of them.

Look in the bottom of the basket. Under the crumbs of dried potato dirt and bits of onion peel are four faded sheets of yellow paper. They are some of Aunt Beatrice's old pamphlets on temperance and chastity. Yes, there is another purpose to Mrs Gilbert's philanthropy. She has grown radical in her old age, and, if the mood is favourable at the end of a visit, she will always offer a few improving words.

'The wonderful thing about poor people,' says Mrs Gilbert, 'is that they really *listen*.'

It is this part that Annabel doesn't like. The villagers seem glad enough to have the vegetables – they are very polite – but it is obvious that they resent the pamphlets. As the pieces of paper emerge from the basket, there is a sudden hard look on their faces, and once, as she was leaving, Annabel turned in the doorway and saw the pages tossed into the fire.

'We're going to see the Smiths today,' Mrs Gilbert says now as they set off. 'They have been very unfortunate, poor things.' But Annabel knows there is no longer any such thing as misfortune in Mrs Gilbert's thinking. It is all consequence. All the bad things that happen to other people are always, somehow, deserved. 'If they would only drink less and have fewer babies,' she says.

They arrive at the cottage, the last in a low terrace, a little rundown but neat enough, with a heartening attempt at window-washing evident in the smeary leaded panes. Mrs Gilbert marches up to the door and knocks.

There is no reply.

She knocks again, harder this time, then peers in at the kitchen window and taps on the glass.

At last, the latch clicks and a woman's face appears at the edge of the door. The woman looks at poor old Annabel, waiting at the gate, and then at Mrs Gilbert, standing on the doorstep with her basket.

'Oh, it's you,' says the woman. 'It's kind of you, I'm sure, but you mustn't come in. We've all been dreadful sick.'

Mrs Gilbert hates sickness, but she is not afraid. She has lived a good life and never drinks. 'I have nursed five children,' she says. 'And I have always found onion broth extremely efficacious.' She holds up her basket of onions and takes a step forward.

'I can make onion broth,' says the woman, keeping a tight hold on the door. 'If you'd be so kind as just to leave the onions there.'

'Nonsense,' says Mrs Gilbert, and presses on into the house.

31

Some Very Small Socks

Come with me again to the attic, past the room where Rosalind's films are kept, right to the end, to the last room in the furthest corner. It is the worst of them, with its cold museum smell and its dim museum light. What a task the hotel people have before them.

It is called hoarding, this insistent keeping of things. People think of it as clinging to the past, a refusal to let things go. I can tell you that it is almost the opposite. It is an attempt to cover the things we cannot bear to look at. It is a burial.

So, you will need to dig . . . beneath the boxes and the mattresses, the piles of newspapers, gardening magazines, seed catalogues, old shoes, wellington boots, riding boots, rugby boots, toys, books, broken sledges, broken tennis rackets, hockey sticks, rugby balls, suitcases, mirrors . . . to the far wall. There, tucked into a corner, is a small chest. The key is already in the lock for you. Go ahead and open it.

I will not have to say much more, I think. It is all quite self-explanatory, this pile of little clothes. There are white cotton sleepsuits, very tiny, very soft. A hat with a knot of fabric on top. Cotton mittens. And all of them with their little labels still attached.

That is enough. Come away.

Now, let us go back to 1953 – a warm spring morning, the pink horse chestnuts all in flower along the drive. The front door is open, and Mrs Gilbert and Annabel are waiting in the hall.

Here is Hugo. He has just returned from the hospital. He is standing very still, staring at the floor, clenching and unclenching his fists.

'How is she?' whispers Mrs Gilbert.

'I imagine she will recover,' says Hugo.

'And . . . and the baby?'

'The baby is dead.'

32

The Scratch in the Dining-room Table

'A contagion of some sort,' says Emma. She is very pale, almost grey, with the set look around the mouth of someone who has decided, silently, deep inside, that they will never smile again. 'Just one of those things.'

'A contagion?' says Mrs Gilbert. 'Just a random contagion that could have been picked up anywhere?'

'Yes,' says Emma. 'Just a random contagion.'

Emma gets up and leaves the room. She is going upstairs to rest.

Mrs Gilbert mutters something about dinner and hurries away. She does not look at Annabel.

A great hush descends on the house, a great holding of the breath. Mrs Gilbert keeps to her room. When she walks around the house, she stays close to the walls, and at meal times keeps her eyes on her plate.

It goes on for two weeks, until one day the front door flies open with a crash, and Hugo cries, 'Mother!' from the hall.

Mrs Gilbert puts down her tapestry and stands. She crosses the gallery and descends the stairs. It is Marie Antoinette going to the guillotine. It is Joan of Arc observing the stake.

'Those peasants you insist on seeing,' says Hugo. 'I hear they are ill.'

'I don't think so, Hugo,' says Mrs Gilbert. 'Not so very ill.'

'Yes, they are very ill.'

'Perhaps a small amount of illness sometimes. You know what these poor people are like . . . with their drinking . . .'

'I told you not to go there.'

'Did you, Hugo? I don't remember that –' She turns to Annabel for support.

'I told you, and you disobeyed me.'

'I don't remember –'

'You have murdered your grandson.'

'Oh no, Hugo. No.'

'Yes. You will leave Thornwalk immediately and never set foot here again.'

An hour later, see Mrs Gilbert pushing a wheelbarrow of personal items up the drive towards the old Chaplain's Cottage on the edge of the estate.

Hugo is watching from the hall, with Annabel hovering in the doorway behind him. As Mrs Gilbert stumbles, Annabel steps forward.

'You wish to assist my son's murderer?' Hugo says.

Annabel stops, and Mrs Gilbert gets to her feet and goes on alone.

And so begins the exile of Margaret Gilbert. I shall say more of the Chaplain's Cottage soon, but for a moment let us stay at Thornwalk.

Six months pass. Spring turns to summer, and summer to a warm day in early autumn. The conker-brown cows are in the meadow at the foot of the hill. Great swathes of purple asters are flowering in the borders.

They have just finished lunch. The windows are open and a

warm breeze is coming in, bringing with it the hum of a lawn-mower and the smell of cut grass.

'I wonder what Mother is doing now,' says Annabel. Who knows what she means by this. Perhaps it is an idle nothing, accidentally said aloud. Perhaps it is a small rebellion, very small.

Hugo looks up from his newspaper. 'You can leave too,' he says. 'Sympathizers and conspirators are not welcome in this house.'

'Hugo –' says Emma.

'No!' says Hugo. He stabs at the table with his cheese knife, and a splinter flies up and lands on the carpet. Annabel picks it up on her way out.

A few minutes later, as Annabel closes the front door behind her, she can hear Hugo and Emma still talking in the dining room.

'Please, Hugo,' Emma is saying. 'Please.'

'What?' says Hugo. 'What do you want me to do?'

'Can't we move on? Can't we let it go?'

'Let it go? Let it go? What can you possibly mean, let it go?'

'Can't we . . . can't we try again?'

'No, Emma. It is a savage world that feeds upon innocent babies. I shall provide it with no more of mine. No. It is all over.'

33

The Way through the Woods

The Chaplain's Cottage is not as deep in the wood as it seems. In the year following Annabel's banishment, Hugo had the paths altered, blocking off the track to the house, so that to reach it would take three times as long. The old path is overgrown, but in winter you can see it still. I will show you.

Go through their grandfather's arboretum, along the edge of their father's overgrown, unfinished rockery, past the summer-house. Two gateposts remain in the hedge there. If you look between them, you can see the cottage. The old path travels almost straight to it, though it is filled now with brambles and holly bushes.

We shall take the other route towards the dairy.

The cottage has, I believe, been earmarked for staff accommodation, but here too they have got their work cut out. The roof is good, but it is full of bats and the ceilings are badly stained. The walls are almost black with mould and there is a thick, airless, mousy smell.

It was here that Mr Higgins took poor Lydia, all those years ago, when she was young and hopeful and thought she was in love.

And here that Mrs Gilbert and Annabel lived for almost five years, dividing their time between that little front room, with its smoky fireplace and damp flagstones, and the little kitchen, with its sunken quarry tiles and cracked white sink. That is the stove that Annabel would struggle to light each morning. That is the outhouse they crept to on frosty nights, huddled in blankets.

'Oh, Annabel, he has done it to you too,' cries poor Mrs Gilbert when Annabel appears at the door with her wheelbarrow. 'My poor Hugo. He has gone mad at last, then.'

The house is very dirty. The servants and estate workers have been told that anyone setting foot in the murderer's house will be dismissed.

'I'm sure he doesn't mean it,' says Mrs Gilbert, 'but naturally people are cautious about that sort of thing. No one has come to see me at all. Only Emma, and she never stays very long. It's not much fun for her, I suppose. I never have any good biscuits. It's not what she's used to.'

The first evening passes slowly.

'They leave crates of food at the end of the path,' says Mrs Gilbert, perched in a very old horsehair armchair, left over from when there was actually a chaplain. 'At first it was bags of flour and potatoes and things like that. But what was I supposed to do with them, when the stove wouldn't light?

'I put a note in the empty crate, asking what I was supposed to do, and they started to leave cooked things instead – pies and puddings and that sort of thing. Horrible, heavy food, Annabel. You know I have never been able to digest pastry.' She lowers her voice to a whisper. 'The pains have been excruciating.'

Mrs Gilbert closes her eyes. 'There are times when I'm sure I'm dying,' she says. 'I know it's just a stage Hugo's going through. I know he just needs a little time to himself. But I think if he knew he was killing me, Annabel, he would realize that it's just not worth it.'

Annabel looks at her mother, so much smaller, her skin dry and red, her hair sticking out in a wild grey halo around her head. She reaches out and puts her hand on her mother's arm.

'There will come a time when he wants his mother,' says Mrs Gilbert, 'when there is need of a grandmother, and I'll hate to have to disappoint him by being dead.'

It is the same thing the next day, and the next. The same terrible stories of her abandonment, the same fears for Hugo's sanity.

'I don't suppose you can tell,' Mrs Gilbert says, glancing down at her dress front, 'but I haven't been able to wash any clothes. Not properly. I mean . . . certain things . . . the essential things I have scrubbed as best I can in the bathtub with soap, but it doesn't help that the water is cold. What a way to live, Annabel! What a way to live.'

She has written to Lydia, asking her to speak to Hugo, put in a good word for her, but there has been no reply.

'I'm sure she's just busy with the children,' says Mrs Gilbert. 'I'm sure she doesn't blame me for anything. Hugo doesn't either, deep down. He isn't thinking clearly, because of grief. That's very natural, but sooner or later he'll see that it was just a random contagion that could have been picked up anywhere. Mad people are so irrational, you see. That's the main problem with them. They tend to blame people for things they haven't done. It happens all the time.'

What else can Mrs Gilbert do? Aunt Beatrice is still worn out and refusing to see them. No one has an address for Jeremy, and, of course, poor Rosalind would be no help to anyone now, no help at all.

And at this Mrs Gilbert collapses on to Annabel's shoulder and starts to cry. 'Oh, Annabel,' she says, 'don't leave me.'

34

The Blotter by the Telephone

No, Rosalind will not be able to help. As Annabel wheels her barrow up the path to the Chaplain's Cottage, her younger sister is lying in a Camden hospital bed.

Poor Nicholas Middleton is sitting beside her, his hands clasped and his head bowed. He is starting to go bald on top.

Rosalind's eyelids flicker open. 'Where am I?' she murmurs.

'Hospital,' says Nicholas. And then, quietly, 'Again.'

Rosalind groans and closes her eyes.

'A policeman is waiting to speak to you,' says Nicholas.

'No. I won't talk to him,' says Rosalind.

'They just need to know what happened. Whether it was just an accident or . . . whatever it was.'

'An accident. Yes, tell him it was just an accident.'

'All right. I'll tell him that,' says Nicholas.

'It wouldn't matter anyway what I told him,' says Rosalind. 'There's nothing he could do. Nothing anyone could do.'

Nicholas clenches his fists until the fingernails draw blood in his palms. He opens his hands and stares at the blood, astonished. So this is what it's like, he thinks. This is how it begins.

He lifts his eyes to the woman in the bed. He can hardly

believe it's the same girl who was so grateful for the three shillings he paid for her breakfast. Even if he killed himself for her now, it would not be enough – not fast enough, enthusiastic enough, sincere enough.

'I just don't understand –' he begins. Then he sees she is crying.

'It was a man,' she whispers. 'A man did it.'

'What man?'

'A man I used to love.'

Nicholas sighs and looks at the floor. 'The same man, or a different one?'

Rosalind's eyes snap open. 'What do you mean by that?'

'I mean, was it the same man as last time, as the other times, or someone else?'

'How should I know?'

'I just thought . . . never mind. So, should I call in the policeman?'

'No. I said no.'

'But if –'

'I said no!'

It is unbearable, Nicholas thinks. He just can't stand it any more. He takes a deep breath. 'Rosalind,' he says, 'it's not that I don't believe you. It's just that I don't –'

'Get out,' she says.

He stands up immediately and goes.

And that is almost the end of Nicholas Middleton. He doesn't visit her again. When she leaves the hospital three days later, she goes home to an empty flat. She stands there looking around. The kitchen cupboards are still empty, and the refrigerator. She had expected food. A pie or a casserole or something, from someone. There are no flowers. She had expected flowers, lots of flowers. There are no cards, no letters, just a note on the table that reads:

It's obvious that I'm doing you no good. I thought I could help you, but I can't. It's just getting worse. This is my mother's number, if you need me.

She sits down at the telephone and dials the number. There is no answer. She calls again and again, but the phone just rings and rings. 'Another lie, Nicholas!' she says. 'Another lie!'

Go down to the morning room, to the telephone on the desk. Next to it is a little blotter covered in scribbles. They were drawn by Emma as she sat here, hour after hour, listening to Rosalind cry. Run your fingers over the page. See how hard the pen was pressed, how deeply the lines have been dug into the surface.

But Emma is not naturally a doodler. Like Nicholas, she is astonished at what is happening to her. She looks down at the page, all these eyes and stacked-up boxes, and wonders if she too is going to go mad.

You will find something similar near the kitchen, where Annabel would answer the phone, much later, when she was here alone with Hugo. The doodles are much worse, in their way, because by then, of course, something worse had happened.

35

The Pile of Bricks on Top of Cley Hill

At around this time, Emma begins to write to Jeremy. She is
the only one who has his address. His replies go to a post office
box in Clifton which she checks every time she goes shopping.
None of those letters have survived.

There is only one of hers. Almost the last one.

I wish you would come home, Emma writes.

*Things are very bad here now. This morning, I found Hugo on
top of Cley Hill with a shotgun and a bottle of whisky. He had
drunk half the bottle and fallen over and the shotgun had gone
off underneath him. He could have been killed.*

You might like to visit this spot for yourself. Cley Hill is the
one on the eastern horizon. The wooded ridge there used to
mark the border of the estate. There is a spot right in the centre
of the ridge where the trees have been cleared and you can see
across the valley back to the house.

The trees were very roughly cut down, savagely almost, and
the trunks dragged to one side. They are still there, after all this
time, rotting in the bushes. There is a distinctive pinky orange
mould on them, smooth and jelly-like, that reminds me of ears.

Between the tree stumps is a pile of red bricks, and it is here that Emma finds Hugo, at around five o'clock on a grey Thursday in October 1954.

'I shall not be going to the office today,' Hugo tells her that morning. 'I shall be here, taking care of urgent business.'

'All right, Hugo,' Emma says. She goes shopping, as usual, leaving him in his study, but, when she gets back, the house is empty.

She sets off into the garden to find him. She searches for almost an hour. It is beginning to grow dark and restless clouds are gathering overhead. Then she sees a crumpled shape, high up on the hillside, and something flapping in the wind.

The rain begins as Emma climbs the path. It patters against the body on the ground. Yes, the crumpled shape is the body of a man. The flapping she saw is the wind blowing one edge of his dark blue waxed jacket back and forth. It is slapping against the man's head, but the body doesn't move.

She reaches him at last, turns him over and sees the gun.

'Oh, Hugo!' she cries.

Hugo groans and opens his eyes.

'What is all this?' Emma says. 'What are you doing up here?'

'I'm building a tower,' Hugo says, struggling to his feet. 'I'm building my father's tower, like I told you, in honour of his memory.'

'You can't build a tower like this,' says Emma, looking around the clearing. 'Not on your own with a wheelbarrow. Where did you get the bricks from? The kitchen garden?'

'I can and I will,' Hugo says. 'Even if it takes a hundred years, I will. I swear it. I swear it.'

The words are slurred. Emma looks down and sees the whisky bottle. 'Oh no, Hugo,' she says, picking it up. 'You promised!'

'Give me that!' Hugo cries, snatching the bottle.

'Why do you want to build a tower?' Emma asks, with tears in her eyes. 'Why is that so much more important than the promises you've made to me? You are breaking my heart, Hugo.' For once, she is being honest instead of careful. She will never do it again.

Hugo gives a roar of fury and waves the shotgun in the air. Emma screams and tries to grab it. Hugo pulls it back and the barrel hits Emma in the stomach. She stumbles and falls on to the pile of bricks.

'That was your fault,' Hugo says, looking down at her. 'I didn't do that. I didn't touch you. You know that, don't you?'

Emma gets up and begins to run back to the house, with Hugo running after her. 'You know that, don't you?' he calls. 'I didn't do anything. I didn't touch you.'

I was thinking that perhaps your mother should be informed, Emma's letter to Jeremy goes on.

Perhaps there's something she can do. I don't know who else to turn to. Also, Rosalind is asking for you. She is very ill now, something to do with her kidneys or her liver. She has told the doctors not to give me any more details, but I think it may be serious this time. It has all taken its toll, as we expected it would.

Poor Emma. Had I been there, perhaps she would have turned to me. Perhaps not. But shortly after she became pregnant, I went abroad for a while. When I finally came home, it was too late.

36

Three Dried Peas

By the time Jeremy gets this letter and returns to Thornwalk, Annabel has been with Mrs Gilbert in the Chaplain's Cottage for almost two years.

'You should have come back sooner,' says Emma, filling the kettle and dropping it on to the stove.

Jeremy looks around the kitchen. 'Where's Mrs Appleford?' he says.

'Gone,' Emma says. 'They've all gone.'

Yes, one by one, the maids and the cook and the housekeeper have been seen thinking about the murderer and told to leave. The last had been poor Ellen, a nice girl from the village. Hadn't lasted a week.

('Not in front of the servants, Hugo. Please. Ellen will be able to hear.'

'Spying, is she? Eavesdropping? Tell her to get out. Go on. Tell them all to get out!)

'You should have come sooner,' she says.

It is the first time Jeremy has heard any reproach from Emma, and he looks at her in dismay. There are short grey hairs sticking up from the top of her head and lines about her mouth. His heart trembles and he feels sick.

'I was travelling,' he says. 'I didn't get your letter until –'

'Never mind,' she says.

The water boils, and the tea things are loaded on to a tray and carried to the library. But it is even worse in here. The fire has not been lit and the room is cold and damp.

'What could I have done?' Jeremy asks.

'I don't know. But at least I wouldn't have been alone.'

'Emma –' Jeremy says, but he doesn't know where to go from there. There is no peace to be found anywhere, he is thinking. No peace and no freedom.

'Never mind,' she says. 'It doesn't matter.'

'Why do you put up with this, Emma?' Jeremy asks, glancing around the room. 'After what you said in your last letter . . .' He shudders. 'How could you stay?'

'I didn't.'

'You didn't?'

'No. I called my mother and she came and took me back to London.' She gives a quick, unindulgent little laugh. 'It was dreadful. I don't think my mother will ever get over it. Hugo was ranting the whole time. Absolutely ranting. There's a box of broken things up in the attic, if you want to see it. He smashed up the whole hall. You remember that nice Chinese vase? That's gone.'

There is a long pause. 'But you're here now,' Jeremy says.

'As you see, yes. I came back. God knows why. He made some promises. I believed them. It's an old story, Jeremy. I expect you've heard it before.' She sighs and begins to pour out the tea, but her hands are shaking and anyway the tea is cold.

'But he doesn't –' says Jeremy. 'He doesn't ever –'

'No,' says Emma. 'Not like that. Let's not talk about it, Jeremy. It doesn't matter now.'

Instead, they talk about Mrs Gilbert, up in the cottage, and how Annabel is there now too.

'I've arranged for someone to deliver Annabel's medicine,'

Emma says. 'And a doctor is going to visit every few months, so don't worry.' She glances at the clock. Hugo will be home soon. It's time for Jeremy to go.

'No,' Jeremy says. 'I need to stay and talk to Hugo.'

Emma clenches her fists and closes her eyes. 'I don't have the strength to fight you, Jeremy,' she says. 'I only beg you not to. Just go, please, before it's too late.'

He stands up. 'You asked me to come back.'

'I know. But it was different then.'

'What do you mean?' Jeremy says.

But Emma only shakes her head.

'I'll be staying down in the village, at the Black Arrow,' Jeremy says, as they walk to the door. 'Come down tomorrow.'

'I don't know if I can. You don't understand.'

'If you don't come to see me in three days, I'll come back here.'

The hall clock begins to chime. He has been here too long, Emma thinks. Why do people have to be like this? So heavy. So hard to move. She pushes Jeremy towards the door, but it is too late. There is Hugo's car on the drive.

Emma grabs Jeremy's arm and drags him back across the hall to the kitchen door. 'You'll have to go out the side way,' she says. 'Wait until he's in the house and then go.'

'Why? What on earth is going on here?' says Jeremy. 'You're that scared of him?'

But Emma has closed the door.

When she turns around, Hugo is standing in the hall, watching her. His eyes are narrow. 'What were you doing back there?' he asks.

Emma stares at him. She can think of nothing.

Hugo is quick to sense that something is wrong. He has been expecting it for years, after all. 'Stand aside!' he says. He pushes past her and flings open the kitchen door. And there is Jeremy.

'My own brother!' he cries.

'What do you mean by that?' says Jeremy. 'Stop being so ridiculous, Hugo.'

'My own brother!' says Hugo again.

Jeremy recoils from the smell of whisky on Hugo's breath. 'Oh, for goodness' sake,' he says, waving a hand in front of his face.

With that, Hugo bellows and launches himself at Jeremy, sending a colander of shelled peas clattering on to the tiles. It is the first of many casualties.

A blow-by-blow account will not be necessary, I'm sure. If you wish to re-create it, you may take a look in the second of the two boxes of broken things that is to be found in the second left-hand-side attic room in the West Wing. The first box, referred to by Emma, contains the Chinese vase from the hall, as well as various objects from the mantelpiece. The second includes the colander, which has lost a handle, three peas, very dry now, scooped up with it, and half the items on the kitchen dresser, which almost topples over when Jeremy is thrown against it.

Generally speaking, it is an ungainly tangle of limbs, as most fights are, but fairly evenly matched. Hugo is bigger, but Jeremy is quicker and not drunk.

At last, Jeremy punches Hugo in the stomach. Hugo doubles over, temporarily unable to breathe, and the fight is over.

Jeremy looks around for Emma, and sees her sitting on the floor, her head bent and her arms wrapped around her knees.

'Let's get out of here,' he says. 'Come on, Emma. Come with me.'

'Come with you?' She looks up. 'Come with you where, Jeremy?'

But he doesn't know.

Emma sighs and shakes her head. 'Just leave,' she says.

Jeremy lifts a hand to his cheek and sees that it is bleeding. 'When I do, I doubt I'll ever come back,' he says.

'Fine,' she says.

Jeremy picks up his bag and his hat, looks once more at Hugo, lying on the kitchen tiles wheezing horribly, and leaves.

There is a long silence after Jeremy has gone, filled only with the sound of Hugo's breathing. Emma gets to her feet. 'Come on,' she says.

Hugo allows Emma to help him through the kitchen door and into the hall, but then he shrugs her away.

'You don't love me,' he says.

'I do, Hugo. God knows, I do.'

'No. It is clear to me that you never loved me. It was all a pretence.'

She doesn't understand. 'Of course, it wasn't a pretence,' she says. 'Of course, I love you.'

'It is a lie,' he says. 'It has all been one big lie.' He drags himself upstairs, to the little room he slept in before he was married – the one that looks like a corridor, with a narrow bed against the far wall, the glass shelf with the toothbrush mug and the cracked tablet of coal tar soap, though they weren't there then – and bolts the door behind him.

37

The Key Ring

From them on, Hugo doesn't let Emma out of his sight.

'We shall spend the day here,' he says. They are standing in the doorway of the library. 'I have laid out all manner of activities for you. There is your tapestry, and there some books, and a notepad and pen in case you wish to write any letters, though, of course, I will need to see them before they are sent.'

Emma turns to look at him. She can't decide if he's joking. Surely, he must be.

'If you wish to use the bathroom, just say so,' Hugo continues, ushering her into the room and locking the door behind them. 'There is no call to be telling your mother that I am keeping you in one room, when you are free to go to the bathroom any time you like.'

'But I suppose you'll come with me?' says Emma.

'Naturally, I will come with you,' he says, 'since you have shown that you are not to be trusted. Surely, you do not intend to blame me for that? You do not intend to suggest that this is in any way *my* fault?'

'I can be trusted to use the bathroom,' she says.

'No. You cannot.'

'Fine.'

Hugo sits down and picks up a newspaper, but Emma remains standing at the door. 'Shouldn't you be somewhere, Hugo?' she says. 'Don't you need to go to the office? Mr Lawrence called yesterday with some questions.'

'You are not to answer the telephone, Emma.'

'I said you were going in today.'

Hugo lowers his newspaper. 'Why this eagerness to get me out of the house?'

'If you need to be in the office –'

'You are waiting to go to him, I presume.'

'Fine,' she says again, and sits down at last. But half an hour later she needs to use the bathroom. 'I need to use the bathroom,' she says. Her voice is laden with protest, but he doesn't notice.

'Very well,' says Hugo.

He unlocks the door and they walk up the stairs together. He goes inside, checks that the window is locked, and waits outside for her to finish.

Emma sits on the toilet with her head in her hands. She can hear him breathing.

'I can't go if you're there,' she says.

'Very well,' he says. 'I shall wait on the stairs, but I shall be watching the door.'

That night, Hugo locks and bolts all the doors and windows, and keeps the keys on a ring under his pillow.

38

The Blood on the Blue-room Floor

It cannot last long. After all, Hugo has no desire to stay in one room, and he hates to hear her crying. If she promises to stay away from the windows and doors, she will be allowed into the rest of the house. Emma promises.

'Do not go too far,' he tells her. 'I will have to keep checking on you.'

'Very well,' she says.

'Emma?' he calls out a few minutes later.

'I'm here, Hugo. I'm just in the kitchen.'

'Emma?'

'I'm still in the kitchen, Hugo.'

The next day, he gives her a hand bell and a pocket watch, and tells her to ring the bell every quarter of an hour. That will save all the shouting.

'Fine,' she says.

But it's no good. He hates hearing the bell, and waiting to hear it. Besides, there's something about the way she rings it that irritates him. There's a sort of accusation in it, which they both know is unwarranted.

As if this were my fault, he thinks. I do my best to address a situation she has created, and once more I am blamed.

'You had better follow me,' he tells her. 'You can use this bag to put your book and your tapestry in, so that you can carry them from room to room, and I have put a little chair and a lamp in the corner of the study for when I am working. You will be quite comfortable there.'

But it is hard to work with Emma in the room. He is trying to write a letter, but always struggles to think of the right words when someone is watching him. He clears his throat, sighs and tries again.

'What is it you're working on?' Emma asks.

Hugo clenches his fists. 'Never mind, Emma,' he says. 'You get on with your tapestry.'

'Perhaps I could help you,' she says. She puts down her tapestry, gets to her feet and slowly, tentatively, approaches the desk. 'I'm quite good at this sort of thing, you know.'

'This sort of thing? What sort of thing would that be, Emma?'

'Oh, letters and numbers. Writing.'

Emma peers at the pages on the desk, but Hugo spreads his hands out over them. 'I don't need any assistance, thank you,' he says.

With a sigh, Emma goes back to her chair, but she doesn't want to read or sew. Instead, she looks around the room. There are papers everywhere, stacked up on either side of her chair, in two cabinets with overflowing drawers.

'Should I tidy up, Hugo?' she asks. 'Should I put all these papers away for you?'

'Very well,' says Hugo. 'If that is the sort of thing that amuses you.'

Slowly, silently, page by page, Emma picks up the papers and returns them to the cabinets.

'Hugo,' she says an hour later, 'is the London branch still in operation?'

'Naturally,' says Hugo.

Emma frowns down at the pages in her hand. 'But look here, Hugo,' she says. 'Look how much money it's losing.'

'The London branch was my father's pride and joy, Emma,' says Hugo. He does not turn around. He does not even look up from his letter. 'It is the heart of Gilbert Enterprises. The very heart.'

'But costs would be so much lower . . .'

Poor, poor Emma. What a fool she is, to keep talking as she does. Yes, like many people who find themselves in holes, she keeps on digging. Just what does she expect to find down there?

'If you don't want to tell them, I could do it for you.'

'Do it for me? You could do it for me?' echoes Hugo. He turns around at last, and his face is purple – an old beef sort of greyish purple, the colour of a dead aubergine.

'If the business is to survive,' she whispers, 'surely something–'

'I see,' says Hugo. 'That's it, is it? Because you have contributed money to the business, you now have the right to dictate how it's run?'

'No, Hugo, not at all. Really. I didn't mean the money.'

'Yes. You think it gives you the right to tell me what to do.'

'Hugo, please, I didn't mean –'

'You pick up a few pieces of rubbish off the floor, and all of a sudden you know more about everything than I do.'

'It's just that I happened to notice –'

'You think I'm incompetent, a failure.'

'No, of course not –'

'Enough!' he shouts. 'Get out! Get out!'

Emma runs out of the room, to sit in the library with her hands pressed over her ears, while Hugo empties the cabinets and throws them against the wall.

At breakfast the next morning, Hugo's face is chalky. It is not the face of a living person and Emma worries he has had a stroke.

When he has eaten his egg and drunk his tea, Hugo gets to his feet. 'Well, Emma,' he says, 'it seems I shall have to work at the office again from now on, since you have made it impossible for me to work here. I hope you are satisfied, driving me from my home. You shall have the place to yourself now, just like you wanted.'

'Hugo, please, I didn't –' Emma says, but it is a half-hearted protest.

'Yes, yes, you will be happy now.'

Hugo checks the locks on the doors and windows, then puts on his hat and leaves, slamming the door behind him.

When he has gone, Emma wanders slowly around the house. It is very quiet without the servants. When deliveries come, she ducks under a table or behind a dresser. It is too awful to hear people knocking and calling, knowing she is there. It is the same with the gardeners. She watches them from the windows, but draws back whenever they look up.

It goes on like this for almost a month. Twice in the first week, Hugo pretends to leave and then comes back suddenly to surprise her. But she has expected this, and both times he finds her sitting quietly, reading or working on her tapestry.

See her there, in the little gold armchair beside the fireplace. 'Yes, Hugo?' she says, looking up as the door opens.

'I forgot my hat,' he says.

'Ah yes,' she says. 'Of course.'

But he soon starts staying away for the whole day, as he did before, and one day, after a solid fortnight of this, Emma gets up from the little gold chair, takes a screwdriver from under the seat cushion, unscrews the lock on one of the bathroom windows and climbs out.

'Where have you been?' asks Mrs Gilbert half an hour later, as Emma appears at the end of the path. 'We're out of almost every single thing.'

'I'm sorry,' says Emma. 'We've been so busy.' She avoids

looking at Annabel, who is watching her very closely. 'For the future, I've arranged for another delivery to come. If Annabel writes a list and drops it down to the pub, they will see to it.'

'Won't you be coming?' asks Mrs Gilbert.

'I may not be able to. I'm sorry.'

'Well, now you're here, you must listen to all our news,' says Mrs Gilbert, ushering Emma into the sitting room.

Emma perches on the edge of an armchair, but her face is very pale and she keeps getting up and looking out of the window. 'I can't stay long,' she says.

'My poor sister-in-law, Beatrice, has passed away,' says Mrs Gilbert. 'It turns out she was ill after all.'

'Ah yes,' says Emma. 'I heard about that. I'm sorry.' She glances at Annabel, who is busy unpicking a line of stitches in her embroidery.

'It is sad,' says Mrs Gilbert. She hesitates, looking at Annabel. 'Death always is. But the good news is that she has left me all her money.'

'That is good news,' says Emma. 'Congratulations.'

'It's quite a substantial amount,' says Mrs Gilbert. 'I wonder why she didn't give it to Hugo, but I think she had some concerns . . .' Her voice falters. 'Anyway, very grateful for it we are too. Of course, I haven't got it yet. There are all sorts of legal bits and pieces first.'

'Yes,' says Emma. 'That's the usual thing.' She looks at the clock. 'I'll need to go soon,' she says. 'It was just a flying visit.'

'Wait a minute,' says Mrs Gilbert. 'I haven't shown you the pumpkin patch. We've done very well this year, haven't we, Annabel?'

Annabel nods.

They go outside and look at the pumpkin patch.

'I'll pick one for you,' says Mrs Gilbert.

'Oh, don't worry about that,' says Emma.

'Annabel, go and fetch the pumpkin knife.'

'No, really,' says Emma.

'It will only take a moment. Hold on.'

'Hugo will be worried if I'm not back when he gets home,' says Emma.

'But he won't be home for ages.'

'He could be. He could get home at any time.'

'Just say you went for a little walk. You know, Emma,' Mrs Gilbert continues while they wait for Annabel to find the pumpkin knife, 'I sometimes wonder if I should just come down to see him. He can't mean all those things he says. He can't still be angry, can he, after all this time?'

'Oh no, you mustn't do that,' says Emma with all the feeling she can muster.

'I'm sure he'd be happier in his heart if he let it all go,' says Mrs Gilbert.

'Perhaps,' says Emma. 'Leave it to me, will you? Don't do anything until I say.'

At last, here is Annabel with the knife. They deliberate over which pumpkin to choose, which one looks as if it will have the most flavour, and struggle for some time over the cutting of the stem, so tough, so hard to get to without damaging the leaves. But at last it is done. Grey-faced and gripping her pumpkin, Emma races away down the track, past the dairy and on to the drive.

Here she stops, for there is Hugo's car, sitting on the gravel. No, she thinks. No, no, no.

She can hear him now. Surely everyone in the village must be able to hear him. She glances back over her shoulder, but it is too late.

With a roar, Hugo rushes out, grabs Emma's arm and drags her towards the house.

'Wait, Hugo. Listen,' she says. 'Please, Hugo. Wait!'

Annabel has followed Emma back to Thornwalk, and stumbles after her on to the drive. 'Hugo!' she cries. 'Hugo, no!'

Hugo turns and stares at his sister. 'What are you doing here, Annabel?' he says.

'Let her go, Hugo,' Annabel says, but something has happened to her throat and only a whisper comes out.

'This isn't anything to do with you,' Hugo says. 'Go home, Annabel.'

'No, Hugo,' she says, clenching her fists. 'No, I won't.' Nothing will make me go, she thinks. Nothing. Whatever happens, I won't leave Emma.

'Get away from here!' cries Hugo. 'Now!'

Annabel turns and runs.

Up the stairs they go, Hugo and Emma – 'Hugo, please!' – to Lydia's room, the one with the bolt on the door, where he throws her inside.

Emma's head begins to throb, there is a roaring in her ears, and blood spurts from her nose. The door is smeared with it, the rug spattered. She cannot find a handkerchief. Instead, she grabs a cushion from the bed and presses it against her face.

Meanwhile, outside, the pumpkin has rolled across the gravel into the bushes, and Annabel crouches under a rhododendron, with her head in her hands.

39

Where the Clock Was

So that is the reason for the blood on the blue-room floor. More blood is to come, but from someone else.

For now, let us go back to Mrs Gilbert and the money left to her by poor dead Aunt Beatrice. She mentioned delays, legal bits and pieces. These will go on for two years.

'This is very strange,' says Mrs Gilbert to Annabel, as they sit at the little kitchen table eating breakfast on a drizzly August morning in 1955. She is frowning at a letter from the family lawyer that arrived in the post that morning. 'Something about somebody contesting something.' She picks a shred of marmalade off the page and hands the letter to Annabel.

Dear Mrs Gilbert

This communication is to give you formal notice of a small matter that has arisen in relation to your sister-in-law's will. I enclose herewith the official documents, one copy of which I would be most obliged if you would sign and return to me as acknowledgement of receipt.

The matter does not appear overly serious, and we are

*confident we can deal with it here with very little involvement
from yourself, but in the meantime, and until the matter is
successfully resolved, the money cannot be released . . .*

Mrs Gilbert opens the enclosed documents and stares at
them, but they are full of dreadful legal words that make her
head hurt. She pushes them across the table to Annabel.

'I don't understand, Annabel,' she says. 'Whatever does it
mean?'

'I think someone else wants the money,' says Annabel, leafing
through the pages.

'Someone else? Surely not Hugo?'

'No. It says Coldwell. Mr and Mrs C. Coldwell.'

'Lydia? I don't think that can be right, can it? They have plenty
of money, don't they? There must be a mistake.'

'Possibly,' says Annabel.

'This is all very strange,' says Mrs Gilbert. 'Oh dear, oh
dear.'

It is a long process. The Coldwells' claims are submitted and
rejected. There are no legal grounds on which to challenge the
will, they are told. No lack of testamentary capacity. No lack of
due process. One cannot challenge a will merely on the grounds
that the beneficiary is unworthy, or that the money would be
better bestowed elsewhere.

The Coldwells appeal, are rejected, and appeal again. At last
they are granted an informal hearing.

'Look at what has been happening at Thornwalk,' says
Cooper Coldwell, opening his attack. 'Madness clearly runs in
the family. Mad people ought not to be entrusted with large
sums of money. That's just common sense.'

They have testimonies from the villagers, full of rumours
of wrongdoing and tales of incompetence, and photographs
of Mrs Gilbert in her pumpkin patch, looking dishevelled and
confused and holding a small knife.

'Look at that,' the Coldwells insist. 'Is that the face of a woman who ought to be entrusted with anything at all?'

'The court doesn't understand why you have brought in these documents,' says the magistrate. 'This kind of evidence is entirely irrelevant. If Mrs Gilbert is of sound mind –'

'Sound mind?' says Mr Coldwell. 'Definitely not.'

'Without evidence to the contrary –'

'Hugo must have banished her for a reason.'

'Not if he is mad,' says the magistrate.

And so the case is lost.

Mrs Gilbert knows nothing of all this. She only waits, month after month, until at last she receives another letter from the lawyer, telling her that the matter has been successfully resolved and the money will shortly be released.

'Hooray,' says Mrs Gilbert. 'Oh, Annabel, saved at last! The very first thing I shall do is have a hot bath. A really hot one.'

But then the letters from Lydia start to arrive.

'Oh, look, Annabel,' says Mrs Gilbert at the breakfast table. 'It's from Lydia. Pictures of the boys.' She squints at a little collection of photographs. 'Well, they are certainly very interesting-looking children, aren't they? I expect they have a lot of character.'

She hands the photographs to Annabel.

'And look here . . . these are some drawings by Sydney.'

Annabel looks at the hasty little scribbles. *Miss you, Granny*, has been scrawled on the back of one.

'They miss their granny,' says Mrs Gilbert, with tears in her eyes.

Annabel sighs, hands the scribbles back to her mother and begins to clear away the dishes.

Over the coming weeks, Lydia writes many such letters to her mother, or, rather, her hand holds the pen.

See Mr Coldwell pacing up and down the room behind her.

'Say you were so overwhelmed at the news of her banishment that you've been in no fit state to write until now,' he says.

'Oh, do I need to say that?' says Lydia. 'I don't think she'd believe that.'

'Yes, she will,' says Mr Coldwell. 'Go on, write it.'

With a heavy heart, Lydia writes. But Mr Coldwell is right – Mrs Gilbert has no difficulty believing it.

'They were overwhelmed, Annabel,' she says. 'Which, of course, they must have been. Yes, that makes complete sense.'

For another month, letters pass swiftly back and forth between the big white Chelsea town house and the little brown Chaplain's Cottage.

'Oh dear,' says Mrs Gilbert, frowning down at another of these. 'It seems things haven't been going too well for them either. Their nice little country estate has had to be sold. That's a shame. They were very fond of it, I know.'

Annabel says nothing.

Back and forth the letters go, until at last, in the autumn of 1957, it is decided that Lydia will defy Hugo, risk his fury and whatever fearful consequences may follow, and come to the cottage. After all, her duty is to her beloved mother, her children's beloved grandmother, not to Hugo, who has gone mad.

'Are we sure about this?' says Lydia to Mr Coldwell, after the visit has been arranged.

'Absolutely,' says Mr Coldwell. 'Your aunt wanted us to have that money. She just forgot to write it down.'

'Yes,' says Lydia. 'I suppose so.'

'Besides, your mother would never spend it properly.'

Lydia sighs. 'That's true.'

'Now, you had better take the children,' says Mr Coldwell.

'Must I?' says Lydia. 'They never do what they're told when it's just me.'

'Yes, yes,' says Cooper. 'I'll make sure they know what to say.'

So, one afternoon a fortnight later, Lydia and the boys arrive at the Chaplain's Cottage at the edge of the woods.

'Ugh,' says Cooper Junior, as they walk down the overgrown lane towards it. 'What is this place, Mother?'

'You know very well what place it is,' says Lydia. She wonders again at Mr Coldwell's decision not to come with them. It could all go very horribly wrong.

'Well, I don't like it,' says Cooper Junior. He looks around and wrinkles his nose. There is a definite no-cake feel about it, he thinks, a decidedly bread-and-butter look to the open doorway, the little tiled kitchen, the grubby green apron tied around this old woman's waist.

'It's sad here,' says Sydney, clutching his mother's skirt. 'Someone doesn't like it at all. He would very much like to leave now, Mother. May he?'

'No, he may not,' says Lydia. 'Now, come along, both of you, and remember to call Mrs Gilbert "Granny" and to say that you miss her.'

The children are dragged up the path into the waiting arms of the old woman in the doorway, who is now crying. Sydney begins to cry too.

'Oh, Mother,' says Lydia, looking around, 'I had no idea it would be like this. No idea at all. If I had known . . .'

'Haven't you been here before?' asks Mrs Gilbert in surprise.

'Oh,' says Lydia, blushing, 'Yes, I suppose I have, but I remember it quite differently. I was under the impression that it was much bigger, much grander. But I suppose I was smaller then.' Her voice fades. She is thinking of Mr Higgins. For some time now, she has been almost certain that he didn't have bad breath.

'What do you think of Granny's house?' Lydia asks the children.

They remember their father's promises. 'I think it's not good enough for our granny,' says Cooper Junior staunchly.

'I bet she doesn't like it,' says Sydney. 'I bet she thinks it's scary at night.'

'They're right,' says Lydia, turning to her mother. 'It isn't the proper place for you. How terrifying all this must have been.'

'Oh, I don't know,' says Mrs Gilbert. She looks at Annabel, who is sitting in the corner, working on a new embroidery of a butterfly in a spiderweb. 'We've been all right, haven't we, Annabel? I'm getting quite used to it now.'

'No,' says Lydia, 'it is not the right sort of thing at all.'

'Why is our grandmother living in a place like this?' says Cooper Junior, warming to the task now that he is halfway to tea at Fortnum's. 'It's embarrassing, that's what it is.'

'Oh dear,' says Mrs Gilbert. 'Is it?'

They sit down to their bread and butter, and the conversation turns to the boys, their education, their clothes. Cooper Junior's have to be specially made, and that's very expensive. 'It's a struggle sometimes,' says Lydia. 'But we muddle through, don't we boys?'

'What?' says Cooper Junior.

'Is it time for everyone to leave?' says Sydney.

'Oh dear,' says Mrs Gilbert again, wringing her hands. 'Here, would this help? You could sell it.' She gets up and takes the little cuckoo clock from the wall. It was a wedding present from her mother and one of the few things she brought with her from Thornwalk – you can still see the dark patch on the wallpaper above the dressing table in Mrs Gilbert's bedroom where it hung all those years – but now she is happy to sacrifice it for Lydia, for the boys.

Lydia holds the clock. She had not expected this. 'How very kind,' she murmurs at last. 'I suppose every little helps.'

Mrs Gilbert blushes. 'It isn't very much,' she says. 'I wish I could do more.'

'Of course, you do,' says Lydia. This is the moment she has been waiting for. 'I know you would give all you have for the sake of your beloved grandchildren, who love you so much. They are your legacy, after all. How better could money be spent?'

'Oh yes,' murmurs Mrs Gilbert. 'That's right.' She thinks of the will, and the lawyer's letter. 'There is Aunt Beatrice's money –.'

'I completely forgot about that,' says Lydia.

Annabel sighs and closes her eyes.

Mrs Gilbert hesitates, glancing at Annabel. 'I haven't got it yet,' she says. 'There was a delay. An objection, I think. Perhaps . . . perhaps Cooper . . .'

'Oh, that,' says Lydia. 'We just wanted to take care of things for you, like Hugo used to, so that you wouldn't have to worry.'

'Oh, I see,' says Mrs Gilbert. 'Well, that was very kind of you, Lydia, very kind.'

Annabel's head sinks slowly on to the table.

'I bet no one else in the family cares about you as much as we do,' says Lydia, frowning at her sister. 'Does Rosalind ever visit?'

'Oh dear,' says Mrs Gilbert. 'Poor Rosalind. My poor sweet Rosalind.'

'Or Jeremy?' continues Lydia. 'No, of course not. It's just us. Of course, you will do everything you can to help us, as soon as you can.'

Annabel gets up and leaves the room.

40

A Fruit Knife

In the top-right-hand drawer of the white kitchen dresser, you will find a fruit knife. It is not the actual fruit knife that we shall be discussing in a moment. That one would naturally have been impounded by the police. When convicts go home, I am aware that they are given back their belongings, but I don't think they would be given a weapon, and besides, she never went home.

No, it is not the actual fruit knife, only a visual aid.

We have come to a critical juncture in the tale. When Mrs Gilbert says, 'My poor sweet Rosalind', it is to this that she refers. So, let us turn our eyes once more in this direction, a bleak horizon though it be.

Nicholas Middleton, somehow, has pieced his life back together. The divorce has gone through, finally, the last judge sympathizing with the decent young professional accidentally dragged into a life of passion and violence. Rosalind is notorious, after all.

'None of the charges laid against you have been given any credence by the court,' the judge says to Nicholas. 'And it is considered strange that Mrs Middleton should be levelling such charges and, at the same time, be refusing to grant the divorce. That strikes the court as contradictory. Therefore, it is the decision of the court that the charges be dismissed and the divorce be granted as of this moment.'

Nicholas leaves the court grim but triumphant. He is grateful not to have seen Rosalind, who was apparently too ill to attend, glad that the single reporter took no photographs and made no attempt to talk to him.

Yes, Rosalind is ill. As Nicholas makes his way out of the courthouse, she is sitting by the telephone, waiting for him to get home. At four o'clock, she dials his number.

He answers on the three hundred and twenty-seventh ring. 'That's it, Rosalind,' he says. 'It's over now.'

'You said you would always love me,' she says. 'Was that a lie?'

'Not a lie,' says Nicholas, 'but surely . . .'

She calls him every day, sometimes ten times a day. 'I don't understand why you're being like this,' she says. 'You've changed so much.'

Then one day the phone goes dead in her hand – not just ringing and ringing and someone finally picking up at two in the morning, but dead.

She goes to his house and sits on his doorstep, waiting for him to come home. She is there for six hours before someone tells her that Mr Middleton has moved. She has been sitting on the doorstep of an empty house.

'Where has he gone?' she asks, but no one will tell her.

'I'm his sister,' she says. 'I'm very ill. He would want to know.'

'You're his sister? Not that crazy ex-wife of his?'

'No, no, obviously not,' laughs Rosalind. 'She's very beautiful. She was a movie star, you know, really famous.'

'Not really famous.'

'Yes, really famous. Anyway, that's not me, as you can see.'

The man looks at her closely. 'All right,' he says. 'Here it is.' And he jots down the address on the back of an envelope.

'I never would have done it, if I'd known the truth,' the man says afterwards at the trial. 'But she lied to me.'

There is a murmur of disapproval from the jury. They hate lying.

Of course, lying is the least of Rosalind's crimes, but it seems significant.

'Clearly there was forethought,' says the prosecutor in the summing-up. 'She knew what she intended to do, so she lied about who she was. That makes it murder.'

See Rosalind a few hours later, back at home in her flat. It is a sordid little place. She has had no work for a long time, and even Mr Aslet is refusing to help her now. See her slowly putting on the ivory satin dress she wore for her wedding to Mr Simms, all those years ago, when she believed in promises and dreams, and slipping a little knife into her pocket.

'Cold-blooded murder,' says the prosecutor.

'With a fruit knife?' cries the council for the defence. 'Come now. It's obvious that she never intended to kill anyone!'

She slips the knife into her pocket, lifts up her skirts and steps out into a struck-by-lightning sky. It is strangely dark. Something to do with the alignment of the stars, perhaps, or an ill wind, blown from distant storms or a dark, dark butterfly's wings.

It has started to rain. How odd to see this woman in a wedding dress coming down the road in the rain.

'Her face was white,' says Mrs Simper of Number 6, Stockwell Terrace. 'How dreadful she looked, like a ghost, like a dead person, like something out of a film.'

Rosalind arrives at Landboat Avenue and wanders up and down for a while. She cannot find the house. There is Number 14, and there is Number 20. It is raining harder now. In the dim light, through the rain, she finally makes out a tarnished number plate against the brickwork.

With her eyes fixed on the door, Rosalind squats on the pavement on the other side of the road. Not sits, but squats. It looks uncomfortable. The way a cat would sit, or a monkey.

At last, a light goes off in the front room of the house and the door is opened. There is Nicholas Middleton, laughing and fumbling with an umbrella. It seems the umbrella is broken. In every gust of wind, half of it turns upside down and a metal bit sticks out.

'May I interject here that my client was also injured in the exchange?' says the council for the defence.

'You must be joking,' responds the prosecutor. 'A spoke in the eye is hardly significant in the circumstances, hardly on a par with the wounds inflicted upon the innocent personages of my clients.'

The council for the defence sinks back into his chair.

Nicholas is not alone. Someone has stepped out of the house behind him. It is the new Mrs Middleton.

'May I point out,' says the council for the defence, 'that my client was until that point unaware that Mr Middleton had remarried? It was this fact that caused her to become temporarily unhinged. Yes, she had a knife, but that was just for emphasis, just to make him listen, which, despite his promises, he had stopped doing. She had no intention of using it until that moment. It was a *crime passionnel*, ladies and gentlemen. It was a moment of madness, provoked by the deliberate cold cruelty of Mr and Mrs Middleton themselves.'

Yes, a woman steps out of the house behind Nicholas. She is laughing too. The umbrella is no good. It was a gift from her father – probably very cheap. How funny.

Rosalind stands. The ivory dress glows yellow under the street lamps.

Nicholas squints into the rain.

Rosalind steps closer, to the edge of the pavement.

'Rosalind? Is that you?' he says.

Rosalind steps out into the traffic. Cars swerve and honk their horns. Rosalind draws the knife from her pocket.

At that, the new Mrs Middleton screams and turns to scrabble with the door, but it has one of those stupid Yale locks and has already closed behind them. She fumbles for the keys, drops them and screams again.

'Of course, I feared for my life,' says Mrs Middleton. 'I will never get over it. The internal scars are almost as bad as the external ones. My life is as good as over.'

Later, when it is Hugo's time in a courtroom, they will refer many times to this, to the sister judged criminally insane and locked away in Broadmoor. Something must have happened, they say. Something, somewhere, must have gone very wrong in this family.

41

The Fire Axe

I am sitting at their father's desk. Beside the window is a set of shelves filled with memorabilia from their grandfather's time and the first Boer War. On the opposite wall, above the fireplace, is a map of America.

From across the gallery, I can hear Emma's voice.

'It wasn't your fault,' she is saying. 'It was just impossible. I see that now. I see that Jeremy was right.'

'Never mention that person's name again,' Hugo says.

'It was outdated. It was all too old-fashioned. The product, the method of production, marketing, everything.'

'I will see it done,' Hugo says. 'I will see it succeed, in my father's name, for my father's honour.'

'Your father had given up on it too, Hugo,' says Emma.

'How dare you say that!' says Hugo. 'He would never have given up on it.'

'My mother found out about it years ago. He was going to take out all his money, close it down.'

'He would never have done that. Never.'

'It's true, Hugo. Ask your mother to tell you the truth for once.'

'I don't believe anything you say. You are not to be trusted. My father was a great war hero –'

'No, he wasn't,' says Emma. 'He wasn't a great war hero.'

'What? How dare you say such a thing!' says Hugo. 'My father died in the war.'

'He didn't die in the war, Hugo,' says Emma. 'Your mother should have told you.'

'How did he die, then?' asks Hugo.

Emma hesitates. 'I think . . . I think he was on a boat.'

'In the war.'

'No, not in the war.'

'Then why was he on a boat?'

'I don't know, Hugo. But it wasn't in the war.'

'You lie!'

There is silence for a long time.

'Let me out, Hugo,' Emma says. She is too tired to talk. She is kneeling on the floor, with her head against the door. She can hear him breathing on the other side, where he sits on the landing with the fire axe across his lap. 'Let me go home.'

'No,' says Hugo.

The brackets for the fire axe are still mounted on the wall to the right of the blue-room door. The axe itself is buried deep in the storeroom behind the kitchen.

42

A Tartan Hot-water Bottle Cover

In the spring of 1958, Mrs Gilbert leaves the Chaplain's Cottage and goes to live with the Coldwells in their nice white town house in Chelsea. It is something she will soon regret, and often in the years to come she will think almost longingly of the little cottage in the woods, the smell of the bats, and the pumpkin patch.

You can still see it, the pumpkin patch, amongst the nettles at the back of the house. Year after year, the pumpkins returned, smaller each time, till they were no more than little orange ping-pong balls in a sea of mildewy leaves, which is what you will find there now.

Shortly afterwards, Annabel returns to Thornwalk. Hugo watches from the library window as she wheels her rusty barrow down the drive, but does not come out to meet her. She lets herself into the hall and finds her own way upstairs to her old bedroom.

It is clear that something terrible has happened.

Emma is gone.

The piles of paperwork in Hugo's study have disappeared and the filing cabinets are locked. That side of things is all over.

There is only one servant, Mrs Chisolm, an ancient woman with a Scottish accent and the pursed lips of the habitual whistler.

'Welcome back, Miss Annabel,' says Mrs Chisolm. 'Aye, I've heard all about ye.'

The hours are long, that first week. Hugo takes his meals alone on a tray in the library. A sign is permanently hung on the door handle, handwritten on a piece of cereal packet, saying do not disturb.

'He does'na mean me,' says Mrs Chisolm, setting off with her tray.

Annabel haunts the passages outside the kitchen. 'Shall I help you with the vegetables?' she asks Mrs Chisolm.

'You should'na be in the kitchen,' says Mrs Chisolm.

'I'm used to kitchens,' says Annabel. 'I did most of the cooking up at the cottage.'

'No' the way I like it done. I'm very particular about ma vegetables.'

'I could just peel the potatoes.'

'You'd best leave it ta me, Miss Annabel.'

'But I'd like to help.'

'I prefer ta work on me own.'

Annabel sighs and turns to leave.

Poor wee mite, thinks Mrs Chisolm, watching Annabel wander away. Must be forty if she's a day, but no more'n a bairn inside. Poor wee mite.

'Aw, go on,' says Mrs Chisolm. 'Peel the tatties, then.'

Mrs Chisolm has brought an armchair into the kitchen for when her hips are bad, and sits down and watches Annabel peel the potatoes.

'It's nothing ta do wi' me what people get up to,' she says. 'My pa was the under butler at Manvers Park in Dumfries. The stories he used ta tell us. Absolutely shockin' they were. What I say is, the disgustin' troubles o' today are the highlight o' the dinner party tomorra.'

On the first Tuesday of the month, Mrs Chisolm allows Annabel to help her change the bed linen.

'People told me he was a bad un,' Mrs Chisolm says, perched on a stool as Annabel turns the mattresses. 'But anyone can see he's a harmless old soul now. He's learnt his lesson. Broken, that's what I'd call him, and there's no man so easy ta pick up and put in ya pocket as a broken one.'

So, it goes on. Until one September evening, perhaps three years after Annabel's return.

Hugo is sitting in the library. A storm is blowing outside, rattling the windows, whistling under the doors. It reminds him of a night long ago, when they were children. The lights had gone out, and he and his brother and sisters had gathered here. There was a full moon, he thinks, just like this, with blue light coming in through the skylight in the hall.

He remembers his mother in a long gown with a great sash at the waist. Lydia, with her hair in plaits, filling the air with that scent she wore. And little Rosalind, so sweet then, holding tight to her mother's hand.

He and Jeremy had stood there at the window, looking out across the valley, and watched a tree go crashing down on Belmont House. And he had run out into the storm to see if anyone was hurt. They had called him a hero.

He takes another swig from his flask.

Little Emma Asquill. She had clung to him, he remembers, her sleepy face looking up at him, her eyes wide and scared. She had slipped on the grass, so he had carried her. Yes, they had called him a hero.

He doesn't see inside the sky-blue Austin 7 as it rolls away down the drive the next morning, doesn't hear Lady Asquill saying, 'What on earth was the point of dragging you both up here?'

Or Emma saying, 'Oh, Mother, he was trying to be kind.'

A hero, he thinks. They forget these things, all of them. They choose to remember the other things.

'Emma,' he says aloud, 'why don't you listen? If we could both just agree that it wasn't my fault.'

He gets up and staggers out into the hall. 'Emma?' Slowly, he begins to climb the stairs.

At shortly after two, Annabel is woken by a scream. She sits up and turns on her lamp.

'Help!' cries a voice. There is a crash and the sound of heavy running feet.

Annabel pulls on her dressing gown and hurries out into the corridor. 'Mrs Chisolm?' she calls out. 'Are you all right?' She rushes along the passage, but by the time she reaches the house-keeper's room the door is shut and locked. 'Mrs Chisolm?' she says, knocking and rattling the handle.

'Go away,' says Mrs Chisolm. 'Keep away from me, all o' ya.'

Annabel turns and runs to Hugo's room. His bed is empty. 'Hugo?' she calls. There is no reply, but from the hall below she hears again the sound of running footsteps and a slamming door.

The next morning, Annabel finds the door to Mrs Chisolm's bedroom open and the room empty. The bed has been stripped – the bedclothes in a pile on the floor with a little tartan hot-water bottle tangled up inside. (For years to come, the hot-water bottle will sit on the scullery shelf, as Annabel thinks about trying to find an address to send it to, until at last she puts it in the cupboard underneath, which is where you will find it now.)

Downstairs, the front door is open, a taxi is waiting on the gravel and Mrs Chisolm is loading her bags inside. Her lips are pursed. She will say nothing, answer none of Annabel's questions, only casts her a terrible look and shakes her head.

Annabel watches the taxi disappear, then turns and goes into the library, where she finds Hugo on the sofa with a blanket over his face.

'I didn't do anything,' Hugo says.

'Of course not,' Annabel says.

'A small misunderstanding,' he says.

'Yes, I know,' says Annabel. 'A small misunderstanding.'

43

Letters from Mrs Gilbert

Other than the small misunderstanding with Mrs Chisolm, these years at Thornwalk are largely uneventful. Hugo goes down to the village almost every evening. Sometimes to my little cottage. Sometimes to sit in the Black Arrow, with the men at the bar scowling and muttering and shaking their heads.

Not long after Annabel's return, some of the outlying woodland is sold, and ownership of Inscombe Farm is transferred to the Kirby family, who have worked it for generations. Such transactions are common enough, but for some reason, this time, Hugo is left very pale and quiet, with a new habit of clutching his hands together suddenly before burying them in his pockets.

Letters arrive regularly from Mrs Gilbert, addressed to Annabel:

4 June 1958
London
Dear Annabel,
Greetings from Château Coldwell!

I must say, I am settling in very well. This morning I had breakfast on a tray in my room. Cooper Junior made the croissant himself. Not really edible, of course, but an admirable attempt. How wonderful it is to be appreciated after everything I have suffered.

Lydia has made me realize that it is not acceptable for a woman of my comparative youth and ability to shut herself away as I had been. Apparently, they had hoped I would come to them a long time ago but assumed I had chosen to go to the cottage because it would be easier. They had thought it a little selfish of me but wanted to respect my wishes so didn't say anything.

How shocked they were to learn that the situation had been entirely the reverse and that I had been for some time – mainly before your arrival, my dear – quite in despair.

Today they have planned an outing to the zoo and lunch at the Carlton. I have insisted that I pay, knowing how they struggle. With some reluctance, they agreed.

Mother

The next letter is dated three months later.

Dear Annabel,

Modern family life is not without its compromises. Last week, Lydia reminded me that I am no longer head of the household and that people won't necessarily be asking for my advice like they used to. They won't be thinking that I know best any more or wanting to hear my opinion on things.

I wasn't quite sure what she meant by that, because, these days, I don't have many opinions left. Lydia said that was good, because she had her own opinions now.

Then yesterday I asked Lydia about what I had perceived to be a new reserve in Mr Coldwell's manner towards me. She

*suggested it might be because of inflation, which meant that
the agreed contribution I was making was no longer sufficient
to cover the cost of my upkeep. She had argued my case with
him, of course, that the benefits I provided went far beyond
monetary considerations, but Mr Coldwell, as the man of the
house, quite rightly has the financial rather than the emotional
needs of the family foremost in mind.*

*They have reluctantly agreed to let me increase my monthly
contribution. It will eat into my capital to some degree, but I
cannot in good conscience allow them to lose out as a result of
their kindness to me.*

Mother

Towards the end of the year, this is received:

Dear Annabel,

*They have asked me not to attend mealtimes until I have done
something about my disapproving manner. Apparently, it is
something to do with my expression – not any particular one,
just the basic underlying arrangement of my features. I wish they
had noticed this before, but apparently it was not a problem then.
It is something that has happened to my face since I went to live
with them. It gives Cooper Junior the most terrible indigestion.*

*I am struggling a little with this, I admit. Having dinner by
oneself in an empty house is bad enough, but not nearly so bad
as eating alone in one's bedroom while downstairs a family
are laughing and having a wonderful time without you.*

*I have been thinking for some time that it might be best if
I used the rest of the money left to me by dear Beatrice to buy
a little place of my own. Just a small flat. I think I should be
very happy with that.*

*It was with some nervousness that I approached the subject
with Lydia and Mr Coldwell, but they were very kind about*

it. They would miss me, they said, but I must feel free to do absolutely as I liked with the remainder of the money. Aunt Beatrice had given it to me after all, and she would have wanted me to be happy.

They kindly took me to see a few places which they judged to be the best of what is currently on the market, but I came away each time feeling quite despondent and not at all certain that my situation would be improved by moving. They were all quite grubby little places in what seemed to me to be not quite the most enviable of locations. On one occasion, I witnessed a man being sick on the street, and the flat was accessed through a shared stairwell that had that same unmistakable odour.

'Are these really all I can afford?' I asked, because, from the little notices in the papers, things had seemed more promising.

'Yes,' they said. 'They are.'

I said, 'Is there really nothing else?'

And they said, 'No, there isn't.'

They could see that I was having second thoughts, and kindly said that, despite all the difficulties I was causing the children, psychologically, they were happy for me to go on living with them, with a small increase in my monthly contribution, in line with inflation.

And I said, 'Goodness, has there been more inflation?'

And they said, 'Yes, there has.'

Sad not to have better news to tell you.

Mother

Shortly followed by:

Dear Annabel,

It is a pretty dismal situation I have found myself in after all.

Increasingly, it has seemed to me that I must try to get away and find my own place, and it occurred to me that, if Lydia and Mr Coldwell were able to repay a little of the money I lent them, I might be able to find somewhere that didn't smell of sick.

I had been thinking back to the places they had shown me, and some of them did not seem quite so impossible. Dirt can, of course, be cleaned away, and I have no need of large light rooms or anything of that sort. I would be quite happy to make do. My only real issue was the smell of those communal stairwells. With a little extra money, I thought, perhaps we could find something in a slightly better neighbourhood.

It was a difficult subject to broach, and their reaction was no better than I feared.

'What?' they said. 'You are asking us for money?'

'Not for your own money,' I tried to say. 'Nothing like that.'

'You know how difficult it has been for us, after that last claim against Cooper. It nearly cleaned us out. Here we are, practically starving to death, and you come to us for money!'

'Not for your money,' I said again, fearing I had not made this clear. 'Just a little of the money I lent you. Just a very little. As I recall, it was only needed temporarily and after that it was going to be returned.'

The look on their faces, Annabel! I felt so ashamed. It was only the thought of more dinners alone in my room that spurred me on.

'That money is being used,' they said. 'You can't just ask for it back any time you like.'

And they went on to say that if it had been a loan, which they actually weren't entirely sure about, then, of course, I might have it back, but not now.

Then they started thinking about it, and said that they weren't sure it had been a loan at all. Hadn't it been a gift? They remembered very well how grateful they had been for it at the time, how much fuss they had made of me afterwards, with breakfast in bed and things like that, and if it had only been a loan, as I said, they couldn't see how they would have been so grateful or would have gone to the trouble of making such a fuss of me.

Did I remember the picture Sydney had drawn called 'My Hero'? That had been a picture of Granny Gilbert.

Well, that's odd, Annabel, because I do remember it, and, unless it was another picture called 'My Hero', it was of his daddy, but they said no, it was you, because you had so kindly given us all that money.

They are so angry, Annabel. Mr Coldwell gets up and leaves the room whenever I go into it, and the children scowl and whisper behind my back.

Mother

In November 1959, a final letter is received:

An update on the small flat idea. It seems that the investment package I chose for the remainder of my capital was not sound and its value has decreased. If I leave it where it is, it may eventually recover. If I insist on withdrawing it now, I must accept a substantial loss. Either way, it seems that in the type of place I would now be able to afford, the smell of sick in a communal stairwell would be almost inevitable.

I am quite in despair, and often wonder what I could possibly have done to deserve all this. I don't think there is anything, really.

Oh, Annabel, when I think of the time we spent in our little cottage, I almost long to return. We didn't have much, did we, and most of it was mouldy, but we were happy in our way.

Mother

44

Saint Catherine of Siena

These are not the only letters to arrive at Thornwalk.

Now and then, things come addressed to Jeremy. In 1960, there is a letter from Giuseppe Cavallo, director of the Street Justice League, thanking Jeremy for his work on a homeless shelter in Madrid.

A few months later, a man called Henrique Pestana writes to pass on the thanks of the three children and one cat rescued by Jeremy from a fire in a Lisbon housing project.

Next is a letter from Mother Seraphina, of the Holy Child in Nîmes, expressing her heartfelt gratitude for all Jeremy's hard work with the orphans, teaching them the rudiments of household sanitation and carpentry, and the improvements he has made in the convent plumbing, the benefits of which are felt by all.

One by one, the letters are opened and read and thrown into the library fireplace.

Thankfully, the fire is rarely lit, and never well stoked, and each evening, after Hugo has gone to bed, Annabel creeps into the room and rescues what she can from the ashes.

*

The last of the letters is a long, official-looking document from the director of the new children's hospital in Rome, which reads as follows:

12 May 1962
Rome

Dear Mr Gilbert,

It is my belief that the Jeremy Gilbert, with whom I recently had the pleasure of some acquaintance, is your brother. This communication is to enquire as to his whereabouts.

The board members here are eager to acknowledge the great debt they owe the aforementioned Jeremy Gilbert for all the hours he worked without pay on the building of the new children's hospital, and also, perhaps more importantly, to apologize for having doubted him, disparaged his work and sacked him.

The board realizes now that it was wrong of them to quibble about the cost of his board and lodging when he would ultimately prove a hero. It was only that, compared with some of the other workers, it did seem as if they were not getting from Jeremy quite the same level of output in terms of units done for units eaten, if that makes sense.

He was so fastidious. It seemed excessive at the time. Some of the other men didn't like it, felt that it cast aspersions on the quality of their work. Of course, in the end, Jeremy was proved right and it has now been almost unanimously agreed that looking like a fire door is not the same thing as being a fire door.

To be fair to the members of the board, however, fuel costs were at a record level at that time, and Jeremy would insist on working through the night. Yes, he was happy to work without heating, but there were the lights to consider.

They had wondered too about the bills for materials. A

few people suggested they saw some disparity between goods ordered and paid for, and goods visibly demonstrable in the completed building. At that point, they didn't know about the sprinkler system he'd made, the components of which were for the most part concealed behind the ceilings. Ultimately, if it hadn't been for Signor Ferrino falling asleep with a cigar in his mouth, they might never have known of it at all and would have gone on indefinitely harbouring their disparaging suspicions.

Thankfully, it all turned out well. A mass has been said in honour of Saint Catherine of Siena, to whom the hospital is dedicated, and it is now our most fervent wish to offer a sincere acknowledgement of gratitude to your brother.

We attempted to hold a simple award ceremony, but at the last minute it seems Jeremy got wind of what was to happen and disappeared. The last possible sighting of him was of a man with a large green rucksack, conspicuous for a set of saucepans dangling from the rear strapping, boarding a bus for Naples. Nothing more is known, though Signorina Bernardi from accounts says that Jeremy often spoke longingly of a small cabin in the foothills of the Alps.

Which is all to say that if your esteemed self would only be so kind as to supply us with an address, the board would be most grateful. Failing that, perhaps you might forward on the enclosed?

With sincerest good wishes,
George Jenkins, FSC, RIJS, BIC

The letter is opened, read and thrown into the fireplace, like the others. After a moment's hesitation, the enclosed medal, with its embossed representation of Saint Catherine of Siena untouched in the centre of a lively conflagration, is placed in the little pot of loose tiddlywinks and paperclips in the cupboard with the *Monopoly* set, where it can be found to this day.

45

Annabel's Duster

After Mrs Chisolm leaves, things are not easy for Annabel. Hugo seems quiet enough, but he cannot be trusted, and, now and then, there is a perilous glint in his eyes that makes her stomach tremble. When she steals the letters, she is sure to leave a little burnt corner or two in the grate, so that he will not become suspicious.

'I don't want to know about ants, weevils or moths,' Hugo tells her one morning at breakfast, 'or anything to do with the roof. You must keep these things from me. That is your job now.'

That afternoon, Annabel moves her belongings up to one of the old maids' rooms in the attic – the one with the yellow sprigged wallpaper, the desk under the window and the patchwork quilt on the bed. Those are her pens in the treacle tin on the windowsill. That is her water glass, with a saucer on top so that nothing will fall in and not be able to get back out, and all her empty bottles of Luminal on the floor beside it.

From then on, she spends most of her time in the kitchen, but she is not a good cook, and at dinner Hugo looks sadly at the little basket of rubbery bread nuggets and his bowl of watery soup with its floating film of raw onion chunks. Mealtimes are short. There is no point lingering on in anticipation of a chocolate gateau or a crème brûlée, or even a treacle tart or bread and butter pudding. Those days are over. If he is lucky, there might be some apple sauce with a blob of yogurt on top.

'That was very nice, Annabel,' he says as he shuffles out of the room. 'Very nice indeed.'

When not cooking, Annabel wanders around, checking on things. She has a duster tucked into the waistband of her apron, as Mrs Chisolm used to, but it is mainly for show. Occasionally, she will look up at a cobweb, think for a moment, and then pass on. It is probably better not to start, she is thinking, because, once started, she has a feeling it would never stop.

That is the duster there at the end of the bed. I believe it is the same one she had for thirty years, miraculously preserved through chronic underuse.

Similarly, she has no idea how to clean an eiderdown, or pillows, and one by one, as these things become yellow and smelly, they are stuffed into binbags and thrown into the courtyard storerooms, and a replacement is found in one of the empty bedrooms.

It is not ideal, but there is no one to notice, until one stormy afternoon when there is a ring at the front door and four tourists are discovered on the doorstep.

Annabel is in the kitchen putting away the lunch dishes when she hears the ring. She looks up in surprise, glancing at the kitchen clock, ticking away slowly on the big white wall. It is half past three. She cannot remember the front doorbell ever having been rung at half past three. Not for years and years. Not since the old days.

The bell rings again.

Annabel hurries out of the kitchen, through the hall and into the porch, tugs open the front door and peers out. On the doorstep, four figures are huddled in dripping macintoshes, their little white faces turned towards her hopefully.

'Yes?' says Annabel.

'Gee, what a place,' says the man at the front of the group.

'We saw the tower from the road and just had to come and see it up close.'

Annabel's frown deepens to a scowl. From across the valley comes a rumble of thunder.

'We sure would love to take a look inside,' the man says. 'I bet you have a whole heap of great old stuff in there.'

Annabel sighs and begins to close the door, but the man holds out his hand. 'We'd be happy to pay for a tour,' he says.

At that moment, there are footsteps in the hall behind and Hugo appears in the doorway. There is a crease on his forehead, where he has been asleep on his book, and a little smear of gravy at the corner of his mouth, left over from lunch.

'What's this, Annabel?' he says. 'Visitors? Well, why not I say! Can't be stingy with the heritage.'

He throws open the door and ushers them inside.

'Welcome, welcome, welcome,' he says, holding out his arms. 'Welcome to Thornwalk.'

Annabel stands at the bottom of the staircase as Hugo leads the visitors into the morning room and begins his tour.

'This is one of my favourite chairs,' he says. 'Very sturdy. That one there? I suppose it may be a Chippendale but it's not very comfortable, I can tell you.'

She can hear his voice as he trails from room to room.

'Great merchants,' he is saying. 'Famous the world over. Later, manufacturers of luxury household goods – the very finest quality. But it's a difficult market. Very difficult.'

The tourists follow Hugo from the morning room into the library . . .

'I am not, perhaps, a natural businessman,' Hugo says, 'but I have done my best. I have done my duty anyway. Unlike some. Some people seek self-glorification by putting the needs of strangers and foreigners above those of family. But not me.'

. . . And from the library, back across the hall to the dining room.

'Some people give out private addresses so that their self-glorification is made known to others. I call that fairly reprehensible.'

On the whole, Hugo seems to be doing well, but when they emerge from the dining room his face is red and shiny with sweat. He digs an old handkerchief out of his pocket, releasing a shower of tiny dried somethings, and rubs his forehead.

'I shall leave you to my assistant now,' he says. 'She is in charge of the upper rooms.'

So Annabel leads the way upstairs, with Hugo trailing behind, twisting his handkerchief and muttering, 'No touching now. This is a no-touching tour.'

'This is the kind of place I like,' one of the tourists says. 'I don't mind dust and cobwebs. They're all part of the deal, aren't they? I call it character.'

Annabel looks up at the dust and the cobwebs. She hadn't realized they were quite so bad.

'Mind if we take some photographs?' another one asks, lifting a camera.

'No photographs,' calls out Hugo. 'This is a no-photograph tour.'

'Gee, what a place,' the tourists say again, as Annabel leads them down the far staircase and past the servants' hall. 'Not many of them left. You guys knocking things down, left, right and centre. A darn shame, I call it.'

At last it is over. When they are gone, Hugo stands for a moment in the hall, looking down at the money in his hand, and then at his clothes.

He clears his throat. 'These days,' he says, 'no one can really tell the difference between a dressing gown and a smoking jacket, can they?'

Annabel looks at Hugo. It is not the dressing gown, she thinks. It's the pyjamas. She will have to find him some new ones.

'Savages!' says Hugo. 'All of them! Going around attacking

people like that. Killing people like that. I try to be kind, but in the end I am always punished for it. Always.'

'I don't know,' murmurs Annabel. 'I thought they were quite nice.'

'Nice?' Hugo says. 'Nice?' He scrunches up the money and stuffs it into his dressing-gown pocket. 'You saw how they came in here and murdered me. Call the doctor, Annabel.'

'Are you sure, Hugo?' says Annabel. She hates calling the doctor. 'Because last time –'

'Now, Annabel,' Hugo says. 'It's clearly an emergency.'

46

The Empty Jam Jars

The doctor comes, and goes, and the next day, when Hugo has recovered, he sits alone in the library for a long while with the visitors' money spread out on the table in front of him.

Money! he thinks. How hideous it is. How disgusting and pointless and sordid. How he would love to despise it and reject it, and not long for it and scavenge for it as he does.

Many hours he spent with me in those days, talking like this. What had happened to the world? he wanted to know. People like him had been made for a different one. That much was obvious. But what was he supposed to do? There must be a way out – surely there always was one. He just couldn't see it yet.

It was almost unbearable. I would have given him everything I had, but he would take nothing from me. I suppose it would have made little difference.

Let us go once more past the kitchen to the still-room beyond, where, as promised, we shall now turn our attention to the jam jars. Admire them while you can, for they will surely fill the first of the skips. The hotel people may dilly-dally over a broken chair or a torn curtain, but a pile of empty jam jars is clearly entirely worthless. Another tragic error. For what we have here is not a thousand empty jam jars but a thousand moments of hope.

It is slow, slow grown, this hope, this plan, agonized over, like a broken toenail. Will it work? Surely it must. At last, in the spring of 1965, having what he considers to be the right amount of jars, Hugo sets to work.

It is a small patch of strawberries he grows – the plants are more expensive than he expected – just one corner of the kitchen garden.

See him bent over, long into the dusky light of evening, tucking them in with straw. There are waterings on dry days, and moonlit slug removals, then tasting, harvesting, cooking, canning and labelling.

'Should we put on a different name?' asks Annabel. 'Not Thornwalk.'

'Not Thornwalk?' says Hugo. 'Why not Thornwalk?'

But Annabel cannot tell him why not.

The little jars with their red-and-white gingham caps and their handwritten fruits of thornwalk labels are proudly displayed in the convenience stores in Wraxley and Wimple. Hugo sends Annabel down every Saturday afternoon to check on sales, but the news is disappointing. In the end, the shopkeepers tell Annabel that they need the counter space for other things and the jam is returned.

'It was probably the jars,' Hugo says to Annabel as he stuffs the two hand-painted banners and the two almost full fruits of thornwalk boxes into the storeroom next to the scullery and closes the door. 'I think perhaps I didn't wash them out well enough. It probably made the jam taste funny.'

But they both know it was not the jars.

Hugo lost heart after that. He never spoke of the episode again, but I think it was often in his thoughts.

'Pickled eggs, that's what did it,' I heard him mutter once or twice, in later years. 'Some people are fussy about that sort of thing.'

Certainly, he ate no more jam.

47

The Pine Cone under Annabel's Bed

Poor Hugo. He doesn't give up. He said he wouldn't, and he doesn't.

In the autumn of 1968, he begins collecting pine cones from around the estate. He takes them up to the sawmill, where he makes a simple picture frame and attaches the pine cones to it with PVA glue.

That evening, he climbs the stairs to Annabel's little attic bedroom.

'What do you think, Annabel?' he asks, handing her the pine-cone picture frame. 'It's rustic, I know, but that's quite fashionable now. And the profits could be substantial – the outlay is practically zero.'

Annabel doesn't know what to say. She never knows what to say, not out loud.

'You can be honest,' he says. 'It's just an idea. Just something to think about.'

Still she hesitates.

'Fine!' says Hugo. He throws the frame on the floor and runs out of the room – see one of the pine cones fly off and go bouncing away across the floorboards. Bend down now and take a look under the bed. Yes, a lone pine cone resides there still, where it was left, all those years ago.

48

Hugo's Wallpaper

It takes Hugo a good three years to get over the pine-cone incident. Outwardly, he has had enough, but secretly he does not give up hope. Secretly, he tries again.

It is a time of some concern for Annabel, with Hugo rifling through the kitchen drawers and disappearing into one of the attics, locking the door behind him. She imagines him looking for knives and plotting to do terrible things with them . . . but, in the end, it is all quite innocent.

Come with me.

We are going to the long attic over the guest bedrooms at the back of the house. The door was kept locked and there was only one key, but Annabel would creep up the stairs after Hugo, stand in a dark alcove on the landing below, and wait . . .

Long hours she waits, crouching in the shadows, until at last she hears the scrape of the key, the creak of the opening door. A moment later, down he comes, in a cloud of some strange, chemical smell, scrubbing his hands with a stained rag, shaking his head and muttering.

'Not sharp enough,' he is saying. 'Just not sharp enough.' He stuffs the rag into his dressing-gown pocket, but, as he turns the corner, in the instant before he switches off the light, Annabel sees a flash of red.

Now, pretend you are Annabel.

Early one morning, Hugo knocks at your bedroom door.

'Annabel?' he says. 'Are you awake?'

He doesn't wait for you to answer, but immediately pushes open the door. His face, bright-eyed, pink-cheeked, appears at the opening. It is clear that the pine-cone incident is forgotten. Pine-cone, what pine-cone? He has never in his life had anything to do with pine cones.

'There's something I want you to see,' he says. 'Come along.'

It is five o'clock in the morning, perhaps four o'clock, but you do not hesitate. You scramble out of bed, grab your shawl and follow him along the corridor. He is whistling, I think, perhaps rubbing his hands together. It is a moment of sudden new-day certainty, a 'Here it is at last, after all these years. It just goes to show . . .' moment. It is his last one.

Down the stairs you go, around the gallery, then up and up again. Hugo unlocks the door at the top and you step after him into a long, empty room with a slanting ceiling and three gable windows along the left-hand side. Hugo switches on the light and gestures ahead.

Between the windows, the bare walls have been newly papered in strips from floor to ceiling. Each strip is two or three feet wide, and each has a different pattern or colour scheme, in combinations of wine-red, ochre, olive and brown.

'It's just ordinary lining paper,' Hugo says. 'The quality won't be the same as the finished product, but you get the idea.'

He gestures for you to look closer. You begin to walk down the room, clutching your shawl, with Hugo hovering beside you, peering at your face.

'You recognize the patterns, of course,' he says.

'Oh yes,' you say. 'Of course.' And then you think about it. The flower motif there, with the five petals and the five sepals, is surely something from the carving in the chapel. And the trellis with the clambering rose perhaps features in the nursery tea set.

'The colours aren't quite the same,' says Hugo. 'But I only had a few to choose from.'

You peer closer. What can you say? The colours are dreadful, all this green and brown and clotted red. There is a thick, drippy look about it all. Poor, poor walls of Thornwalk.

'What paint did you use?' you venture to say, your tone light and inquiring, not at all despairing and accusatory.

'Wall paint,' he says.

'Wall paint?'

'Yes.' His voice is impatient. 'From the tins in the storerooms.'

'Oh yes. I see. And . . . what happened here?'

'Ah, that's where I tried to mix them. The very shiny ones were a particular problem. I think some separation has occurred there.'

'And for the stencil . . . it is a stencil you've used?'

'Yes. A stencil here, and over there a print block.'

'What did you use for the stencil?'

'The lid of an ice-cream container.'

'Really?' Still light and enquiring. Naturally curious. Not at all pitying, no hint of 'Oh, Hugo, what next?'

'Yes,' he says. 'I cut it out with a Stanley knife. Obviously, there's only so much you can do with a Stanley knife. I had to sacrifice a little of the complexity of the design.'

'And to apply the paint?'

'A sponge. You know, from the kitchen. I found one in the sink.'

You continue to nod as you make your way slowly down the room. Behind you, Hugo has stopped for a moment and is staring at a particular pattern. He tilts his head to one side, then the other. Then he shrugs and turns away.

'And for the print block?' you call from the other end of the room.

'A potato.'

I shall leave you to think how you will get out of that one.

49

The Greasy Window

In between Hugo's efforts with the pine cones and the paint, there are phone calls from Rosalind.

If you go out into the corridor between the kitchen and the housekeeper's room, you will see the place where Annabel stood. There is no paper blotter, as there is in the morning room, to be covered with frantic doodles, but Annabel's finger draws endlessly on the window.

Look carefully beneath the general dimness, there at the subtle thickening of dirt at just below head height. That is the mark of Annabel's forehead as she leans against the glass. Her spine gives way when she is talking to Rosalind. Her legs turn to Play-Doh.

Hear them now. Go into the passage, cold and dark though it is, and listen.

Bring-bring, bring-bring. It has an old-fashioned tone, this mustard-coloured Bakelite telephone. *Bring-bring.*

Here is Annabel, in a long green dress, very faded, with a wide collar of ancient lace. Her greying hair reaches almost to her waist and is very wild, held back by an old green ribbon that might once have adorned a pony's tail, tied in a bow on top of her head.

Bring-bring, bring-bring.

Annabel rushes along the passage. 'Hello?' she says. Her voice is suspicious, cautious, by now a little afraid.

'Yes, hello,' says a voice. 'It's me again. You probably hoped it would be someone else, but it isn't.'

'I didn't hope it would be someone else –' begins Annabel.

But Rosalind isn't listening. 'I just called to say goodbye,' she says. 'I really am dying this time. The doctors pretty much all say so.'

'Oh no, Rosalind,' says Annabel. 'Are you sure?'

'I'll be glad to go. Glad to go before I'm completely bald. That's all I want now. I don't want them laughing at me in the coffin.'

'They wouldn't laugh at you in the coffin, Rosalind. I'm sure they wouldn't do that.'

'Yes, they would. That's what they're like here.'

And she tells Annabel, again, what it's like there, and how unfair it is. How strange it is that Nicholas isn't there too, after everything he did to her. And that it was her birthday last week.

Annabel closes her eyes and lifts a finger to draw a circle over and over on the dirty black window pane. 'I'm sorry, Rosalind,' she says. 'I'm very sorry.'

'Oh, I didn't expect *you* to remember,' says Rosalind. 'I've given up expecting that. But him! After everything he used to say. It makes me sick that people can be like that.'

And she starts to cry.

Annabel's finger draws the side of a face and a closed eye. Perhaps in the right light you will be able to make it out, the face she drew that evening. She had been in the kitchen boiling a chicken when the telephone started ringing and only had time to wipe her hands quickly on a dirty tea towel. There will be chicken juice in those greasy window lines, and onion juice and carrot-peel juice.

50

The do not disturb Sign

What a time of it Annabel has in these years, with the phone calls from Rosalind, and Hugo wandering around the estate with his shotgun, and taking to his deathbed, again and again.

The old cereal packet do not disturb notice scarcely leaves the library door (you will find it in the hall cupboard, fluffy with age, the words rubbed almost to nothing). When Hugo is not wandering around with his shotgun or on his deathbed, he will be here in the library, thinking about shotguns and death, with the notice hung on the door and Annabel standing outside with a tea tray of cold Darjeeling or a bowl of cold chicken soup.

One morning, Annabel is startled awake and hurries downstairs to find the front door open and autumn leaves rattling against the tiles. It is still dark outside. She pulls on her coat, grabs her torch and dashes out.

'Hugo?' she calls, her tiny voice lost against the wind. 'Where are you, Hugo?' But he is not in the glasshouse, or by the lake, or in the sawmill.

When she gets back to the house at last, she finds a pair of muddy slippers discarded in the hall and the do not disturb notice hanging once more on the library door.

Later the next night, Hugo rings his bell.

Annabel pulls on her dressing gown and hurries to his room. There he is, lying like the top of a sarcophagus, his hands clutched to his chest, his eyes closed, his face deathly pale.

Perhaps he has had a heart attack, Annabel thinks. Perhaps he is dying.

Hugo stirs, and the fingers of his right hand creep across the eiderdown towards her. 'Annabel?' he whispers.

She takes his hand. 'Yes, Hugo.'

'Annabel . . .'

'What is it, Hugo? What's wrong?'

'I . . . I've shot a cow.'

'What? When?'

'Today. This morning.'

'But why, Hugo?'

He tosses and turns against his pillows. 'Steak, Annabel. Steak.'

'Steak? But Hugo –'

'It didn't die!'

'Oh, Hugo!'

He hears the dismay in her voice and flings away her hand. 'It was *my* cow!' he says, kneading the edge of the eiderdown in his fists. 'People shoot things all the time . . . Man is a hunter, Annabel . . . You hypocrite! Get out. Get out!'

The next day, Hugo doesn't leave his room, and the next. Annabel paces up and down the corridor outside. Perhaps, after all, she will have to call a doctor again. But which one? They are none of them very polite any more.

She stands at his bedside, watching him breathe slowly in and out, in and out. Is this it, then? she thinks. Finally? Is this it?

'Shall I . . . shall I call Maximus?' she whispers at last.

Hugo opens his eyes and stares at her. 'Maximus? Who's Maximus?' he says. 'I don't know anyone called Maximus. I don't know what you're talking about.'

Ah, Hugo, my dear, dear friend. If only you had been able to say yes.

Late the next night, once more Hugo rings his bell. There he is, grey-faced, the same little bit of dirty eiderdown pinched and twisted between his fingers.

'I'm afraid I'm taking a long time about this, Annabel,' he says. 'I thought I was ready to go a while back – that's why I rang the bell. I didn't mean to disturb you – I just wanted to say goodbye. But now –'

She reaches out and takes his hand.

'It makes me think of the cow,' he says. 'How long it must have taken to die.'

'The cow!' she says. 'I'm so sorry, Hugo, I forgot to tell you. It didn't die at all. It was fine.'

'Fine?'

'Yes.'

'How do you know?'

'One of the farmers came and told me. He said we ought to know that someone was going around taking potshots at the cattle, but that the cow was fine . . . Just a graze, I think he said.'

'No, Annabel. I am quite sure I gave it a mortal wound.'

'He said you just skimmed it.'

'I was twenty yards from it, Annabel! I could hardly have missed a cow at twenty yards!'

'Oh.'

'It must have been a different cow.'

'Yes.'

'Mine would have died a terrible death.'

'Don't think about it,' she says, squeezing his hand.

He sighs and nods. 'No. I'm not going to think about any of these things any more.'

51

Bertie's Rag

I realize that in all this, I have said almost nothing about dogs. It is a major mistake, and, recognizing this, I acknowledge the possibility that I may have made others. It is a little disheartening.

Well, we shall just have to make the best of it. You will need to insert into all the past scenes a certain doggy smell, dirty pawprints on the Minton tiles, that sort of thing. When Annabel sits crying in the attic, see Nugget, the new Labrador puppy, trying to eat her ear. Every time you cross the hall, you must imagine a fat old Labrador in the corner, whining softly. Dinnertime has been forgotten again, but they will remember it three times tomorrow.

I have not said much about the pet cemetery between the yews at the back of the chapel. Let us go there quickly now. They are all buried here – the pets, I mean – goldfish, hamsters, a canary. It is very overgrown, but you can make out some of the headstones. The last of them was Bertie, a smaller-than-average Miniature Schnauzer with slightly crossed eyes. Yes, there is the little stone with bertie on it.

Linger a while. Linger, linger. Absorb a little pain.

Now, go to the front door. There is a dirty rag on a

wrought-iron hook on the side of the dresser. You might pause for a moment and admire the dresser (commissioned from Crace, measured precisely for the room, the carved emblems all deeply symbolic to the first generation of Gilberts, less so to future ones), but I am more interested in Bertie's foot rag. It has been cut from the centre panel of an old flannel dressing gown, formerly cream-coloured, now brown. The darkest marks are from the mud between his toes.

There is a walk they liked to go on around the estate, Hugo and Bertie, up through the north wood and around to the east.

In the year of 1987 there was a great storm, which I may have mentioned before, and into this, as usual, they set out. Hugo often went walking in storms. He was never afraid. He did not think it would be his fate to be killed by a falling tree.

The rain was coming down heavily, on this walk in 1987. See Hugo in his waxed jacket and flat cap, and Bertie in his fluorescent yellow dog coat, heads bent, soldiering on through the wind.

Suddenly, there is a roaring, crashing, sploshing sound and a tide of flood water sweeps down the hillside. Bertie is knocked off his feet and swept up into the torrent. Hugo plunges in after him. Had there been a moment's hesitation, the dog would have been lost, but there is not. Hugo grabs Bertie's collar and hauls him out of the water. With Bertie pressed against his chest, Hugo is carried down the hillside until the water disperses at the bottom. Hugo suffers some superficial wounds to legs and elbows. Bertie is miraculously unharmed.

The rag utilized after that incident would most likely have been washed since then. This may be the same rag – there were some half-dozen, cut from the same dressing gown, that were rotated – but the mud on it is probably not the toe mud from the storm of '87. Bertie died in 1992. I shall not go into details. The lifetime of a man is just so measured as to allow him never to forget a lost pet.

52

The Empty Hair Cream Pots

I fear we may have drifted into something of a montage, for the events of the passing years are hard to order. And it is possible that all these little scenes may have given you the impression of activity, but they are not much, spread out over the years.

Hugo preferred it that way. He counted it a good day when there was nothing to be done and nothing happened, because it was less likely to make anything change.

He hated change.

For instance, there was a certain hair cream that he liked. Fearing it might suddenly stop being manufactured – such things had happened to him before with shampoo and marmalade – he purchased a large amount of it and stored it in a box under his bed.

Despite this, he realized one day that he was indeed running low. Enquiries were made and thankfully the brand found still to be in existence. Short was his relief, however, for the recipe had been 'reformulated'.

Let us cast an eye once more into the dining room, and see Hugo and Annabel there, at the far end of the table, having breakfast.

Hugo is very subdued. For a long while, he doesn't touch his Weetabix.

At last, he clears his throat. 'Have you any knowledge of chemistry?' he asks, handing Annabel a small white pot. 'The ingredients are there on the back. I imagine it's all fairly basic.'

Annabel stares at the pot, but, of course, she has no knowledge of chemistry. She doesn't understand any of the words on the label at all.

There are tears in her eyes as she shakes her head and hands the pot back to Hugo.

'Ah,' says Hugo. 'Never mind.'

It was a dark day, at the threshold of many more dark days. Just as he had struggled with the world after the war, so Hugo struggled for the rest of his life with the smell of the reformulated hair cream. He soldiered on, but many was the night he wept, overwhelmed with the sense of all being not quite as it should have been.

53

The Empty Shelves in Aunt Beatrice's Cabinet

Sadly, more change was to come, for, shortly after the cow incident, Cooper Coldwell dies and Lydia begins her campaign of thievery at Thornwalk.

Here she is, on her first visit since the afternoon tea the Coldwells accidentally shared with Rosalind, all those years before. She parks her car in the side courtyard, and Annabel shows her into the house through the kitchen.

'I'm sorry about Mr Coldwell,' says Annabel, as they step into the hall.

'Oh, don't worry,' says Lydia. 'People in the public eye are always demonized, but for every person who says something horrible there are a hundred people, probably, who are thinking something nice and just don't say it.'

'But . . . he is dead?' says Anabel.

'Oh, you meant that,' says Lydia. 'Yes, it's very sad. I miss him very much, of course. We were extremely happy together. Extremely.' She looks up at the paintings around the stairwell. 'Have these ever been valued, do you think?'

Behind them, the library door opens an inch and an eye is pressed to the gap.

'Let's go upstairs,' says Annabel.

'Upstairs?' says Lydia. She is very large now and stairs are the bane of her life.

'I have a tea tray ready,' says Annabel. 'With Bourbons.'

'Bourbons?' says Lydia. 'Oh, very well. Lead on.'

Up they go, to the little attic room with the yellow sprigged paper, where Lydia lowers herself into an armchair with a sigh. She looks around at the desk, the narrow bed, the treacle tin on the windowsill . . . An odd place for Annabel to be sleeping, she thinks, but each to their own.

'So, what about that Mrs Chisolm?' Lydia says.

'An accident,' says Annabel. 'A small misunderstanding.'

'Oh yes? Well, accident or not, Cooper had to pay out a great deal of money to keep her quiet. He claimed it back from the estate, of course, but was never reimbursed for his time or the stress of it all. We probably should have added on something for that.'

'I'm sorry,' says Annabel.

'Oh well, never mind,' says Lydia. She considers her sister for a moment – the ridiculous long dress, the apron, the duster. There is a distant, fixed look about her, as though she were studying everything very carefully but from somewhere far away. Then she notices the water glass and the bottles of Luminal. Probably takes too much of it, she thinks. Fair enough.

'So, you can manage?' Lydia says.

'Yes,' says Annabel. 'I can manage.'

'Quite right,' says Lydia. 'Why not? Just chuck some dust sheets about and close a few doors. Easy-peasy. I imagine he doesn't mind what he eats. I suppose you can handle that?'

'Yes, I can handle that.'

Lydia looks again at her sister. It is an odd habit she has of parroting everything back. It gives Lydia an uncomfortable, watched sort of feeling, as if everything she's saying were being stored up very carefully, word for word, to be used against her later.

It is a fleeting thought.

'What about asking that friend of his in the village to help out?' Lydia says. 'Is he still around?'

Annabel blushes and looks at the floor.

'No need to be like that about it,' says Lydia. 'Happens all the time. Cooper too, I think, now and then. Goodness, if I didn't mind, I don't see why you should. Well, then, that's settled.'

Lydia sips her tea. From the woodland outside comes the dull bickering of rooks, and, somewhere deep in the storerooms on the other side of the corridor, a broken carriage clock begins a mistimed chime.

'These are pretty cups,' Lydia says, holding hers up to the light. 'I've not seen them before, have I?'

'They were in Aunt Beatrice's room,' says Annabel.

'Oh yes. In the glass-fronted cabinet. I imagine they must be quite valuable. What happened to the usual ones?'

Annabel tells her that the usual ones were broken some time ago when the kitchen dresser nearly fell over.

There is a short pause. But Lydia doesn't ask why the kitchen dresser nearly fell over, she only says, 'You see? That's just what I wanted to talk to you about. Things like this ought to be kept somewhere safe. Fortunately, I happen to have a few crates and some packing paper in the boot of my car. I can easily take them today.'

'I'll have to ask Hugo,' says Annabel.

'No need,' says Lydia. 'How can he be expected to make that kind of decision? Didn't they all agree that he's mentally incapacitated? Legally, I mean. I should have had that done with Mother, really. It would have saved a good deal of trouble.'

So talk turns to their mother. 'You've heard she's in a care home now, have you?' Lydia says. 'A severe stroke. Very sad. I blame Hugo and Rosalind. They quite broke her heart. Poor Mother.'

'Poor Mother,' says Annabel. 'Yes. Poor Mother.'

'It's not a bad place,' Lydia goes on, 'except for the constant ringing of those bloody bells, and the smell, of course. I must say, I wouldn't want to end up in one myself. Thankfully, the boys are determined to have me stay with them, whatever happens. They're devoted to me. Absolutely devoted.'

Lydia puts down her cup and eats five chocolate Bourbons very quickly, one after another, as Aunt Beatrice used to, then licks her finger and wipes up all the crumbs.

'We've got power of attorney for Mother now,' Lydia says, 'me and the boys. Obviously, if she runs out of money, then it's down to us, but, considering the condition she's in, I'm not overly concerned. We put her on the "Small Meal, No Activity" plan, which she would have wanted – she being such a light eater and never very sociable – and that makes it much more affordable.'

On their way back down the stairs, Lydia stops outside her old bedroom.

'Goodness,' she says. She peers around the door at her old dressing table and mirror, and thinks of Higgins. How on earth would Aunt Beatrice have known if he had bad breath or not?

'I'm so glad things worked out the way they did,' she says. 'I've been tremendously happy. Tremendously.' She closes the door and turns back to Annabel. 'Now, let's see about those cups.'

Downstairs, the cups and saucers are carefully removed from Aunt Beatrice's cabinet, packed into a crate and carried out through the rear corridor and the kitchen to the boot of Lydia's green Morris Minor estate.

'I've had a wonderful time,' says Lydia, waving a gloved hand out of the window as she reverses away down the drive. 'I shall certainly come again soon.'

54

The Tin-can Chains

Come again soon she does. The visit is repeated every few weeks, and never does Lydia leave Thornwalk empty-handed.

Finally, perhaps a year or so later, Lydia makes her last sortie to Thornwalk, declines tea with Annabel in the attic (she has put on so much weight, the stairs are almost impossible) and goes straight for the silverware in the bottom of the morning-room dresser. What a painstaking endeavour it is, the silent extraction of each item, tiptoeing with it through the hall and loading it into the car, with Hugo napping in the library next door. Annabel marvels at how quietly Lydia can manoeuvre her great bulk when she has to.

'Hasn't this been fun?' Lydia says, leaning her head out of the car window as she reverses away. 'See you soon!'

But she does not see Annabel soon. Three days after this last visit, Lydia has a heart attack which puts her in hospital for a month. No permanent damage has been done, the doctors say, but she will probably never drive again.

So, it is up to Cooper Junior and Sydney, now in their late twenties, to take up the banner and go on with the crusade.

At first, they knock at the front door, which is answered by Hugo in his shooting tweeds.

'Tea and cake are no longer being served at Thornwalk,' says Hugo.

'Dear Uncle,' they say, 'we just came to see you.'

They sit with Hugo in the cold library for half an hour. Then Cooper Junior elbows Sydney in the ribs.

'I say,' says Sydney, 'aren't those our mother's plates?' He gestures to the wall above the morning-room door. 'Yes. I think they are the ones described in the legal documents for her dowry.'

'Everything in here is mine,' says Hugo.

'Are you sure? They seem awfully similar. Perhaps . . . perhaps we could just take them along for safekeeping, then. They must get awfully dusty there.'

Hugo slowly gets to his feet and shuffles out of the room. There is the sound of a door opening and closing in the hall.

'I say,' says Sydney, 'do you think he's getting a ladder?'

But Hugo is not getting a ladder. They hear the hall door open and close again, then the shunting of slippers on the hall rug, and Hugo appears in the doorway with his gun.

'Out!' he says.

And out they go.

It is a small triumph, and Hugo chuckles softly over his cocoa that evening. But it is not the last they have seen of Cooper Junior and Sydney. Three nights later, there are noises in the kitchen, and, when Annabel goes downstairs to investigate, she discovers that a small ormolu clock from the library mantelpiece and the three blue-and-white plates from above the morning-room door are gone.

For the next twelve hours, Annabel hides in her room while Hugo rampages through the house below.

At last, when it is quiet, she creeps downstairs to find the billiard-room door barricaded with an old writing bureau and the taxidermied moose head. The other doors have been hung with lengths of string, threaded with empty tin cans.

Hugo is camped out in the back of the hall, with the door

to the servants' quarters wedged open with a folded cornflakes box. He has dragged his leather armchair out of the library, and is sitting there with the tartan rug around his shoulders and the shotgun across his knees.

'Let's see them sneak in here now,' he chuckles to himself. 'Come on. then, my boys!'

The next two nights are the same – Hugo sitting silently in his armchair, waiting.

On the third night, a torch flashes in the courtyard, and a key scratches against the lock of the courtyard door.

The door inches open, and through the gap squeeze Sydney and Cooper Junior.

'I say, what's this?' says Sydney, spying the tin cans.

'What's what?' says Cooper Junior, pushing forwards.

Sydney squeals as he trips over the string and collapses in a heap with Cooper Junior on top of him. At the same time, the string breaks and the cans clatter to the floor.

Hugo reaches out and switches on a lamp. 'Nephews,' he says.

'Uncle,' they say. 'What a nice –'

Hugo lifts the shotgun.

Only a single shot is fired. It is high above their heads and causes no dramatic shattering of ceiling plaster, for by now, of course, Annabel has replaced all the cartridges with blanks, but it is enough. It is a sorry sight, this scrabbling and shoving of Cooper Junior and Sydney – pushing each other into walls, snatching at each other's ankles, clambering over each other as they try to get away. It takes them a full minute to finally crawl out of the door.

'We'll get you for this, Uncle Hugo!' weeps Sydney as they disappear into the darkness outside.

'You can try, my boy!' says Hugo. 'You can certainly try!'

How magnificent he is. I can see him there now, exactly like that. I can see, exactly, the look on his face as he turns to

Annabel, triumphant . . . But a moment later, the gun clatters to the floor and Hugo sinks down on to his knees.

Annabel helps him slowly up to bed, where he will stay for some time. 'Shall I call the doctor?' she asks.

But Hugo shakes his head. 'No, Annabel. Either it's the end or it's not. Either way, the doctor cannot help me now.'

55

Annabel's Manuscript

I am standing in the hall, at the bottom of the stairs, with the vast domed skylight high above my head. It has been leaking for years. The beautiful green wallpaper below is streaked with damp and mould. It will be repaired soon, I suppose, but I will remember it like this, when it looks as if the walls are crying.

The time has come for me to show you something else, something I have deliberately delayed until now. Go back up to Annabel's room and look once more beneath the bed. Right at the back, near the pine cone, is one of those thick office files, a box file I think it's called. Bring it out and open it. It contains a manuscript, Annabel's story of her brothers and sisters.

Yes, remember Lydia's sudden insight when she and Annabel were drinking tea together? She had noticed something about Annabel's eyes, the watchful, remembering expression. It is the only sensitivity to her sister that Lydia has ever shown, but it is correct.

Return to that day, if you will. Watch Annabel wave goodbye to Lydia. Then see her turn, climb the stairs and come back here to her room, where she sits down at this little table under the window and starts to write.

It is a sad story she tells. The housekeeper has just left and she is alone with Hugo. There are heartfelt descriptions of dusty pot plants and dying flies, spider webs and sunsets, and crescent moons like toenail clippings in the sky.

This is an example of the kind of thing she writes:

'Would you like the last piece of cake, Annabel?' Hugo asks.

'No, Hugo,' I say. 'You have it.'

'No, no,' he says. 'I insist.'

We are sitting together in the library, with a single slice of Jamaica ginger cake on the plate between us.

'No, really,' I say. 'I'm full up.'

'You can't possibly be full up,' he says.

'I am, honestly.'

'No, no. Now, you must have it. Go on.'

'Please, Hugo,' I say, 'you have it.'

'No. Absolutely not.'

'Yes, do. Please.'

'No.'

'I don't want it, Hugo. Really, I don't.'

'Well –'

'Please do take it.'

'Very well, then, I shall.'

He takes the cake, which crumbles on its way to his mouth, and brushes the crumbs off his lap as he chews.

'A fine day,' he murmurs when he has finished the cake. We look out at the garden. 'Cold,' he says, 'but clear.'

'Oh yes,' I say. 'Very fine.'

We sit in silence a moment longer, and I am just thinking about getting up and clearing away the tray when he says, 'I feel guilty now.'

I turn quickly to look at him. 'Oh no, Hugo,' I say. 'Why?'

His face is grey, his expression sad. 'I shouldn't have eaten the cake,' he says.

'But you mustn't feel bad about that!'

'Yes, I must. I'd already had three pieces and you'd only had one. I shouldn't have eaten it.'

'But I insisted.'

'That should not have been enough to sway me from what I knew was right.'

'Please, Hugo –'

'No, Annabel. It's too late.'

'But I didn't want it, Hugo. Honestly, I didn't.'

'Unfortunately,' he says grimly, *'that is irrelevant.'* And with that he gets up and leaves the room.

Feel free to read the entire manuscript, but if you didn't find the above extract interesting, then perhaps the book is not for you.

There are some poignant moments as she recounts her time with Simon in the hayloft, in much more detail than I have done. She describes at some length the pores in his nose and the scar on his cheek, things that do not interest me to the same extent.

She is kinder to Rosalind than I have been. She remembers a trip to the seaside, and how that night she found a note from Rosalind on her pillow saying, 'I'm sorry I took your boots and left you the ones with holes in. You can have my best shell,' and there beside the note is a little pink shell.

She remembers Jeremy setting off on walks with his rucksack and his stick, and returning five minutes later with Rosalind, knees grazed, dress torn, clinging to his back.

'You can't come on walks with me any more, Rosalind,' he says.

'I didn't mean to fall over, Jeremy,' Rosalind says between her tears. 'I'll be braver next time. Honestly, I will.'

Later on, there is the letter to Mr Kellogg about the cornflakes, and various other day to day trials – concerns over ants and moles, for example – but nothing that would constitute a 'plot' according to the standard definition. It is from this manuscript that I have my account of the pine-cone incident, the wallpaper scene and the tragedy of the wounded cow. Of course, her style is different, substantially more ponderous, but then she had a great deal of time on her hands and you and I have almost none.

At a certain point in the manuscript, Annabel begins to invent things: a campfire on the hill behind the house, someone breaking into the kitchen to steal raisins and Hugo wandering around in a curtain toga with a wreath of bay leaves on his head (though, in fairness, this last may have actually happened). She decides to write to Emma, who arrives one stormy night and tells Annabel that she is still in love with Hugo and will use all her money to help them save Thornwalk.

While they are considering their options – an animal park like Lord Bath has, perhaps more jam-making or pig breeding – a fire breaks out in Hugo's study. Annabel sounds the old tower bell and Jeremy and Simon rush to the rescue, revealing an ingenious sprinkler system housed in the roof (we heard the inspiration for this earlier, if you remember, in that letter about Jeremy's exploits in Rome). Yes, it was Jeremy camping out in the woods, keeping an eye on things, and Simon has come back to marry Annabel and take her away to France, or at least Cornwall.

Even Lydia and Rosalind make an appearance, near the end, and together they come up with a plan inspired by Hugo's efforts in the attic: thornwalk walls, traditional wallpapers – heritage and hope. Jeremy quickly knocks up some printing presses. Lydia, being skilled in the art of positive self-representation, plans a publicity campaign. And Rosalind, accompanied by a warden, sits in a corner of the sawmill, whittling woodblocks.

In the midst of this activity, Mrs Gilbert arrives. Yes, in Annabel's poor lonely imaginings, Hugo welcomes the old woman back to Thornwalk at last. There is a tender deathbed scene, as Mrs Gilbert apologizes for everything that has been done to them – for ignoring Jeremy, spoiling poor dear gentle little Rosalind and giving Hugo such ridiculous ideas about himself. She has some confessions to make about their father. It is possible that in the past she may have misrepresented things slightly . . .

'And you, Annabel,' she whispers, clutching Annabel's hand in her own trembling fingers. 'I'm sorry. I shouldn't have let her take you away.'

Annabel looks at her mother for a long moment. 'Don't worry about it now,' she says at last. 'You did what you thought was best at the time.'

'I did, Annabel,' says Mrs Gilbert. 'I did what I thought was best . . . at the time.'

Poor Annabel. I can see her writing all this . . . The little table is too low and she is hunched up over it, her long grey hair brushing the page. She has grown thin. See her turn and reach for a roll of toilet paper. There are tears running down her face.

56

The Tower Bell

But, of course, none of that is true.

No, it is an expert piece of imagining, better than I would have thought Annabel capable of, in the circumstances. She believed in happy endings, you see. She felt it was the writer's duty to conjure sense from chaos and uncertainty. A happy ending, she thought, was far more realistic than an unhappy ending, because in life the happy ending was to come, and that reality had to be incorporated into the book. Yes, she believed in heaven. She had strong faith in an afterlife, as people will who have not really lived.

Perhaps she wrote to Emma, but there was no reply and Emma never came back. No one came back. Their mother died in 1972 in a nursing home in Chew Magna. She never apologized for anything and never told anyone the truth about their father, which was left to Jeremy to discover (more of this soon).

There was a fire at Thornwalk at around that time, and no doubt Annabel rang the bell, but no one came to the rescue. No Simon. No Jeremy. Jeremy hadn't been home since the fight with Hugo in 1955, and there was certainly no magic sprinkler system in the roof. By the time the fire engines arrived from

Clifton, a great deal of the East Wing had been destroyed, as you have seen. Simon was married with three children and living in Liskeard. He didn't even go to Annabel's funeral.

That is all I have to say about her manuscript. She sent it to a London publishing house, hoping to make enough money to mend the roof, but was told it was too slow for modern tastes. She ought to start with a murder.

A murder! See her sitting there, chewing the end of her pencil. She remembers many things . . . many terrible things . . . perhaps the publisher would like to hear about them. But, no, they are too terrible. She cannot even bear to think of them.

Well, Annabel tried her best, added a few little Gothic bits and pieces – mainly owl noises and more stormy weather – but it wasn't fooling anyone.

'It's not quite there yet,' said the publisher. 'Could one of the brothers and sisters be killed off? Could it be hinted at early on to get the reader interested?'

Annabel didn't reply, only sighed, crossed out the silly Gothic bits, then placed the manuscript in this box under the bed, which is where it has stayed ever since.

57

A Book of Poetry

So, no, Lydia does not come back to Thornwalk to help Hugo run a wallpaper business. She gets gradually older and fatter, and less and less inclined to go anywhere. Now and then, she sends Cooper Junior and Sydney along to see what they can find, but Hugo is always waiting with his gun.

In the autumn of 1988, after slipping on a glacé cherry from a Danish pastry and twisting her ankle, Lydia is admitted to Wyke Manor Care Home.

Wyke Manor is a large white Georgian building, five miles from Thornwalk on the Nailsea Road. No doubt you have seen it. Cold and uncomfortable but impressive-looking. All the best people go there to die.

'It's just for respite,' Cooper Junior tells his mother. 'Just for a week.'

'It's just for respite,' Lydia tells the manager, Mrs Briggs – a large woman in a black wig with a no-nonsense this-is-a-business-first-and-foremost attitude – handing her a very small suitcase. 'Just for a week.'

'Of course,' says Mrs Briggs. 'Just for a week.'

'Just respite,' Lydia says to the other residents at dinner. 'Just for a week.'

'Right,' says a woman called Priscilla. 'That's what they said to me and I've been 'ere three years.'

How sad, thinks Lydia, for this poor woman to have been so shamefully deceived by her family, and she looks pityingly at Priscilla.

The week passes quickly. Cooper Junior was right – Lydia enjoys having her food made for her and someone else do the washing-up. She likes to ring her bell and ask for things, to send the carers running off for little bits and pieces – a knitting needle, a book, a cardigan, a different cardigan – but there is no denying the smell of the place, even in the wing reserved for respite care.

'I have enjoyed my stay,' she says to the receptionist at the end of the week. 'But I'm ready to go home now.'

'You won't find it so easy, going back to doing everything for yourself again,' says the receptionist.

'I shall manage,' says Lydia.

'You're better off staying here,' says the receptionist.

'No, thank you,' says Lydia.

'If you go now, you might not be able to come back,' says the receptionist. 'I won't be able to keep your room for you.'

Lydia smiles contemptuously. A strong, independent woman such as herself will not be that easy to catch.

'If you could call my sons and tell them I am ready to be collected,' says Lydia.

'To be honest,' says the receptionist, 'I have nothing in the diary about your going home today.'

And that, to cut a long story short, is that. It turns out that while Lydia has been away, the Chelsea house has been sold and paperwork drawn up for her permanent admission to Wyke Manor Care Home.

'We've opted for the "Small Meal, No Activity" plan,' Cooper Junior tells Mrs Briggs, 'because she was always a light eater and never very sociable.'

'A very affordable option,' says Mrs Briggs.

*

Now, let us skip forward a while, to the summer of 1993, when Mrs Briggs calls the activity coordinator into her office.

'We need some stories for the newsletter,' Mrs Briggs says. 'Bob in Room 23 was once the Dean of Somewhere, and Lydia in Room 6 used to live in that big old house on the hill. Those are the kind of people I want you to focus on.'

So, the activity coordinator climbs the stairs to Room 6, a small attic room at the back of the building.

'That's kind,' says Lydia, when the activity coordinator tells her what they want. 'It's kind of you to care.'

'Did you really grow up in the big house on the hill?' asks the activity coordinator – let us call her Annie. Annie has often glimpsed the house behind the trees on her way to Bristol and wondered who lived there.

'Ah yes,' says Lydia, leaning back against her pillows, 'Thornwalk.' She is almost bald and still large, with a massive soft chest sliding into a massive soft stomach. On the wall behind her, a little red lightbulb is flashing to show that she has rung her bell for assistance. It is almost half past ten in the morning, but she is still in her nightdress, a grubby pink nylon thing with cheap brown lace at the neck. 'Yes, that's right,' she says.

'What was it like?' asks Annie. She has no outdated reverence for rich people or anything like that, but she loves beautiful things and big houses.

'I don't know,' says Lydia. 'It was just the way it was. Most of the time I just wanted to leave.'

'It's very beautiful,' says Annie.

Lydia shrugs. 'I suppose so. I could never see it. But it was where I met my first real love, the man I should have married.'

'Ooh, tell me about that,' says Annie, settling into the armchair by the bed with her clipboard and her pen.

'His name was Mr Higgins,' says Lydia. 'They said he had bad breath, but he didn't.'

'What did he look like?' asks Annie.

'He was tall, with curly brown hair and dark eyes. Glasses. Nice ones. He used to talk about poetry a lot. *Glory be to God for dappled things – for skies of couple-colour as a brinded cow* . . . Now, how did I remember that?' There is a sudden look of wonder on Lydia's face and tears in her eyes.

'How lovely,' says Annie. 'I love poetry.'

'We would go walking around the arboretum together,' Lydia continues, with a dreamy, faraway expression. Yes, despite the dim light of the room, the smell of the unemptied commode behind her, and the relentless beeping of the alarms in the corridor outside, she is back at Thornwalk, sitting on the grass under the trees on a summer day.

'*Though aloft on turf or perch or poor low stage,*' Higgins is saying, '*both sing sometimes the sweetest, sweetest spells, yet both droop deadly sometimes in their cells, or wring their barriers in bursts of fear or rage* . . . Do you know what that means, Lydia? Can you feel it? Do you understand what he was talking about?'

'I think so, yes. I think I do,' says Lydia.

'You are so young,' he says, 'but I sense deep understanding in you of an almost adult kind. Well, I am prepared to wait. I will spend the time earning the respect of your family by becoming a great poet myself.'

'How long will that take?' asks Lydia.

'Oh, not long, I shouldn't think,' he says. 'I have lots already. For instance, here is one entitled "Ode to Procreation":

'Have your pheasant babies
Pheasant man, pheasant lady
Breed noble eagle
Fill the world with your people
Grow wild rose
Spread thorny hedge
Every leaf find a lover
And life take over.'

'Oh,' says Lydia, 'is the ending quite right?'

'That's what is called poetic licence,' says Mr Higgins.

Of course, not everyone recognizes his genius. Jeremy is very disparaging, particularly of what Higgins considers to be his finest work, 'Ode to Tuberculosis', which I shall not reproduce here, the subject matter being somewhat heavy and not to popular tastes. The general gist is that Keats was fortunate to die as he did, in company with all the other great writers and artists.

Better a sweep of the scythe than mildew and blight, it concludes.

'Tuberculosis? A sweep of the scythe?' Jeremy says. 'Prolonged hacking with a blunt potato peeler more like.'

But then Jeremy is disparaging of everything. Lydia has learnt to take no notice of 'the children', as Mr Higgins calls them.

'I think it's wonderful,' she says. 'So funny.'

'Funny?'

'Not funny. I meant sad.'

Lydia sighs. The beeping outside stops, and then starts again.

'The younger ones were a total nuisance – I remember that,' she says. 'Especially Rosalind. She would spy on us. I think it was her that told on me.'

'Told on you?' says Annie. She has picked up on the note of intrigue in the old woman's words.

'Yes,' says Lydia. 'How I hated her. After that, they locked me in my room.'

'Locked you in your room?' echoes Annie again. It is all very shocking and sure to make a brilliant article for the newsletter.

'Yes,' says Lydia. 'From then on, until Aunt Beatrice came, I had to be escorted to the bathroom by one of the gardeners. It was so embarrassing.'

At that moment, there is a quick knock on the door and two carers come into the room.

'Personal care,' they announce, and Annie has to leave.

'I'll come again on Thursday,' she says.

But Thursday is not so good. Annie comes into the room to find Lydia crying.

'They've taken my things,' she tells Annie. 'Someone has been in here and taken all my things from under my pillow.'

'I'll find out what's happened,' says Annie. 'Don't worry.'

'This isn't something for you to get involved in,' says the nurse, when Annie goes to investigate, 'but yesterday she was found in Peggy's room, going through her cupboard. We searched Lydia's room and found all sorts of missing bits and pieces under her mattress.'

'I thought she couldn't walk,' says Annie.

'She can't. But there you are. There was cutlery under her pillow too. Just goes to show, doesn't it? It's always the rich ones, isn't it?'

Annie climbs the stairs back to Room 6. 'Perhaps we should go on with the story,' she says.

'I think that's my watch,' Lydia says, pointing at Annie's wrist. 'I used to have a watch just like that.'

'This one's definitely mine,' says Annie.

'Are you sure? I think it might be mine. Did you find it on my table?'

'I'll come back later,' says Annie.

The next week, Annie tries again.

'Mr Higgins?' says Lydia. 'How do you know about him?' Once more, she tells Annie about the trees in the arboretum, the sunshine, and the poetry. 'You know, I think he gave me a ring. Yes, I think . . . I think I remember a ring. I don't know where it is now. I think someone has taken it.'

'He gave you a ring?' says Annie. 'What kind of ring? Was it an engagement ring?'

'I think it might have been, yes.'

'So, you were engaged to someone else when you got married to Mr Coldwell?'

'I think I might have been. Dreadful isn't it?'

This is the story Annie finally submits to the manager:

> *I was born at Thornwalk House, where I lived with my two brothers and two sisters. When I was eighteen I married Mr Cooper Coldwell, a wealthy businessman from Chelsea, but he wasn't the man I loved.*
>
> *The man I loved was called Mr Higgins, who was our tutor. We had to keep our love a secret, because I was too young, but we were planning to run away together as soon as I was sixteen.*
>
> *Unfortunately, one day my younger sister Rosalind, consumed with jealously because I was so much more beautiful than she was, betrayed me to our mother. I was locked in my bedroom until my aunt arrived. She took me to a special hospital in London where I was scrubbed with caustic soap and made to drink terrible medicine. When I got back, I found that they had sent Mr Higgins away. They must have told him that I didn't love him any more.*
>
> *They made me marry Mr Coldwell, but I never loved him. I probably never really loved my children either. They always seemed like not quite the children I should have had.*
>
> *I never saw Mr Higgins again. But at night I still dream about him, the man I should have married, and wonder where he is. I used to go around old bookshops sometimes, looking for his poems, but I never found any.*
>
> *He didn't have bad breath. They lied about that.*

'That's not the kind of thing we want at all,' says Mrs Briggs. 'You need to focus on positive things – where she used to go on holiday, if she had any sporting achievements. That kind of thing.'

Annie puts the story in the bottom drawer of her desk and doesn't submit another one.

The next weekend, Annie visits a local bookshop and asks about a poet called Geoffrey Higgins.

'He used to work near here,' she says, 'a long time ago. But I don't know where he went after that.'

'I'll ring around for you,' says the shopkeeper, 'see what I can find.'

Two weeks later, Annie climbs the stairs to Lydia's attic room carrying a small green-and-gold hardback book.

'It's a collection of Higgins's poetry,' she tells Lydia.

Lydia turns the book over in her hands. 'How wonderful,' she says. 'Thank you so much, my dear.'

'Look at the flyleaf,' says Annie. 'It's got a dedication.'

Lydia turns to the flyleaf.

'*For Lydia*,' she reads. She presses her fingers to the words. 'That's me.'

'I know,' says Annie. 'Good, isn't it?'

Over the coming months, Annie visits Lydia as often as she can, and listens many times to the story of the arboretum and the poetry and the caustic soap. The collection of poems is always on the bedside table or sticking out from under Lydia's pillows.

'I like it when you come and see me,' Lydia tells Annie. 'It's very kind of you.'

One afternoon, Lydia points to a small round tin on the table. 'You can have a sweet, if you like,' she says. 'Go on. The yellow ones have sherbet in. They're the best. Have one of those.'

'There's only one yellow one left,' says Annie, looking in the tin.

Lydia hesitates. 'That's all right,' she says. 'You go on and have it.'

In January 1995, at the age of eighty-two, Lydia dies of pneumonia. Her body is manhandled down the narrow attic stairs and cremated at the Ashton Crematorium on the Bridgewater Road. Annie goes to the service and is the only one to cry.

'Not very professional,' says the receptionist, handing her a tissue.

Not long afterwards, Hugo received a package from Wyke Manor containing the little book of poems and a note from the activity coordinator:

> *When Mrs Coldwell's sons came to clear her room, they left this behind. I thought perhaps someone there might want it . . .*

You will find it on the bedside table in the blue room. Turn to the flyleaf and see the inscription – smudgy with fingerprints, slightly sticky and smelling of lemons.

58

Rosalind's Paper Bag

No, Lydia does not come back to Thornwalk, and Rosalind is never allowed home either. Really, who could have read the end of Annabel's story without laughing? Broadmoor patients, convicted of attempted murder and judged criminally insane, are not generally escorted home by a personal guard, to sit in the corner of a carpentry workshop with a chisel, whittling woodblocks for wallpaper presses.

But she does come home, very briefly, in 1977, when she escapes from the secure unit of St Andrew's Psychiatric Hospital in Northampton, where she has been held under section for the past fifteen years, and walks and hitches the 110 miles to Thornwalk.

She arrives on a rainy afternoon in April, wearing a large yellow rain mac, much too long in the arms. She is small and pale, hunched under her hood a bit like a snail, as though she were carrying something heavy on her back, and her forehead is very big, where she has pulled out the fringe. She is nearly sixty years old, but for some reason she looks much younger, almost like a child.

'Rosalind!' says Annabel, stepping out into the rain to help her sister inside.

'Yes,' says Rosalind. 'It's me. I know you were probably expecting someone better, but there you are. That's life, isn't it?'

Annabel helps Rosalind take off the mac and the soaking wet tennis shoes, and shows her up to the attic. Then, leaving Rosalind crouched in an armchair, wrapped in a patchwork quilt, she goes down to the kitchen, makes some soup and some tea, and carries them up on the little brown tray.

Rosalind eats in silence, her head bent almost to her knees.

'I know you never liked me, Annabel,' she says when she has finished, pushing away the tray, leaning back and closing her eyes. 'No, not ever. Well, I guess that's just how it is sometimes. I guess that just happens.'

Annabel tries to think of something to say, but it takes too long.

'So, it's true, then,' says Rosalind. 'I thought it was.'

Annabel stares at her sister. 'Rosalind –' she begins.

But it's too late.

'When I'm gone, you can have my pearl necklace,' says Rosalind. 'It's in my bag.' She gestures to a crumpled paper bag in the corner (which can be found now in the bottom of the bedside cabinet in the next room).

'I think it was my pearl necklace –' Annabel says.

Rosalind sighs. A tear escapes from under one of her eyelids and slowly rolls down her cheek. 'Well, then,' she says, 'you can have it back.'

Annabel makes up the next room and sits by the bed, smoothing her sister's hair. She looks down at Rosalind's face, slightly swollen and heavy around the jaw, and thinks of the films she was in, the cuttings she used to send home to Hugo. She remembers the trip to the seaside, the boots with the hole in and the pink shell, and how Rosalind called all the Christmas trees Norman.

She sees Rosalind standing in front of the house with Jeremy. She has a canvas rucksack on her back and is carrying a walking stick, just like his.

'The rucksack isn't too heavy?' asks Jeremy.

'No,' says Rosalind. 'I can do it. Don't worry, Jeremy.'

'Your shoes don't hurt?'

'Nope.'

'You're ready to go, then?'

'I'm ready!'

'You're sure? You don't need the toilet? Because last time we only got to the end of the field. I want to go much further than the end of the field today.'

'I don't need the toilet. Honestly, I don't. I'm ready to go, Jeremy, really I am.'

Annabel watches them set off down the drive, but half an hour later here they are again, Rosalind with grazed knees and a tear-stained face, clinging to Jeremy's back.

'I'm sorry, Jeremy,' she sobs. 'I'm sorry I fell over. I won't do it again.'

'You always do it,' says Jeremy, dropping her at the front door and marching away. 'You can't come with me any more, Rosie.'

It is a long night. Rosalind wakes often and calls out for her sister. She tells Annabel, again, about the hospital, about the pain she's in, and the dreams she has, night after night, of cliffs and crocodiles and struck-by-lightning skies.

'I came back to say I'm sorry,' she says. 'I know that's what you want me to say, but to be honest I don't mean it. I never decided anything. I never chose to do any of the things I did. They just happened. And look how I'm being punished. Is that fair? Every day is agony for me. They say I'm lucky to be alive. Lucky! They say I have a liver of iron. But what's the good of having a liver of iron, Annabel, if you've got kidneys of jelly?'

Towards morning, Annabel wakes to the sound of running footsteps back and forth along the corridor outside her room.

It is Rosalind, with a sheet clutched around her shoulders

like a cape. Back and forth she runs, back and forth, the sheet flying out behind her.

'Look, Annabel, look,' she cries, seeing her sister in the doorway. 'I'm a bird again. I'm a bird!'

The police arrive at the house that afternoon. They tell Hugo that they believe he may be harbouring a dangerous criminal.

'Nonsense,' says Hugo.

They have a search warrant, they say, but would prefer not to have to use it.

'Search away,' says Hugo.

The police take a long time searching the house, but, of course, they cannot find her. By that time, Rosalind is in a trucker's cab heading down the M5.

They catch up with her at last, at a Little Chef on the side of the A30, where she is trying to hitch a lift to Weston-super-Mare. She would like to see the sea, she says.

'Come on,' says the younger of the two police officers. 'Let's just take her to see the sea. It's not that far.'

'No,' says the older one.

They discuss it for a few minutes, back and forth.

'Fine!' says the older man at last.

It is starting to get dark by the time they reach the seaside. The policemen buy ice creams from a kiosk and watch Rosalind running up and down the beach.

'She's supposed to have been a film star,' says the younger man.

The older man peers at Rosalind, standing there in the dusk, holding out her arms to the seagulls. 'Now that you mention it,' he says, 'she does look a bit familiar. Maybe I saw one of her films.'

'My dear friend!' cries Rosalind, running over and clasping the older man's hands. 'How wonderful! If I have touched just one life, it will all have been worth it,' and her eyes are shining with tears.

They don't stay long. The ice cream is soon finished, the sun goes down, and Rosalind is bundled into the police car and driven back to Northamptonshire.

In 1991, after re-evaluation, Rosalind is removed from the secure unit at St Andrew's and placed in a small flat in Abington Vale, where she dies five months later, at the age of seventy-three, attended by a community nurse.

'Who is Wilfred?' the nurse asks Hugo, when she calls to deliver the news. 'She was asking for him at the end.'

59

Annabel's Notebook

And, no, Annabel does not set off around the world with Simon Greenway. She never lives with him in one of the Blacksmiths' Cottages, never leans out of a bedroom window on a moonlit evening, to watch him ambling down the drive towards her . . . That is one of the saddest things about her story, I think. The publisher called it 'poignant', said it deserved to be told. If only she would cut out the boring bits and murder someone.

The manuscript was put away, as I said, but it was not forgotten. It was a habit of hers in the following years to walk around the kitchen garden, talking to herself.

'I wanted them all to be remembered,' she can be heard to say. 'I wanted it all to count for something. Of course, I know that it doesn't, count for something, I mean. Nothing really does, does it? It's the same for everyone, even the famous people. All the lights go out in the end. But still, that's what I thought I would try to do.'

She pauses, while an imaginary interviewer asks a question.

'Yes, but those things are just on the surface,' she says. 'The broken bits. All the ivy and the lichen, and the holes where the woodpeckers have buried their beaks. I could still see the little acorns, trying so hard. It is impossible not to love the tree, broken and covered in bird poo as it is, when you see the acorn, trying so hard. Oh, don't you love them? It is so important that you do.'

Sometimes her walks take her too close to the village, and the children in the playground catch glimpses of her between the trees. She no longer has attacks like she used to, but sometimes she will stop and stand quite still, staring up at the sky, even when it's raining or starting to get dark, and, when the children call out, she doesn't seem to hear them.

Other times, in the dim light of a misty evening, she can be found standing in the courtyard with Simon. The present moment has grown thin from neglect and the past is pressing in upon it, like wind against a clingfilm window.

Yes, Simon is there, standing right in front of her in his checked shirt and corduroy trousers. He smells of sweat and sawdust. There is a piece of hay in his hair.

'If there's something I'm doing wrong –' she hears him say. 'Something you need me to do.'

'No,' she whispers. 'Nothing.'

If you listen hard enough, on an evening like this, you can hear a little echo. 'No, nothing,' it says. 'No. Nothing.'

And, now and then, at night, Annabel will sit on the stairs to the old chauffeur's quarters. She is thinking of a scene I have not shown you yet. I shall put it here.

We must go back to the day she listens to her mother and Aunt Beatrice plotting in the library, to the moment she realizes she is in danger. Once more, see her run across the hall, out into the courtyard and down the drive. Once more, see Randall stepping out of the bushes and wrapping his arms around her.

'Hold still, Miss Annabel,' he whispers. 'Hold still.'

Annabel, sitting on the stairs, presses a hand to her stomach. After fifty years, sixty years, she can still feel his arm. She can still feel the terrible hollow inside her. In her fist, in a tiny velvet bag that once held a set of silver *Monopoly* pieces, is the little tangle of nothing.

'Hold still, Miss Annabel.'

See her wrestled into the car and driven away.

And now, three months later, see her coming back. The car pulls up in front of the house and Annabel clambers out. She looks at Randall, sitting in the front seat, both hands gripping the steering wheel. She looks at Aunt Beatrice, standing on the other side of the car. 'Annabel –' Aunt Beatrice says, but Annabel turns and runs away.

That much, I have already told you. Now, we come to the new bit.

That night, Annabel sits under the desk in her father's study, watching the doorway to the servants' quarters on the other side of the gallery. Shortly after one o'clock, she hears the softest pad of woollen socks, sees the liquid streak of a candle flame as Lizzie turns the corner of the stairs.

Annabel gets up and follows.

Softly, softly, the kitchen door opens and closes. Outside in the courtyard, a fine mist hangs in the moonlit air, as Lizzie picks up the ends of her dressing gown and tiptoes over the cobblestones to the bottom of the steps.

Up she goes, to tap on the door, very gently. No answer. More insistently now. Nothing.

Lizzie pushes open the door.

'Oh, it's you,' says Randall, turning towards her. He is sitting in the armchair in front of the window, his elbows on his knees, his head in his hands.

'Of course, it's me,' says Lizzie. 'Who else would it be?'

'Oh, never mind,' says Randall. 'What do you want?'

Lizzie stares at him, then scowls. She turns and closes the door behind her.

Up the steps creeps Annabel, to press her ear to the door.

'What on earth is the matter with you?' says Lizzie.

'You know what,' says Randall. 'You know very well what.' There is a creak of leather and a clink of glass.

Lizzie wrinkles her nose. So, he has been drinking again, she thinks. That explains it.

'You've been drinking,' she says. 'You always get like this when you drink.'

'It has nothing to do with that,' says Randall.

'It definitely does.'

'No, it doesn't. It's her. It's Annabel.'

Outside, Annabel leans closer to the door and holds her breath.

'What about her?' says Lizzie, never more lemon-hearted than now.

'I don't know. I don't know,' says Randall. He draws a hand through his thick dark hair. It is standing on end a little bit now, and Lizzie, for all the lemon in her heart, thinks she is going to suffocate with love. 'I had no idea,' he says, 'no idea what was going to happen, what they were going to do to her.'

'Didn't you?' Lizzie says. 'That's strange. Everyone else did.'

'I'm not going to put up with it any more,' says Randall. There is a thud and a crash. The little chipped Chinaman has fallen over and his head has come off.

'Hush!' says Lizzie. 'What do you mean you're not going to put up with it? Put up with what?' There is a tiny trembling of fear in her voice. Perhaps, after all, he is going to escape.

'All this. Her. I've had enough.'

'You always say that.'

'I mean it this time. I'm going to sort all this out. I'm going to make it up to her.'

'To who?'

'Annabel, of course. I'm going to make it up to her.'

'How?'

'I don't know. I'll think of something.'

'I don't know why you're worrying about it,' says Lizzie. 'She won't care. She probably hardly even noticed.'

'Hardly even noticed?' Randall blinks and turns to look at her. 'What do you mean?'

Lizzie shrugs. 'People like that don't. Like cows. They don't feel things the same way we do. Anyway, I think they were right to do it. You can't let people like that breed all over the place any old how. It's unhygienic.'

'Get out!' he shouts.

Randall picks up the Chinaman's head and throws it, as Lizzie runs for the door.

That night, Annabel can't sleep. Early the next morning, she hangs around the courtyard, waiting for Randall to come down, but he doesn't.

Soon, she thinks, soon he will come and see me.

'I'm sorry,' he will say. 'I didn't know.'

And she will say, 'I know you didn't. Don't worry. It's not your fault.'

And then he will tell her his plan, what he's going to do to make it up to her.

But he doesn't come. He doesn't even look at her when that afternoon he loads Aunt Beatrice's bags into the boot of the car and gets into the driver's seat.

In all the months to come, on all the visits he makes to Thornwalk, he says nothing to her at all, and he does not leave Aunt Beatrice as he said he would, not for some years yet anyway, not until Lizzie is pregnant and Aunt Beatrice tells them both to go . . . but still, as she sits there on the steps, in another moonlit mist, clutching the tangle of nothing to her stomach, Annabel is waiting for Randall to make it up to her. She has been waiting all these years. No, she never understood, not even at the very end, that it is just something people say.

★

As Annabel gets older, the imaginary interviews stop, and she no longer stands in the courtyard or sits on the steps to the chauffeur's quarters. Instead, she is found wandering on the lane to the sawmill.

See her there now, a little old lady in a ragged nightdress, long grey-brown hair, skinny arms and legs and a little round belly, clambering up the rickety ladder to lie down in the powdery hay with her hand stretched out to an invisible body beside her.

By then she was dying. She had some sort of autoimmune disorder. Her hair was falling out, and she had rashes all over her hands and face. She'd had it a long time, but recently it had got into her kidneys and lungs.

She wasn't scared to die. She was quite religious, in her way, and that helped. It wasn't something she was comfortable talking about, God, but small things had happened in her life that made her believe there was a pattern to it all. For example, she knew she was meant to be ill, because that's what had kept her at Thornwalk with Hugo. Every time she had ever even thought about leaving, she had had another attack – another dizzy spell or blackout. It was a sign.

And things had sort of worked out, one way or another, not in any way she could have imagined or planned for herself, but for every small act of faith, there had been a corresponding sense of walking on water. Every time she just said, 'It'll be all right,' somehow it had been.

She stayed with Hugo as long as she could, but was finally admitted to hospital in 1989, at the age of seventy-three.

When the ambulance came to collect her, she told them to call me and refused to leave until I arrived. 'Your turn now,' she whispered, and pressed this key into my hand.

She left me her notebook, full of recipes that Hugo liked, things it was better not to mention, how much water to put in the whisky bottle, where his winter pyjamas were kept, that sort of thing. But most of it I already knew.

There are no rats, she wrote.

That is quite important. If there is any noise in the storerooms it is only squirrels. His eyesight isn't that good now, so, unless you are standing right on top of a rat, it should be fine.

Equally, no moths. And don't mention the moles on the lawn, or the ants.

He likes to feed the birds but make sure you keep the lid down tight on the bird-food container (the rat thing again).

I visited her a few times, but wasn't with her at the end. She had hoped to die quietly, without asking anyone for help. I hope she did.

60

Slippers from Norway

And then, of course, there is Jeremy, of whom so little is known and so little physical evidence remains.

His book *Me and My Penknife: A Whittling Journey* appears in 1957. After that, he has a series of articles published in various periodicals under a variety of names, from Wilson J. Wilberforce to Johannes Gandalf and Jeremy Tree. Copies or cuttings are sent to Thornwalk regularly in brown envelopes with French stamps, but they are not addressed to anyone in particular and there is never a note.

Hugo throws them all into the library fireplace, from where they are rescued by Annabel.

In 1966, a package arrives addressed to Hugo containing a photograph of a middle-aged woman and two children. *The woman is Birdie Long*, writes Jeremy, *who was our father's mistress.*

At the time he knew her, she lived in London, which is where they met, but some time afterwards she moved back to her family in New York. As you may already have worked out, Father didn't die in the war. He died some years later, in an outbreak of what looked like Spanish flu on a passenger ship crossing the Atlantic, probably on his way to see her.

After his death, Birdie wrote to our mother, explaining her situation, but sadly she received no reply.

The two children are our half-sisters, Elsa and Irma. Elsa is a librarian in a suburb of Boston and Irma is married with three children and lives in Baltimore. Birdie passed away in 1963, but the girls would very much like to come to England and visit Thornwalk. I have enclosed their addresses, should you wish to contact them.

This letter too, after a day resting on Hugo's desk, is thrown on the fire and rescued by Annabel. It can be found as an appendix to her manuscript in the bottom of the box file under her bed, along with a number of drafts of letters to the two half-sisters, finished copies of which I doubt she ever sent.

It would be lovely to see you, she writes. *But you mustn't come to Thornwalk.* In some, she has added, *Would you like any jam?*

In 1967, Jeremy sends a pair of slippers from Norway with a label saying 'For Mother' attached. Hugo takes off the label and keeps the slippers, which can still be seen under the edge of his bed.

The last postcard from Jeremy is dated October 1968 and postmarked Cairo.

Nothing more is known of the fate of Jeremy Gilbert, but rumours tell of a certain wise man in a hut at the foot of the Alps, living on honey from a hive of rare black bees and milk from a herd of wild mountain goats.

When a famous journalist, fleeing a religious fatwa, becomes lost in the mountains, he finds shelter in the wise man's hut.

'Teach me the key to enlightenment,' pleads the journalist, envious of the wise man's air of peaceful acceptance. There is not a trace of restless idealism about him.

'The unexamined life is worth diddly-squat,' says the wise man, 'but whereof one cannot speak, thereof one ought to shut up.'

The words seem faintly familiar, but undeniably true, and the rest of the journalist's stay is passed in happy silence.

'Don't you ever get lonely?' asks the journalist as he prepares to leave at last. He gazes out over the mountains. It is still summer, but the threat of snow is already somewhere in the air.

'No, I don't think so,' says the wise man. His eyes become distant. 'Which is not to say —' But the sentence is left unfinished.

The journalist glances around the little hut. 'You've always lived here alone?' he asks.

'Always,' says the wise man.

'But before this,' pursues the journalist. 'You weren't married?'

'No.'

'You were never in love?'

'There was someone once,' says the wise man. 'A long time ago.'

'What happened?'

For a long while, the wise man does not reply. Then at last, in a voice filled with pain, he says, 'Nothing.'

A description of the encounter is published in the *National Geographic*, accompanied by a photograph of the wise man. He is turning away from the camera and shielding his face with a small whittled ostrich. All that can be seen is a long grizzled beard, tousled grey hair and, in the corner of the one visible eye, surely, the unmistakable glint of the Gilbert.

Yes, I know I mentioned a tragic demise. It was a ruse to pique your interest. Jeremy's death, if death there has been, is most likely a quiet affair, wrapped up in an air of soft inevitability, as of the loosening of a bronzed rhododendron flower in an autumn breeze or the crumbling of dry wood beneath a reindeer's hoof.

61

The Missing Model Ship

We are approaching the last part of this story, but, before we move on, I ask you to pause for a moment here in the library and consider Hugo, sitting in front of the fireplace, holding Jeremy's letter about Birdie Long and the two American half-sisters. Everything in it is true, of course, and I think Elsa and Irma are both still alive, should anyone wish to clarify things further. I have not.

Until this point, Hugo has believed all their mother's lies about their father – her awkward tales of valour and bad luck, the mislaid letters from the Admiralty and the War Office, and the stolen medals. He has despised Emma for her words in the blue room, her foul and idiotic attempt to blacken his father's name. And even now, somehow, he still believes his mother and despises Emma.

Slowly, Hugo crushes the letter in his fist, then the photograph, and presses them down into the ashes.

Then he gets to his feet and climbs the stairs to his father's study, where, all this time, a half-made model ship has sat upon the mantelpiece and slowly thickened with dust – string rigging, hand-stitched calico sails, little blobs of rabbit skin glue between the boards, dried to the colour of ear wax, the name *Bluebird* sketched in pencil along the prow.

A labour of love it was, this ship. The work of a great questing mind, a mind dreaming of adventure, of heroism on the high seas. Symbolic of a life cut short, hopes dashed, potential robbed. How much Hugo has admired it, and mourned the loss of its maker.

Hugo looks at the ship for a moment, then he picks it up, throws it on the floor and stamps on it. He continues to stamp on it until it is almost dust – dust and tangled bits of string and cloth. Then he bends down to pick it up again and spends the rest of the morning on his hands and knees, digging the splinters out of the rug and stuffing them into the bottom cupboard of the left-hand cabinet, where you would have been able to find them now, had the door not been locked and the key thrown into the lake.

62

Concrete Lions

No, Emma does not come back to declare her undying love for Hugo and use all her money to help them save Thornwalk. There would never have been any hope of this, and Annabel must have known it.

And so it is that we approach, at last, the darkest heart of the story.

How to begin? Let us take another walk. This time, we shall leave the grounds of the estate as they are measured now, and go down the road past the turning to the village and along the lane posted south hamm and wraxley, to the fields to the west of Hamm Wood and Inscombe Farm.

The events I am about to narrate have been alluded to before, if you recall, when I mentioned that shortly after Annabel's return to Thornwalk, Inscombe was transferred into the hands of the Kirby family.

It was a subtle foreshadowing, for I knew this moment must come.

It was one of Hugo's saddest moments, the loss of this farm. It had been part of the outlying estate for more than a hundred years, purchased by Nathaniel Gilbert himself for the housing of a fine Jersey herd.

In order to understand, you must see it as it was then – a rustic farmhouse, the clay-tiled roof bowed in the middle and heavy with moss, the red-brick walls dusted with sage-green lichen and crumbling at the corners. There were yellow roses around the door, blue shutters at the windows – with the five-petalled passionflower, emblem of the Gilberts, cut out of the centres – and an old oak door with flaky blue paint. The barn behind the house was golden with age, soft with woodworm, and fragrant with summer dusts and autumn moulds.

You must imagine a cobbled courtyard, a foot deep in mud, armless runner ducks and glass-eyed chickens waging war over a hay bale and a soupy water trough, and the smell of a flowering daphne, there by the garden wall, filling the cool winter air with thick sweet scent.

As we watch, the old oak door opens and out comes a young man, short and stocky in the way of the Kirbys, his face ruddy from hard work outdoors since the age of four. His name is Percy. He throws a pitchfork into a wheelbarrow, grabs the handles and sets off for the big house. He has promised old Jupiter that he will help out at the dairy . . .

Are you able to see any of this?

I realize that not everyone has my imaginative skills. Perhaps you can see nothing beyond this moment's reality, this impressive, expansive, 'fully renovated and modernized former farmhouse' with its double-glazed PVCu windows and clean grey synthetic roof slates. The soft yellow barn has been converted into a triple garage, as you see. Inside the house, I can tell you now, having perused the brochure (another act of misguided curiosity, very much regretted), that the kitchen has an island, granite worktops, state-of-the-art fitted appliances and inset spotlights. The old cabinets – handmade by Percy Kirby's grandfather, Ernest, in 1905 and left behind for the enjoyment of the new owners, who had admired them greatly at the viewing – were ripped out soon after the sale, along with almost everything else. Three skips were filled in a month.

It was a sorry sight for poor Percy (the young man we just met coming out of the old farmhouse door), who had moved into the little bungalow he had built at the bottom of the drive, from the kitchen window of which he could see the passing skip trucks. Ah, well.

We shall go there now – to the bungalow, I mean. Brace yourself.

As we walk, we will remind ourselves of the last time we saw Emma (before Annabel's romantic account of her miraculous return, I mean). Yes, we left her locked in the blue room, if you remember, with Hugo squatting outside, the fire axe across his knees.

Now let us go back a little further, to Emma's ill-fated visit to the Chaplain's Cottage. See her there, perched on the edge of the old horsehair sofa, turning often to glance out of the window.

'I must go,' she says.

'But you've only just got here,' says Mrs Gilbert.

'Actually, I've just remembered something I have to do,' says Emma. She gets to her feet and hurries to the door. 'Urgently.' It is all she can come up with.

'Oh, I see,' says Mrs Gilbert. 'Well, you must take a pumpkin. They've done so well this year. We have ever so many.'

'No, really,' says Emma. 'Really, don't bother.'

'It will only take a moment. Annabel, where's the pumpkin knife?'

Annabel finds the pumpkin knife and the pumpkin is finally cut.

'Thank you very much,' says Emma. 'Goodbye.'

'Hang on,' says Mrs Gilbert. 'I have a recipe here for a soothing tea. You must make it for Hugo. Now, where did I put it?'

'I'll get it next time,' says Emma. 'I've got to go.'

'Hold on,' says Mrs Gilbert. 'Hold on.'

The recipe is found. Emma grabs it and rushes away. But as soon as she is gone, Mrs Gilbert sees the pumpkin on the table beside the door.

'Oh no!' she cries. 'The pumpkin.' She presses it into Annabel's hands. 'Annabel, run after her.'

'Perhaps she left it on purpose,' Annabel says. 'They probably have their own pumpkins.'

'Nonsense,' says Mrs Gilbert. 'Off you go!'

So it is that Annabel follows Emma back down to Thornwalk. So it is that she is there at the edge of the clearing in front of the house when Hugo rushes out. She sees Emma run, and fall, and scramble to her feet. Hugo grabs at her shoulder. Emma ducks free. He grabs again, and again. Finally, Hugo catches hold of Emma's arm and drags her into the house and across the hall.

'Please, Hugo,' Emma says. 'Please.'

Annabel looks around for some sort of weapon. There is only the pumpkin.

'Let her go!' she cries, lifting the pumpkin and hurling it at Hugo. Of course, it doesn't get anywhere near him, just lands with a thud on the porch tiles. Hugo stops and turns.

'Go home, Annabel,' he says.

'No,' she whispers. 'No, I won't.'

'Get out of here. Now!'

Poor Annabel turns and runs.

'Please, Hugo. Please,' Emma says.

With another roar, Hugo heaves Emma over his shoulder, while Annabel stumbles away into the bushes, where she stays until it is dark.

It is here that we left them before – Emma with a nosebleed, clutching a pillow to her face, Annabel hiding in the bushes. I alluded to more blood, someone else's blood, and now the time has come to tell you whose.

★

Days pass.

'Let me out,' says Emma.

The weather is unseasonably hot and the room is suffocating. The smell of the chamber pot is dreadful, and the window has been nailed only an inch ajar.

'Please let me out.'

Hugo is sitting outside the door with the axe across his lap. 'If I let you out, you'll leave me,' he says.

'Hugo . . .'

'You will, won't you?'

'Please, Hugo. Let me go home.'

Hugo leans his head against the door and closes his eyes. 'No,' he says.

On it goes, until the day Percy has agreed to help out at the dairy.

Here he comes, with his wheelbarrow and his pitchfork. He has been told not to go within sight of the house, but the other path, the one that used to run past the Chaplain's Cottage, has been closed for years. There is nothing for it but to go the long way, past the kitchen garden and the stables.

Percy is just turning the corner, when he stops. A branch is lying across the path, with an old door propped against it. On the door, someone has painted road closed – go this way and an arrow, pointing towards the house.

It is the best Annabel can do.

Percy pauses for a moment, then sets off along the edge of the arboretum. He will blame the sign, he thinks, should anyone say anything.

A few minutes later, as he crosses the end of the yew walk, a fluttering white thing catches Percy's eye. It is a handkerchief, tucked into a crack in a window frame. He comes closer.

'So,' he whispers, 'it is true after all.' Because, of course, there have been rumours.

Percy leaves his barrow at the edge of the trees, snatches up his fork and approaches the house. See him creeping along the path and in through the old conservatory door, tiny clumps of manure dropping now and then from the prongs of his fork on to the gravel behind.

Past the door to the servants' quarters he tiptoes. From the hall ahead comes the tinny chime of the grandfather clock. He smells cold stone, floor polish and manure.

From somewhere above comes a voice. 'Please, Hugo. It doesn't have to be like this. You don't have to do this, Hugo.'

'Do this?' says another voice. 'Do this?' It is Hugo, coming down the stairs, dragging the axe behind him. 'Do what? What have I ever done? Nothing, nothing at all. As if she wasn't the one who did everything. All of it. Every single thing.'

Hugo crosses the hall and disappears. As soon as he is gone, Percy runs up the stairs to the door at the corner of the gallery.

'Mrs Gilbert?' he whispers. 'Mrs Gilbert, are you in there?'

'Percy? Is that you?' says Emma.

'Yes, it's me,' says Percy. 'Don't worry. I'll get you out of there.'

'No, Percy, go away,' cries Emma. 'Get out of here right now.'

'Hang on,' he says. 'It's just a little bolt.'

For a few breathless moments, Percy struggles with the bolt. It is not so little after all, and he is not quite tall enough to get a good grip on the handle of the shank. There are soft footsteps on the stairs behind, but Percy's attention is fixed on the bolt and he doesn't hear them.

'You!' cries Hugo, appearing at the top of the stairs. 'So, it's you, is it? All this time! You disgusting, creeping, miserable rat! You filthy snake in the grass!'

Hugo rushes forward, lifts the axe and swings it at Percy's head. There is an almighty crash as the axe hits the door. Hugo tugs it away, leaving a splintered gash in the middle panel, and swings again. This time, the edge of the axe catches the side of Percy's head. Blood gushes, as Percy turns and runs – the fork forgotten – back down the stairs and through the hall, screaming for help.

Well, we have arrived at Percy's little bungalow now. Stop at the end of the drive, beside these charming concrete pillars topped with concrete lions. If you wait here, you will soon see Percy himself. You can't miss him – old man, white hair, one hand.

63

The Wounded Oak

I should like to move on now, leave it at that, but, of course, you will have questions. Where is this missing hand? Why didn't Hugo end up in prison? What happened to Emma? Yes, yes, I suppose we must look at all these terrible things.

For that we shall leave the bungalow and go back to Thornwalk – past the dreadful renovated farmhouse and up the lane, along the edge of the arboretum, through the courtyard and down the drive towards the stables. There is Hugo, just in front of us, swinging the fire axe.

'Enough!' he cries as he runs. 'Enough! You will not kill my children and steal my wife and cut down my trees!'

And there is poor Percy, fifty yards further on near the edge of the wood. He is a short man, as I think I mentioned before, stout, all body and no legs, and his desperate sprint is a pitiful thing to behold.

'What was that?' he shouts back over his shoulder. 'I haven't done anything, Mr Gilbert. I haven't killed anyone or stolen anything. It wasn't me!'

Hugo is moderately large but surprisingly fast, and he catches up with Percy just as he enters the trees. There is a great deal of grabbing and twisting free, dodging behind trunks and ducking under branches. At last, Percy is cornered, his back to a mighty oak. He raises his hands. If Hugo will just give him a moment, he will be able to explain. There has clearly been some horrible mistake. 'Hang on a moment!' he says, trying to catch his breath. 'Just hang on a moment!'

But Hugo does not hang on.

And so, the terrible deed is done. The scream is heard as far as Wimple, so they say. Down in the village, people lift their eyes to the hillside and see a cloud of rooks rise up out of the trees and sweep away to the north, while in the house, the ancient grandfather clock gives a dreadful groan and stops dead, never to start again. So they say.

In the Chaplain's Cottage, Mrs Gilbert is startled awake from her nap and hears the rooks pass overhead. 'Bloody poachers,' she mutters, and falls asleep again. Annabel, at the kitchen sink, tugs off her apron and sets off at a run towards the house.

And the hand? It was searched for by the police and the ambulance crew, but never found. I imagine it was most likely snatched by an opportunistic fox and resides still, in much depleted form, in the corner of some subterraneous larder. And when in the end the woods are cut down and the diggers move in – for Thornwalk must surely, one day, have its fair share of the bungalows – no doubt it shall at last be discovered and pondered over and placed, as a crowd pleasing curiosity, in a display case in the local museum, beside the knapped flints, the reproduction Roman amphora and the nugget of possible meteorite discovered by little Johnny Moss in the roof of the Moss privy in 1965.

64

The Estate Map

Hugo was arrested, of course, but almost immediately transferred to the psychiatric unit at Barrow Gurney. There were plenty of people ready to testify to his increasingly strange behaviour, his long mental decline. No, he wasn't in his right mind, they said, hadn't been in his right mind for a long time. There was talk of his war years, some sort of trauma. Along with the shrapnel in his leg, perhaps a small piece of shrapnel had been lodged in his brain. That sort of thing was turning out to be quite common.

There were negotiations. Talk of reparation. The Kirbys accepted a preliminary verdict of diminished capacity, and Inscombe Farm was signed away. Not long afterwards, work began on the bungalow (which we have just seen), the pride and joy of a surprisingly dextrous and cheerful one-handed Percy.

'I always said I'd give me right arm for a place of me own,' Percy still regularly declares, perched on a bar stool at the Twisted Willow. 'Turns out, I only had to give me left hand.' It always gets a good laugh.

Neither Hugo nor Annabel ever again set foot on Inscombe land.

Well, that covers it, I think. I am aware that I have been brief. I hope it will suffice.

One last thing I can show you, which may help you to understand. If you take a look in the middle drawer of Hugo's desk, you will find a large, roughly folded sheet of parchment. It is a map of the Thornwalk estate. Once upon a time, it had pride of place in their father's study – you can still see the four screw holes left in the wall over the fireplace where it was taken down, replaced by a slightly smaller map of America – but many years ago it became a thing of shame.

One by one, the cottages marked upon it emptied, as one by one the tenants left. There were those who never came back from the war, and those who came back and left again, because there was no money to keep them. Families who had worked the land and loved the house for generations, scattered to the wind like so many dandelion seeds, like so many diamonds in a Romanov crown.

One by one, as they are sold, the farms are drawn around and blotted out. A stretch of forest here, a pasture there. Until Thornwalk is left in the middle, teetering on a tiny white island, like a polar bear on an icecap.

65

The Wedding Ring

And Emma.

Of course, she cannot stay at Thornwalk. Of course, she does not.

And now the time has come for me to show you my little village house. We shall go there together – down the hill, across the road, past the pub and left along School Lane. There is the school – what was once the school – converted into two residential flats, the way they do, with that ridiculous chopping in half of beautiful windows. We will avert our eyes.

Mine is the last house at the end of the lane – thatched roof, white walls, an old yellow door. I think perhaps I've said that already.

Come inside. There is only one main living space, as you see, much cluttered with books and painting paraphernalia. The kitchen is there at the back. Just a little electric cooker, kettle, toaster, all the basics.

There is a slight smell of mould – I forget to keep the fire in and the damp quickly creeps back out of the walls – and the usual issues with slugs, hornets, spiders, dead mice slowly decomposing under the floorboards, blocked drains, frozen pipes, leaking chimneys, etc.

It was here that Emma came, the third day after the terrible deed, with Hugo at Barrow Gurney and Annabel at the cottage with her mother. Down the hill she came, and across the road, as we have done, to knock upon that yellow door.

See her there in her tweed skirt and felt hat. Neat but badly coordinated. There is something entirely inoffensive, even endearing, in the correctness of her clothes and her complete lack of style. She will never be either envied or despised.

But it is no time to notice her clothes. Her face is pale. Worse than pale. She looks ill. Old and very tired. The circles under her eyes are so low on her cheeks that they might almost be called jowls. Her whole face has sunk, gone down with her hopes and dreams.

There she sits. On the same chair in which Hugo spent so many hours, staring into the fire.

'I must do my duty, Maximus. We can't all be like Jeremy. We don't all get to choose.'

She perches on the edge of the chair, clutching her gloves and the handle of her handbag, and looks slowly around the room.

'I can make her happy, Maximus. You mustn't worry about that.'

Her eyes fix on a small painting of Thornwalk above the fireplace. It is an early work of my own. Not technically proficient but containing something my later work has lost.

Emma stares at the painting, and tells me she will do what she can for Hugo, legally, financially. Her father will help. He has a certain amount of influence, her father, and money isn't a problem. As long as Emma promises never to see Hugo again, her father will help.

Finally, she looks at me, and her eyes are searching and sad.

'I must leave him to you now, Maximus,' she says. 'You and Annabel. I hope you do a better job of it than I have done.'

And that is that. I suppose it is not much to show you, to

have come all this way for. It had seemed bigger, somehow, in my memory.

No, she does not stay long. She waits a moment, thinking, sifting through all the things she has meant to say, wanted to say, all these years. But, no, they have disappeared, been swallowed up by the big thing, and that is too big and too terrible to talk about.

As she gets up to leave, she tugs the wedding ring from her left hand and places it carefully on the arm of the chair. I think perhaps she meant me to return it to Hugo, but you will find it where I have kept it all these years, in the enamel pill box on the mantelpiece.

That afternoon, a taxi arrives at Thornwalk and takes Emma away, never to return.

And after that? I think I mentioned the philanthropy and the politics already. That is all anyone knows for sure.

Of course, Hugo keeps his scrapbook, with the glued-in photographs and articles which, again, we have already seen. They are quite hard to find in those early years. Every time something comes up about Emma, everyone talks about Hugo and Rosalind, so perhaps she is careful not to let things come up.

Eventually, it doesn't matter any more. It is old news and there are worse things going on in the world. But she keeps her promise to her father and never sees Hugo again.

Around 1975, the photographs suddenly stop and Emma disappears entirely from public view. It is said that she has gone abroad, possibly to her parents' house in Cannes, possibly to Buenos Aires or Italy. On her abandoned desk they find a copy of the *National Geographic* and a receipt from a Bond Street store for a map of the Alps and almost three hundred pounds' worth of camping equipment.

Make of that what you will. I like to think that there was, in the end, a little glimmer of light for her.

66

The Gramophone

And so, I was alone with Hugo.

For a long while after Annabel left, he did not speak, hardly moved from the sofa in front of the fireplace, where he sat huddled in blankets.

He ate very little at first, refused everything I made. I can still see him now, shuffling away to the kitchen, to struggle with the instructions on a pot noodle or a packet of dried soup. I can still feel it in my heart.

Somewhere in the second week, it began to rain, a relentless strumming on the skylight, which was leaking even then. On and on it went, for three days without stopping. It gets into the eyes, such rain. It gets into the mind.

On the afternoon of the third day, I left Hugo alone in the library while I went to make some cocoa. When I came back, his blankets had been dropped in a heap on the floor and the room was empty.

I searched the house, but somehow I knew he wasn't in it.

I went outside and saw him standing at the edge of the lake. I started to run, but was still only halfway down the lawn when he stepped forward and toppled into the water.

'An accident,' he said, as I dragged him back out. 'I slipped. It's so goddamn muddy there at the edge.'

From then on, for some months, I didn't leave him alone for long.

And so, our days went on. I cooked mushroom stroganoffs and winter stews. He preferred his pot noodles. When his green velvet dressing gown got thin and stained, I bought him a new one for Christmas, but he put it aside with a smile.

I don't really know now how our days were spent. They passed so quickly, more quickly than it is possible to express. It was as if we had already reached the end of the land and all that was left for us to do was to slip down the cliff. That's how it seems, looking back.

Mornings were spent eating breakfast, drinking tea and reading the local newspaper, and quietly became lunchtime.

Every afternoon, we went for a walk around the estate, but never too far from the house.

Don't go further than the holly tree to the west, Annabel had written in her notebook, *and to the east, no further up the hill than the corner with the three oaks.*

These were the points beyond which Hugo would have been able to see the new bungalow at Inscombe and the clearing at the top of Cley Hill where Emma found him with his shotgun.

And avoid Shute Lane when it's been raining. He'll want to pick up all the snails and it will take you forever to get back.

He loved gardening. Warm days were spent pottering about the beds below the terrace and in the kitchen garden. In the evenings, we looked through his seed catalogues, and I filled in the order forms. You wouldn't think it now to look at them, but for many years the borders were full of wonderful things – pulmonaria and hellebores and narcissus in spring, roses and cornflowers and nasturtiums in summer, and asters, so many asters, in autumn.

In April, you will see the lilacs he planted, but not much more survives from that time.

We picked flowers and brought them into the house. I haven't shown you the flower presses yet, or the cards he made.

Sometimes, we would read. He liked his little spy stories, but not much else. He had tried proper literature, he said, but found it disappointing. John Irving, for instance, was too deliberately shocking, had lured him in and assaulted him, made him feel used. He knew where he was with Ian Fleming.

I told him about a memoir I had discovered, about a beautiful Italian orphan living on a remote farm in Norfolk. He had always wanted to go to Norfolk, and wrote down on the back of an envelope all the places mentioned in the book – Aylsham, Drabblegate, Erpingham churchyard . . . You will find the envelope in his desk.

'One day,' he said. 'One day.'

The first winter, I fetched the little 1920s Bakelite gramophone from the morning room and set it up on one of the tables in the library, and we often spent our evenings going through his old record collection. Annabel had told me which ones to bring out, which ones to leave in the cabinet.

You will find the gramophone there still, and the pile of records we used to play. Feel free to take a look. There was a lively rendition of Rachmaninov's second that we grew to love – a cheap little pressing, worthless to the Cooper Juniors and Sydneys of the world, thankfully, but precious beyond measure to me. There is some decent Vivaldi, some Tchaikovsky. Listen to them, if you will, and think of us here.

67

The Television

I remember one evening in early spring. We had spent the day in the garden. He was tired and suggested watching a film.

'Nothing post-1960,' he said. 'I despise modern films. Anything pre-1960 has a ninety per cent chance of being better than anything post-1960.'

'Why 1960?' I asked.

'That's the date when films got worse,' he said.

'But why?' I said.

'How should I know?' he said. 'I'm not a filmmaker.' He seemed annoyed, but still I pursued it.

'Ninety per cent?' I repeated.

'Yes.'

'Why ninety per cent? I mean, how did you come by that number?'

'It's a high number,' he said. 'How very obtuse you're being.'

We ended up watching *My Fair Lady*. 'It's 1964,' he said, 'but I'll make an exception.'

I remember it so clearly. We had Annabel's little VHS machine on a stool under the television set, and he was sitting in the leather armchair with the tartan rug across his knees. He was getting so thin. His face was pale, hollow under the cheekbones, and his hands trembled.

'Isn't she wonderful,' he said, when Audrey Hepburn came down the stairs for the ball, and there were tears in his eyes.

Increasingly, he liked to watch television. They were putting on lots of village police dramas then, and he liked those. There were a number of soap operas that he followed too, and it soon seemed that every evening there was one or another of them.

'I never watch television,' he would say, 'except this and this and this.' And the list would get longer and longer. 'I prefer listening to Rachmaninov,' he would say, 'but there's never enough time for Rachmaninov, after this and this and this.'

But I had to be careful. He had loved his little eighties television programmes – *Magnum P.I.*, *The A-Team*, all the Miss Marples and Poirots – but the modern shows had started to distress him. He couldn't stand to see suffering.

For the same reason, we didn't walk near the village any more. He hated to hear children playing. They were so innocent, he said. They had no idea what was coming. And whenever a baby cried, he heard agony in it.

I had convinced him to stop driving some time before. It had become so erratic – emergency braking for birds, swerving for butterflies or leaves that looked like butterflies. In autumn, when the lanes were full of little flocks of pheasants and partridges, he would get out and usher them into the verges. In the end, he drove so slowly, just in case, that cars would back up behind him, the drivers honking their horns and swearing. And once, at the sight of a livestock carrier on its way to the abattoir at Trent, he stopped dead in the middle of the road with his eyes closed and his hands pressed to his ears.

I took over the driving, with Hugo sitting in the passenger seat beside me, until one evening, when we were heading to the supermarket on the Nailsea Road (it was always quieter then and he could take as much time as he liked at the checkout), he suddenly shouted 'Hedgehog!' and grabbed the wheel. It was not a hedgehog. It was a crisp packet. From then on, he sat in the back.

Anyway, it was the same thing with television, those modern remakes of things. The gritty ones. Why anyone would choose to have something gritty when they could have it not gritty was beyond him, made him despair for the modern world. So, then I would turn off the television and he would talk.

He reminisced about his schooldays, the camaraderie of the boys, his prowess on the cricket field. He wished he hadn't burned all his old reports. Some kind things had been written in them, which he would have liked to read again now.

But mostly he spoke about his brother and sisters in this big old house: Jeremy sawing at the bars of the nursery window with his little pocket penknife, Lydia saying, 'Being loved is better than loving, isn't it, Mother?', Rosalind smuggling half her breakfast up to the little fat pony in the stables and Annabel in his arms, clutching a cricket ball.

He loved them so much. Too much.

'To be able to love is a luxury,' he said. 'That's why it is always balanced exactly with loss. It is another of life's great justices.'

It was terrible for him to see them change and age. How selfish they all became. How strange. He could hardly bear to look at them at the end.

Of course, much has been said about them, over the years. 'The Infamous Gilberts' they were called by one newspaper. I think perhaps 'Infamous' is a little strong.

Another newspaper described them as 'a bunch of lunatics'. Well, that is a gross exaggeration, but there is some truth in it. And why not? Life drives us all to madness. In every cavernous longing for something we cannot have, something we have lost, something that was rightly ours and of which we have been cruelly, disastrously robbed. In the relentless propulsion of time that launches our bodies onwards into death while our dreams linger in the past with our childhood books and toys. In the disparity between the elevated soul that longs to soar, and the work of gravity that keeps us down below, washing dishes, eating and going to the toilet. It tears us apart. Those who most long to fly are most torn apart by having to go to the toilet. It becomes unbearable.

Yes, life drives us all to madness. Or it should. People who stay sane haven't been doing it properly. But, as I say, it is terrible to see.

Towards the end, there were long illnesses, then periods of recovery, but he grew weaker each time.

He didn't sleep well. Now and then, he would wake in the middle of the night and go down to the kitchen to make himself some cocoa. When he switched on the light, the white walls would be speckled with the woodlice that each evening crawled out of the cracks around the kitchen door.

'Ah ha, here you are again,' he would say to them. 'Don't mind me.'

Then one night he came into the kitchen to find a fat black spider on one of the woodlice. He tried to save it, but it was too late. It was this that brought on the last collapse, from which he would never recover.

'I have been worn down, Maximus,' he told me, his eyes red, his pillow damp with tears. 'Like a snail with a very thin shell. Life has battered me, like a snail in a sandstorm. I am very close to being entirely made of the inside part of the snail. The jelly part. That is how it feels.

'And there is no medication for it. You can go to the doctor and say, "I feel like a snail whose shell had been sandpapered, a snail who has been lost in a sandstorm," but they will not know what to do. You can say to them, "Every time I see a newspaper stand, I think I'm going to faint; every time I see a rendered concrete wall with mastic joints and weep-hole vents, I almost throw up," and they look at you as though you were mad. They offer you Valium and Temazepam, but never do they say, "What is the nature of the sandpaper? Tell me about the storm."'

68

A Squashed Blackcurrant

'What will become of it all, Max?' Hugo said to me then. 'What will become of this place, when I am gone?'

Poor, poor Hugo. What an enormous death he had, surely larger than most. He held so much. There was so much to let go.

'We shall be forgotten,' he said. 'We shall be lost. They will scrub us away like a set of dirty fingerprints on a plastic kettle.' He was holding a small photograph, much buckled and faded, of the five of them as children, standing in a line in front of the old cedar that was lost in the winter of '87.

'I feel them here, Maximus,' he said. 'There is a great deal of Annabel's hair in the drains, and I can still smell Rosalind in the green corridor – probably that bottle of perfume she threw at Lydia. Jeremy's socks have been home to many moths, over the years, and will never again be useable as socks, but they are dear to me.

'They say that dust is mostly made up of tiny bits of skin. People don't like that, I know, but I find it comforting. They are still here, on the lampshades and the light switches, in little grey snowdrifts on the backs of the doors and the skirting boards.

But what will happen to them when I am gone, Maximus? People are so keen on dusting these days.'

What could I say? In a voice choked with tears, I swore to him that as long as I lived no dusting would be carried out at Thornwalk.

It was not enough. He only looked at me sadly and pointed to a small dark stain on the rug at my feet. 'It was there that Annabel stepped on a blackcurrant,' he said. 'When I look at it, I think of her. I have told you much – I have tried to tell you everything – but not that, I think.'

'No, not that,' I said.

'Who will see it and think of Annabel, when I am gone? It will be just a stain on a rug, and people are suspicious of stains, Maximus, when they don't know what made them.'

With tears in my eyes, I swore to him that the stain would remain, that I would not rest until the whole true story of the Infamous Gilberts had been told, until the dust and the stains had become so beloved to strangers that they would be preserved as carefully as the Sèvres dinner service and the Aubusson tapestries, until the entry in the Historic England handbook read thus:

Interior entirely unaltered. Stain on bedroom rug from the squashing of a blackcurrant, circa 1930. Twentieth-century dust throughout . . . etc.

I have done my best.

69

A Piece of Jade

The chapel was built in 1872, designed by John Norton and paid for by great-grandfather Nathaniel Gilbert.

It is cold and empty now. The mosaic floor and jewel-filled windows, meant to be marvelled at, gloried in, are unseen by anyone but me. I sit here and think of the rise and fall of civilizations, and the shapes made by heartbeats and tides and particle waves. Everything goes up and down.

Over the years, I often found him here, thinking about his great-grandfather – the grim face with the long white whiskers in the paintings around the gallery – and how, back then, building churches had been on a par with feeding the poor. It is hard to imagine, is it not? But every age has its delusions. The eyelids of man are heavy indeed.

I can see him here now, his hands in his dressing-gown pockets, staring at the ceiling. 'Man does not live by bread alone,' he is saying. And then, after a moment, 'Though, realistically, bread is a large part of it.'

The crosses along the walls are each dedicated to an ancestor, but he knew nothing about most of them. It was a tragedy, because soon he would never know.

Each cross is studded with semi-precious stones, as you see – garnets, amethysts, jasper and aquamarine. Sometimes he sat here and ran his fingers over them. They were so beautiful, he said, and there were so many of them. There was just too much of everything. It made him dizzy. If you couldn't hold it in your hands, if you couldn't put it in your pocket, it was too much.

One day, I found him holding one of the pieces of jade – see, there, the little bald spot in the cross closest to the altar?

'It fell out,' he said. But that evening, I discovered a small screwdriver in his pocket and knew the truth.

He carried that piece of jade with him for many years. I think it gave him some comfort. He said many times that he wanted to be buried with it, but near the end he gave it to me.

'Something to remember me by,' he said.

Yes, he often sat here in the chapel, but he could not pray. He had no faith. Or, rather, he had a deep faith, deeper than normal. It was so deep it never came close to the surface and no one ever saw it. He would never have presumed to pray. It was that deep.

Outside is the graveyard, with its pitiful scattering of tombstones. None of the family are buried here, except Hugo, and they had to get special dispensation for that. It hadn't been consecrated ground for a long time.

Yes, he is buried here, but the grave is still unmarked. I believe they are arguing about who will pay for it.

'It's your graveyard,' Cooper Junior is rumoured to have said to the hotel people. 'Why should we pay to enhance your property?'

Let us not linger here now.

70

The Empty Bed (Part Two)

Let us return then, at last, to the small bedroom – the narrow corridor-type room between the blue room at the back of the house and Aunt Beatrice's room at the front.

Come in this time. Yes, come in. But breathe even more carefully than before. It is the rarest air of all and the smell is already fading.

What is it? I have written down the recipe. Two parts coal tar to one part lavender, chintz curtains, nylon carpet, cedar mothballs, cigar smoke and Aquafresh minty gel toothpaste, with background notes of mould, damp, cold stone walls, bat droppings, taxidermy and cheese sandwiches. That is as close as you can get. One day, I will make a bottle of it and keep it on a chain around my neck.

Yes, that is the bed he died in. He died in it many times, though only once finally and actually, in the usual sense. So many goodbyes he said. The doctors gave up coming in the end. They never could find anything really wrong with him, except his eagerness to claim the tragic moment.

'I feel it. It is here,' he would say, with a hungry searching look. A romantic delusion, because the real moment is not a wisp of fragrance or the murmur of angel wings. Far from it.

I had a camp bed that I unfolded here beside him. You will find it now in the attic, next to the chest of baby clothes. The dents of its rubber feet can perhaps still be seen in the carpet. No, perhaps not.

Here we had our last moments. Not moments. Months they were. It was a gentle slope he slipped down, while I clung to his hand. It is all one can do, in the end, this clinging, to prevent the terrible thud of a body hitting the final barrier at speed.

The death of a human being is not the running down of a fly that spins on its back a while then stops, dries to a powder, blows away in a puff of wind. It is not the death of a spider that crisps in its perch and drops, the old deer that quietly succumbs to the winter, nor the fox, descending a little further from sleep in its hole. No.

Sometimes I take my head in my hands and squeeze. It is impossible to crush oneself. I feel the enormity of the act of living, of the distinction between life and death. Of breath itself, in and out, in and out. Sometimes it feels like a hurricane, so immense are even these last gusts of my existence. How I envy the fly.

I shall not describe the end. There is no need. We are all familiar with the fall of a man and it will be no different here. His walls were no mightier, his towers no higher, the ransacking of his keep no more terrible. We are all the ruins of castles. Enough.

I have taken some souvenirs: one of Annabel's empty biros, Jeremy's first hand-whittled spoon, the wisp of hair from Sparklefoot's tail that Rosalind once wore in a locket around her neck (the locket is sadly long gone), Lydia's half-finished cross-stitch heart, so determinedly, so painfully, executed, one stitch at a time with her eyes on the window, as she sits in her bedroom waiting for Aunt Beatrice to arrive . . . and, lastly, Hugo's Dennis the Menace Weetabix bowl, for which he saved up so many tokens. How distinctly I remember the tap of his spoon against its rim. It was a child's bowl, really, very low, and each morning he had to fill it three times.

The Weetabix bowl shall be returned on the condition that it be on permanent display in the dining room, with an explanatory text. I can supply them with an original packet, plus three spare tokens. They have only to ask. But, until this is agreed, the bowl is mine.

There is so much more to be said, but I cannot say it.

I had planned to handcuff myself to the banisters when they came, to stand upon the tower with a loudspeaker.

'Depart, you thieves and usurpers!' I was going to say. 'Begone, you philistines and tomb defilers, etc.' I had compiled a long list of aspersions and derogatory terms of address, but I do not have the heart for it any more.

Well, then, I think the time has come for me to bid you adieu and return to the village.

I leave behind a single object. You shall find a new tombstone in the chapel graveyard, etched in the naive style with angels and Miniature Schnauzers, and the words (in my still amateur but promising calligraphy): here lies hugo gilbert, beloved of maximus.

Lock the door behind me, if you will.

Acknowledgements

[Acknowledgements to come]